DIZZY WORMS

For 25 years MICHAEL HOLMAN reported on the continent for the Financial Times, and continues to visit regularly. Brought up in Gwelo, Rhodesia (now Gweru, Zimbabwe), he took his first degree at the University of Rhodesia before he taking up a place at Edinburgh University, where he completed an MSc in Politics. From 1977 to 1984 he was based in Lusaka, Zambia, for the Financial Times as the paper's Africa correspondent; he moved to London in 1984 when he became the FT's Africa editor. In 2002 he took early retirement to write books. His first novel, *Last Orders at Harrods*, was published in 2005, the sequel, *Fatboy and the Dancing Ladies* followed in 2007.

Michael Holman lives in London, and writes for a range of papers in the UK, Kenya and South Africa; *Dizzy Worms* completes the Kuwisha trilogy. He is currently working on a play – *Missing Apartheid*.

Praise for *Last Orders at Harrods* and *Fatboy and the Dancing Ladies*

"It is not easy to write a novel which combines humour with an understanding of the serious issues facing contemporary Africa. In this delightful novel, Michael Holman, a writer who has for many years commented on African affairs to a world-wide readership, has produced a book which is not only an entertaining and amusing read but also a profound comment on the political and economic landscape of Africa. The style is engaging, the characters lively, and the end result is a superb novel born of years of engagement with Africa."

Alexander McCall Smith,
author of *The No. 1 Ladies' Detective Agency*

"Charity Mupanga is an African heroine in the spirit of Alexander McCall Smith's Precious Ramotswe – big hearted, township-wise and self-reliant."
Peter Godwin,
author of *Mukiwa: A White Boy in Africa*

"In this satirical feast, Holman hits his mark every time as he exposes the humbug and also the humanity of life in modern Africa. With a Dickensian cast of characters in the troubled nation of Kuwisha and a plot worthy of Waugh, this is a cracking fictional debut . . . Full of humour, home truths – and anger simmering beneath it all – this is a book that must be read."

Aidan Hartley, author of *Zanzibar Chest*

To Anne,
with best wishes &
my... all you
... hope. love, M

DIZZY WORMS

An African Tale

Michael Holman

Polygon

This edition first published in Great Britain in 2010 by
Polygon, an imprint of Birlinn Ltd

West Newington House
10 Newington Road
Edinburgh
EH9 1QS

www.birlinn.co.uk

ISBN: 978 1 84697 153 2

British Library Cataloguing-in-Publication Data
A catalogue record for this book
is available on request from the British Library

Typeset by IDSUK (DataConnection) Ltd.
Printed and bound in Great Britain by Clays Ltd, St Ives plc

In loving memory of my dear brother
Peter David Holman
12/4/50 – 11/11/73

ACKNOWLEDGEMENTS

My heartfelt thanks to: Gabrielle Stubbs, whose loving care continues to sustain me; to the friends who encourage me, in particular: Alan Cowell and Sue Cullinan; the Orr family and the staff at Jinchini, Kenya; Peter Chappell; Chris and Janet Sherwell; Quentin and Mary Peel; the late J. D. F. Jones; and Ann Grant; Dr Patricia Limousin and her colleagues at London's National Hospital for Neurology; Hugh Andrew and Neville Moir at Polygon, my publisher and editor respectively; Judy Moir, whose sharp editing spotted errors and inconsistencies – those that remain are mine; Michela Wrong and John Githongo, who have long been my guides to the "real" Kuwisha; and I am indebted to my god-daughter Lilly Peel, who braved my bad temper to perform wonders; and to Sandy McCall Smith for his long-time support. Above all, I am grateful to my inspirational and indefatigable mother who has lived through a revolution in Africa.

Rye Barcott and Salim Mohamed continue to bring hope to the children who live in an all-too-real Kireba (http://cfk.unc.edu/).

The land of Kuwisha and the characters in this novel are the products of my imagination. Nearly everything else is true. No goals were harmed in the writing of this novel.

A nightmarish air of normality greeted me when I flew into the shell-shocked city of Kinshasa. President Mobutu sese Seko had reshuffled his cabinet for the thirty-fifth time in ten years, and I was determined to find out why. My first port of call was the United States embassy, where the laconic ambassador was an old friend of mine. What was the significance, I asked him, of the reshuffle? Could it mark, I suggested, a paradigm shift in relations with the country's fractious opposition?

He drew on his cigar and puffed the smoke towards the rumbling air conditioner, and together we watched as it drifted away. He turned my question back on me.

"What do you get when you shake up a can of worms?" he asked: "Dizzy worms, Ekim, dizzy worms."

And so it proved . . .

In Search of Africa: A Foreign Correspondent Looks Back
Ekim Namloh
Polyglot Press, 1998

PROLOGUE

Peep! Peep! Peep! Peep! Peep! Peeeep!

The vintage Braun radio at the foot of the plain coffin beside the altar flickered into life. A bulb within the old-fashioned receiver lit up and illuminated its tuning panel, aglow with the names of fortresses and outposts of a colonial world long past. Luanda and Lourenço Marques, Elizabethville and Nairobi, Cape Town and Johannesburg, Pretoria and Grahamstown, Pietermaritzburg and Bloemfontein, Bulawayo and Salisbury, Blantyre and Gwelo . . .

The BBC time signal, which marked the formal opening of the service, echoed around the granite walls of the crematorium chapel, built many years before the east African state of Kuwisha won independence from Britain. The sound of the pips cut through the murmurs from the world outside. Muffled car horns, cries of street vendors and the tinkle of bicycle bells blended with the shouts of *matatu* boys as they drummed up passengers for their buses, which in turn merged with the laughter and chatter of children from the nearby school as they began their mid-morning break.

Just as the last *peep* faded away, an old man entered, wearing a pin-stripe suit, dark glasses and a fresh rose in his buttonhole, a solicitous aide by his elbow. His unexpected presence was greeted with an almost tangible combination of fear and loathing, fascination and awe, as if a malign spirit was made manifest, Victorian in appearance but *voodoo* in its impact.

As the late arrival took his seat in the front row, the chirpy Irish jig, "Lillibullero", signature tune of the BBC World Service, burst out, relayed by loudspeakers wired to the organ loft, high above the congregation. It was out of the usual sequence. The composition, which began life two hundred years ago as a Northern Irish Protestant marching song, normally comes first, but the deceased had left specific instructions that the order should be reversed. Indeed, not long before his death he had personally helped splice the tape that was now playing to the congregation.

Just last week, a couple of days before he passed on, he had summoned Boniface Rugiru, senior bar steward at the Thumaiga Club, to receive detailed instructions about the settlement of his estate and the disposal of his mortal remains.

Word of the terms of the will had spread through Kireba like wildfire. The endowment was enough to cover the clinic's running costs for years. More than that, it was enough to cover the fees that would allow Mercy Mupanga to achieve her long-cherished ambition – to complete a diploma in public health.

From his vantage point in the organ loft, Rugiru looked down on the congregation. There was not a seat to be had, he noted with satisfaction. A dozen or more street boys, displaying their appreciation of the deceased's insistence that they be given free dough balls to mark his passing, took up the best part of a row, scratching their intimate crevices with nonchalant indifference, peering at the rest of the gathering with befuddled curiosity.

The distinctive smell of ripe boys, a powerful mixture of wood smoke and burnt tyres, acrid sweat and a whiff of *bhang*, made those who were sitting downwind wrinkle their noses, while those who were upwind gave thanks for their good fortune.

One boy stood out among the fidgeters, however, sitting immobile but for a forefinger that constantly traced the left orb of his nose, his eyes fixed on a bull-necked man wearing the mayoral chain of office, staring at the back of his head with single-minded intensity.

"Rutere!" hissed a woman in her forties, sitting a few feet from the boy. "Behave!"

Boniface Rugiru took out his handkerchief, wiped beads of sweat from his brow, and shifted in the chair that would normally be occupied by the organist. To his delight and relief, the makeshift system that connected the radio to a tape recorder and on to the speakers, operated by switches on a panel in front of him, had passed its initial test.

Rugiru, an imposing figure in his freshly pressed uniform of bow tie, black jacket and trousers – the Club committee had given him permission to wear the outfit off-premises – loosened his collar. It was too early to relax. But for the first time since that painful evening at the Club, he dared to hope that he would successfully discharge the heavy responsibilities placed on his shoulders by his old friend.

He stopped holding his breath and inadvertently let out a strained noise, somewhere between a moan of satisfaction and a cry of triumph, which carried to the front rows of the packed congregation sitting below him . . .

What a turn-out!

Under one roof, the movers and shakers of the slum called Kireba had come together. Clarence "Results" Mudenge, proprietor of the Klean Blood Klinic, source of sound advice and dispenser of herbal potions, sat next to his friend Philimon Ogata, whose Pass Port to Heaven Funeral Parlour was doing a thriving trade. Mudenge took out the cloth he carried for the purpose and wiped his eye. Were he not in church, he would have removed it altogether and given it a good rub. Dust and a glass eye did not go together.

Ogata coughed, a racking persistent cough, disquietingly similar to the one from which his late wife, Beatrice, had suffered in the months before her death.

Alongside Ogata sat Mildred Kigali, devoted wife of Didymus, house steward by profession, senior elder of the Church of the

Blessed Lamb by vocation, two septuagenarians who were pillars of their community; Charity Mupanga, owner and manager of Harrods International Bar (and Nightspot), a well-known eating house on the edge of Kireba, sat at the end of the bench, keeping a maternal eye on the street boys.

She looked up towards the organ loft, concern and compassion on her face, and turned to a middle-aged white man alongside her. Edward Furniver, manager of the Kireba People's Co-operative Bank, whispered in her ear, giving her hand a squeeze as he did so.

Some distinguished outsiders were also present. Mrs Bunty Benton, chief housekeeper at State House for as long as anyone could remember, had firmly turned down Rugiru's invitation to take a place in the front row. Instead she sat at the back, next to the young army officer who had escorted her to her seat.

Boniface Rugiru bowed his head and resumed his prayers for the soul of the man who had been his thirstiest customer, his most generous source of tips, and the family benefactor who had paid the school fees of the surviving four of the six children with whom he and his wife Patience had been blessed.

Boniface also gave thanks to the Lord for helping him resist a terrible temptation. How he had longed to take the radio for himself. Instead he had honoured his late friend's instruction that the Braun, which Rugiru had coveted ever since he had been a youngster, should accompany its owner into the flames. In a few minutes the receiver would be gone forever. Together with the coffin, it would disappear through the sombre brown curtains that concealed the furnace from the packed congregation.

With the radio would go a chunk of Rugiru's childhood, for it had been a cherished companion of his teenage years as the Thumaiga Club's "small boy", a friend to whose voice Rugiru had listened as he had dusted the owner's bedroom.

Even then, at the tender age of thirteen, he had dared to hope that one day the Braun would be his. Alas, it was not to be . . .

4

Rugiru's limbs twitched as he reached back into these memories. He had not danced for the radio since he was a *toto*; regrettably he had failed to persuade the bishop conducting the service to let him perform the ritual dance before the altar, in a final act of friendship.

A thought occurred to him: although the space around the organ was cramped, there was room enough to pay a private tribute, accompanied by a silent rendition of that song in honour of the radio, which he had composed nearly fifty years ago.

While the congregation was absorbed in prayer, Rugiru got to his feet. He double-checked that he could not be seen from below, and began to limber up with a couple of moves. They were tentative at first, for his joints were stiff. Then as he got into his stride, he showed how he had won the Northern Transvaal Ballroom Dancing championship when still in his twenties.

Silently and with great agility, knees raised impossibly high, elbows jutting towards the heavens, torso bent parallel to the ground, Boniface Umfana Rugiru *toyi-toyi*'d his tribute to the radio and to its master, singing under his breath:

Jo'burg, Cape Town and Salisbur-eee.
The world is watched by the BBC . . .
Pretoria, Bulawayo, Nairob-eee,
Wherever in Africa you may be
Bloemfontein, Gwelo, even Umtali,
You cannot keep a secret from BBC . . .

With a final silent stomp, the chant ended. Boniface mopped his brow. In less than a minute, the service would be over.

Then a sudden movement caught his eye. As the Bishop of Central Kuwisha delivered the final blessing, and the coffin began to move out of sight, the bar steward watched with horror and anguish an act that was sacrilegious, truly offensive to his Christian soul and demeaning to the reputation of the country called Kuwisha.

Spotted only by Rugiru, thanks to his elevated position in the organ loft, an arm appeared from behind the curtain, ripped out the wires that led to the radio, and withdrew, clutching the Braun. Although it weighed several kilos, the receiver disappeared from sight in an action that seemed almost as fast as the tongue of a chameleon plucking a fly from the air.

When Rugiru's involuntary gasp of pain, fury and anguish reached their ears, members of the congregation, moved by what they believed was an uninhibited display of raw grief, gave out a collective murmur of sympathy.

Charity Mupanga spoke for them all when she whispered to Edward Furniver: "Poor Rugiru! His heart is very sore. My goodness, how he loved that old man."

The Kireba Youth Choir led the singing of "Nkosi Sikele' iAfrika" and the congregation prepared to leave their seats.

Rugiru looked on, helpless and incredulous.

As the chapel emptied, he took a solemn oath, swearing in the name of the deceased that he would track down the thief, and make the scoundrel rue the day he had interfered in the last rites that marked the final journey of his old friend.

"Welcome to Kuwisha!"

The immigration officer at the international airport handed back the passport to Digby Adams, Senior International Profile Co-ordinator and Cross-cutting Media Expert for WorldFeed, the Oxford-based aid agency.

Digby took a deep breath. At last! Within five years of leaving university he had arrived on the front line of the battle against poverty, trained to serve as a development professional as dedicated as any soldier. He was ready to take on the curse of illiteracy, to confront the scourge of poverty, and to play the role of guide, mentor and spokesperson for the stakeholders of Kuwisha.

The clammy heat had enveloped him like a steaming hot towel as he stepped out of the plane, and he took a lungful of what he was sure was the "real" Africa.

Digby wiped his brow as he waited in the arrivals hall and kept an eye open for his travel companion. The battered luggage-carousel wheezed into life.

Although early morning, it was already hot. So hot that in the city the feral street children, who normally flocked around visitors like predatory skinny birds, their beak-like fingers dipping into pockets of jackets and carrying away wallets, merely looked on at the passing scene, lacking the energy to throw stones at the mangy dogs that lay panting under whatever shelter they could find.

Even the spindle-legged marabou storks stopped delving in the piles of decaying refuse and sought the shade, abandoning their duties as the city's garbage processors.

Digby had not known Dolly for very long, but he had already become more attached to her than was perhaps wise. As he picked his case off the conveyor belt, he spotted his companion, receiving VIP treatment, being escorted across the hall by two airport officials.

The paperwork was completed in minutes, and together the travellers headed for the exit, past the customs inspectors and into the massed ranks of taxi drivers in the arrivals hall.

"So far so good," said Digby. "All gone smoothly, wouldn't you say?"

Dolly was silent.

Looking back, Digby wondered if some instinct, some sixth sense, a premonition perhaps, was warning her about the perils that lay ahead . . .

It had been a stroke of luck that Digby Adams met Cecil Pearson, former Africa correspondent for the London *Financial News*, the night they both left for Kuwisha.

Digby had noticed that a passenger immediately ahead of him at the check-in queue at Heathrow had been behaving rather strangely, alternately paging through a book the size of a novel and looking with an odd intensity at the check-in desk.

Digby turned his attention to the other passengers, and passed the time trying to guess their occupations. About half of them he classified as tourists, concealing their professions with outfits that were deemed suitable for their East African destination. They either wore khaki-coloured trousers, equipped with numerous pockets; or sported safari suits with epaulettes, and pouches for camera film, a feature which had long been a sartorial anachronism.

In a huddle of their own were a group of American evangelists, wearing cheerful bright-toothed smiles and T-shirts emblazoned with the claim that they were "Bringing Love and Hope to

Kuwisha". About half the rest, Digby decided, were visitors on business of one sort or the other.

The balance was made up by a category in which he could now include himself, someone who worked at the sharp end of international assistance: aid workers. As he listened in to their conversations, places that once seemed obscure and remote came alive – Kisangani and Goma, Darfur and Entumbane, while acronyms such as UNWFP, Cafod and UNICEF had life and romance breathed into them.

Digby could not help eavesdropping, fascinated by locations that were now going to become more than spots on wall-sized maps, with tiny flags representing the offices of UN agencies, or Oxfam, Save the Children, or UKAid. It was an intoxicating world of conferences and workshops, of breakaway sessions and consultative processes, of reports back and stakeholder participation, a world that Digby was about to enter.

He had the feeling he was joining an exclusive club, a club whose members carried themselves with a confident diffidence, with an air of modest authority, appropriate to a profession that occupied the moral high ground, accepted into the ranks of practical dreamers, united in their determination to serve the interests of a continent that needed their help.

He, too, would now proudly declare his occupation, his vocation, his very calling in life: "I work for an NGO."

As he moved slowly towards the check-in desk, he overheard conversations and exchanges of information about destinations that made his heart beat faster.

"Your first visit to Kuwisha?"

Two aid workers were exchanging credentials.

"Yes, really looking forward to it . . . Live in Denmark . . . going to a workshop, in Kuwisha?" The words ended with an interrogative lilt. "Urban youth?" she continued, the pitch of her reply slightly more assertive.

Her fellow passenger looked impressed.

Urban youth was a subject of growing concern, and an even faster growing source of funds.

"Presenting a paper on street kids? . . . Got a copy if you're interested."

She rummaged in a bag, made of hemp, that hung on a leather strap from her arm.

Digby looked over her shoulder.

"Africa's future or Africa's problem: finding jobs for urban youth."

Digby resisted the urge to introduce himself.

The odd behaviour of the passenger who had first caught his attention meanwhile continued. Digby decided to break the ice.

"Got the time?"

He replied civilly enough, but continued focussing his attention on the check-in desk.

"Ten past seven."

As the man, mid-thirties, fair-haired, wearing a crumpled linen suit, checked his watch, it gave Digby the chance to take a closer look at the book. It turned out not to be a novel, or a handbook on Kuwisha, their East African destination, but the *Airline Travel Guide.*

Just as Digby was about to ask why it was being studied so attentively, the passenger reached the check-in desk. He watched as the man, whose luggage consisted of a single wheeled case that was small enough to be treated as hand baggage, exchanged a few words with the woman behind the desk.

Digby was next, with an old-fashioned suitcase that was a much-loved survivor of his boarding-school days, and a carry-on canvas bag containing a surprise for Dolly, including some mini Mars bars, one of her favourite snacks.

"Keep chocolate away from her. If she gets as much as a sniff, she goes crazy," her minder had warned Digby at the hand-over in Oxford.

Digby, ever the professional media manager, had stored the information. Perhaps this fondness for chocolate could be turned into a joke for the press conference that was due soon after their arrival in Kuwisha.

Rather to his surprise, his fellow-passenger had waited for him.

"Sorry if I seemed rude. I was concentrating. Keeping an eye on the check-in staff. Watch their body language. If the plane is overbooked, you can tell before any announcement, provided you've been looking out. For a minute or two things looked dodgy, so I was using the guide to work out alternative routes. For example, there is an Emirates flight to Kuwisha which leaves tonight, gets you in three hours later than BA."

"So what?" Digby was inclined to say, but decided to hold his tongue – Cecil was clearly a seasoned traveller. Instead he raised a subject that preoccupied economy class travellers the world over: "Any tips on how to get upgraded?"

"You need to work at it. Wear a jacket, dress the part."

He gave a disparaging glance at Digby's outfit of trainers and multi-pocketed trousers.

"I'm Cecil, by the way, Cecil Pearson. Pearson of the *Financial News*."

The two shook hands.

"Seen your by-line," replied Digby, the traditional response from a journalist, or indeed anyone in the information business who wanted to flatter a hack, but who had never read a word of what they had written.

"See we're on the same flight to Kuwisha. I used to be based there when I did Africa for the paper. Great job, but a dead end. So when the accountancy job came up, I threw my hat in the ring. At the heart of the *FN*."

He sounded a trifle defensive.

"And you?"

"Digby Adams. WorldFeed, media consultant, profile manager. I'm going out with Dolly, a sort of goodwill ambassador, to sharpen the WorldFeed image. Trip is sponsored by UKAid. Actually the idea came from the chap in charge of the East Africa operations in Kuwisha. Got his name somewhere . . ."

After a brief search, he located a notebook in one of his pockets, and lifted a rubber band that was attached to the moleskin cover and which held the pages in place.

"It's the sort that Hemingway used," he said.

Turning to an earmarked page, he read out a name.

"Podmore, Dave Podmore, head of UKAid, at the British High Commission. Good sort, been one of our supporters for ages. He'll keep an eye on Dolly once I've handed her over."

"I bet he will," said Pearson, with an edge in his voice.

Digby shrugged.

"Don't mind. Really. I'm not jealous. Though I know what you mean. It's all too easy. One gets close, gets used to one other, gives them a few chocolates, and before you know it, they're eating out of your hand."

Although what Digby said may well have been perfectly true, Pearson felt a shiver of distaste for the matter-of-fact tone. His disapproval must have been picked up, though the cause was misunderstood.

Digby added, apologetically: "I know it's a bit of a stunt, but it's got a serious purpose."

Pearson nodded again and decided to change the subject.

"What were you doing before 'Feed?"

"Had a spell with TAF after an internship with HARE. Once I get Dolly off my hands, I'll be advising on an audio-visual project for DanAid, about the redevelopment of a slum – place called Kireba. You probably know it . . . Think we'll call the film *A Future Called Hope* . . ."

He saw the look on Pearson's face, and hastily added: "It's just a working title. Suggestions welcome."

"How long have you been with WorldFeed?"

It turned out that Digby's current job was the latest in a list of attachments to some of the blue-chip aid agencies – Take Africa Forward, Helping Africa Recover Economically, Securing Africa's Future by Enterprise.

"Gosh!" said Cecil, impressed despite himself. It was the aid industry equivalent of a decent Oxbridge degree, topped off by a spell at Harvard. What was more, the chap looked absurdly young.

The conversation moved on to other topics.

"Tell me more about your time with HARE," said Pearson. But as Digby began to reply, the public address system broke in.

"This is a security announcement . . ."

". . . make stakeholders aware . . ."

". . . *will be destroyed* . . ."

". . . and will hand over tomorrow morning. Quite a relief . . . though I'll miss her . . ."

". . . *last call* . . ."

". . . so the best way was to take Dolly out to Africa myself. A sort of trail-blazing effort. Link up with WorldFeed, get some publicity."

"Expect you'll meet my friend Lucy Gomball," said Pearson. "Resident representative of WorldFeed . . . My companion, partner thingy . . ."

Pearson seemed about to say more, but must have thought the better of it. Had he not been keeping an eye on the check-in counter, Cecil might have asked Digby to repeat his side of the exchange that had been made unintelligible by the security announcement. But his uncertainty about the flight, his effort to get upgraded and Digby's mention of a female companion all combined to inhibit him. Instead he played safe, and followed the long-established rule of the foreign press corps in Africa.

Should a colleague refer to a member of the opposite sex, or appear in public with one, it was best to assume that questions about the relationship were seldom welcome and never sought.

The female companion could be a fiancée, mistress, daughter or wife – or more likely than not, someone else's wife.

So Pearson, though curious about Dolly's credentials and history, limited himself to a simple question:

"Has Dolly checked in?"

"Oh yes, couple of hours ago. Press briefing, photos and so on. We'll have another, proper session in Kuwisha, and introduce her as an ambassador for African growth."

He was going to say more but just then a BA official called out.

"Excuse me, Mr Pearson . . ."

"See you on the other side," said Pearson, grabbing his green canvas wheel-on bag.

"Where are you heading?"

"Been upgraded – business class," said Pearson. "Tell you what, let's meet tomorrow at this bar I go to. In that place called Kireba – Harrods. Every taxi driver knows it. Bring Dolly, if you like. About ten. I'll see you there," he added.

He handed Digby his business card.

Cecil Pearson, it read, *Accountancy Editor, Financial News*. He had scribbled a few words on the reverse of the card.

"Here, show this to Charity, Charity Mupanga, she owns the place. Her mobile number is on the back."

Pearson then disappeared through the Fast Track entrance.

"What's your phone number?" Digby called out after him, but it was too late.

2

The sun was well above the horizon when Charity Mupanga, manager and owner of Harrods, the most popular rendezvous in Kireba, spotted the two boys, legs like sticks and with the pot-bellies of old men, glue bottles strung from their necks, rummaging in a pile of rotting vegetables.

She put two fingers into her mouth. The piercing whistle reached the pair, and the taller of the two held up a hand in acknowledgement, while the other boy waved a large manila envelope.

They broke into a trot.

"We have it, mama!"

"For sure!"

"The stamp is from Zimbabwe."

"The post office woman wanted 50 *ngwee* . . ."

"Too much . . ."

"Dough ball! We have earned a dough ball!"

Titus Ntoto and Cyrus Rutere raced towards her, bare feet slapping as they deftly hopped from stepping stone to stepping stone, placed where the mud was thickest.

"Furniver!" she called excitedly. "I think they have come. The plans, my rats have brought the plans."

Edward Furniver, former London banker turned manager of the Kireba People's Savings and Investment Club, looked up from his newspaper. He took a sip of coffee, and replaced the mug on the plastic table in front of him.

"Hang on a mo. First listen to this. It will make Harrods famous . . . or should I say, more famous. It's by *The Nation*'s restaurant correspondent," he said. "Half-way through the article there is something rather nice."

He read from the newspaper:

"But for a surprisingly good meal, which is excellent value for money – indeed it puts many establishments in this city that charge several times the price to shame – I heartily recommend lunch at Harrods International Bar (and Nightspot). If you try the avocado soup you won't be disappointed. The bar is run by Mrs Charity Mupanga, widow of the late and great Bishop Mupanga. And a word of warning: her dough balls are exceptionally, mouth-wateringly good."

Charity seemed lost for words and then declared: "Please, Furniver. Read that again. Wonderful! Harrods is the very best place to water your mouth. That is now official. I will write that now, on the menu board."

The boys, still panting from their exertions, looked on as Charity took delivery of the envelope they had collected from the post office.

"Come, Furniver! Come and read what's inside. I think there is something special. You will remember that I told you about my plans for good toilets in Kireba?"

Furniver nodded. If the truth be told, Charity had a thing about toilets.

"Well," she said, "there is a man in Zimbabwe who is a first-class expert on toilets without water, but with no flies."

She shook her head in wonder. "Just think, Furniver. No flies."

Charity opened the envelope, confirmed the contents and broke into a celebratory shuffle around Furniver's table, hips swinging, bottom swaying, in a manner that left Furniver slack-jawed with appreciation.

She brandished a magazine in front of him.

"*Bush Latrines Monthly*, the best in the world on bush toilets."

"Not much competition, I would have thought," said Furniver, but not so loud that she could hear.

Charity, hands shaking with excitement, flipped through the contents of the magazine and then pointed to a page.

"Read this, Furniver. Read this. You will see my name, Mrs Charity Mupanga. Twice in one day we see the name of Mrs Charity Mupanga. In writing! First in the newspaper, now in the magazine. Official. Truly, it is a day when letters are red."

Furniver took the proffered magazine and examined the contents. There was a letter to Charity from the editor himself, as well as the blueprints she had ordered for the construction of the Zimbabwe toilets.

Furthermore, the journal had printed a note submitted by Charity suggesting a modest but useful change in the construction of the Mark Two Latrine, involving a slight adjustment to the filter.

Charity stabbed her forefinger at a headline: " 'The VIP, an invention from Zimbabwe'. Please read, Furniver."

He obeyed her instruction:

"One smart idea is the Ventilated (Improved) Pit Latrine, in short: the VIP – which was developed as the 'Blair Latrine' by Peter Morgan, who has been living and working in Zimbabwe for over 35 years, researching and developing water and sanitation technologies."

"Thirty-five years! A toilet specialist! My, my, what a fine man! I would like to meet this person. Do you know him? Mr Peter Morgan?"

Charity seemed to believe that *mzungus* in Africa all knew each other, and she looked surprised and disappointed when Furniver admitted he neither knew of Mr Morgan nor his admirable work.

Charity clucked, sighed, shook her head and continued.

"Anyway, there is a drawing of this first-class latrine."

They spread out the blueprint on a Harrods table.

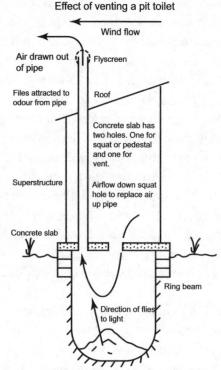

Effect of venting a pit toilet

Wind flow

Air drawn out of pipe

Flyscreen

Files attracted to odour from pipe

Roof

Concrete slab has two holes. One for squat or pedestal and one for vent.

Superstructure

Airflow down squat hole to replace air up pipe

Concrete slab

Ring beam

Direction of flies to light

<u>Diagram showing effect of vent pipe on functions of pit latrine</u>

"How exactly does it work?" Furniver asked.

"Listen, just listen."

She took back the magazine article, and read aloud, all the while prodding with her forefinger the illustration that accompanied it.

"The major advantage of the VIP over a normal pit latrine is that it comes with a ventilation pipe" – she looked up – "which of course is covered with a fly screen on top. This means fewer flies and less smell."

She continued to read, but slowly and more loudly than necessary, as if instructing a dim street boy.

"Over half a million VIPs have been built in Zimbabwe. They work without water, are cheap to build, and have low maintenance costs."

She paused.

"And flies are trapped. I hate flies. Much worse than worms, which are harmless, as you know. But flies . . . Now Furniver, I must tell you, I have ordered materials for six VIPs. They will arrive any day. But first, we must finish digging the holes . . . and cement, we must lay the cement, just as the instructions say."

3

Life President Dr Josiah Nduka, Ngwazi Who Mounts All the Hens, graduate *magna cum laude* in econometrics, whose University of Edinburgh doctorate thesis, *Money Supply in Authoritarian States*, remained the definitive work on the subject, was in a reflective mood as he sat in his study at State House.

He watched the beams of sunlight move across the carpet as the morning advanced. This was his inner sanctum to which only his personal secretary and Bunty Benton, the chief house-keeper, enjoyed the privilege of regular entry, together with his head of security and the kitchen *toto*, whose presence was taken for granted.

The room was dominated by an old sofa and two armchairs, newly covered in a floral print, and an oak desk, its top bare except for the day's newspapers, and with silver-framed signed photos of Queen Elizabeth, Prince Philip and Margaret Thatcher. On the side table by the desk stood a cut-glass vase holding a single fresh rose. A fireplace, the wood laid but unlit, gave out the fragrant scent of smoke.

Nduka looked with satisfaction at the pattern on the cloth of the sofa, just back from its bi-annual change of cover, carried out by a family firm in Godalming, Surrey. They had been doing it for years.

The firm was cheating, Nduka soon realised, when he studied the latest bill. They either thought he was a stupid native who could easily be duped, or regarded him as a lazy native, too lazy to check the bill. They did a good job on the sofa, though . . .

But I am not stupid, and I am not lazy, he thought to himself. He passed a few happy minutes devising a suitable punishment. Perhaps he would invite them to Kuwisha, as his guests, hinting that they would receive an honour for their services to the State; then confront them with evidence of over-invoicing and double invoicing.

"Oh yes, I know these tricks, all too very well," he muttered.

Nduka summoned the *toto* with a ring of the service bell, set into the wall behind his desk.

"Where is my honey water?"

In his seventies, fast approaching eighty, Nduka was finding that his memory was letting him down. He could not remember if this was the first or the second time he had tried to order his honey water.

He called again: "Where is my honey water?"

This time a small boy, bare-footed, in khaki shorts and a white T-shirt, appeared in the doorway, shaking slightly from nerves – or it could have been malaria.

"It is on your side table, suh."

There it was, below the main flower arrangement by Mrs Benton. Every day except Sunday the housekeeper set out a mixture of carnations and freesias in a silver vase on the mantelpiece above the fireplace.

The single rose, placed in exactly the same spot on the side table, at exactly the same time each day, displayed in a slim crystal glass, had been picked that morning from the State House rose garden, established by his old friend, adviser and jailer, the last governor of the former British colony.

The building had been neglected since independence, and had long been showing the strain. At first glance, and from afar, State House looked like wedding cake on a bed of green, sitting amidst daubs of red bougainvillaea and purple jacaranda blossom. The surrounding lawns, with a nine-hole golf course running through them, were watered and trimmed by a team of elderly gardeners.

On closer inspection, however, all was not as it should be. The greens – especially those on the 5th and 7th holes – needed professional attention, for termites had created several brown patches.

Within State House itself, the seat of government built in the 1920s, cracks could be seen below the white paint. The French doors that opened from the ballroom onto the rose garden, let in the rain. And the stuffed lion in the entrance hallway, shot by a previous governor less than 500 metres from where the beast now stood, was starting to moult, while its tail, tugged by generations of visitors, had been sewn back on by Mrs Benton several times.

The air conditioners creaked and groaned to little effect, and the ceiling fans spun sporadically and erratically, and did no more than move the heavy warm air around the poorly lit rooms.

It all would have been far worse were it not for the efforts of Mrs Benton, who had devoted her life to the service of the president. But as she approached forty years in the job, its constant demands were proving too much for her . . .

Nduka savoured the sweet scent of the rose, and then pondered the statement he had made at the press conference the day before.

Kireba to be reborn, declared the newspaper headlines.

Kuwisha teams up with donors.

The editorial in the *Standard* concluded with a question:

"Is this the long overdue end of an eyesore called Kireba?"

The president rose with the aid of an ebony walking stick, moved slowly round the desk and reached the mantelpiece, where he adjusted one of the freesias.

According to the papers, within hours of the announcement, cement prices had soared. His ministers had moved fast and cornered the market. Some had called their lawyers, instructing them to "discover" title deeds to plots in the slum, for which they could claim compensation when the state issued compulsory purchase orders.

Where was that *toto*?

"Boy! Bring me my honey water."

Hardwicke Hardwicke looked out of the window in his office at the Washington headquarters of the World Bank and dug his heels in.

"Nduka made me look stupid and naïve on my first visit. I'll never forget sitting in the State House waiting room drinking warm orangeade. Finally saw him after waiting an hour. Told myself: Never again. Meant it then, mean it now. I won't set foot in Kuwisha as long as he is in charge."

Jim "Fingers" Adams, the long-serving senior adviser on interaction with stakeholders, stopped chewing on a toothpick.

"But this is no ordinary crisis. As president of the World Bank you should really be there, if only to represent the international donor community."

"It is precisely because I am the president of the World Bank that I will not be there," fumed Hardwicke. "All it would do is add to the credibility of a nasty piece of work."

Fingers flicked the toothpick in the direction of the wastepaper bin and thought hard. It was precisely this situation in which his skills were best employed.

He owed his nickname to the speed with which his stubby forefingers raced over the keyboard of his laptop, and the phrases that emerged invariably won him the respect of donors and debt-burdened delegations alike.

The unacceptable features of governments throughout Africa were described in language that was inoffensive yet accurate. Thus "pre-humanitarian assistance" had allowed international donors to turn a blind eye to the re-arming of half the continent's armies, most of whom had experienced what he termed "dysfunctional military activity" – or coups, to use a term generally regarded as unhelpful. Government delegations that took offence at crude references to corruption, did not object to expressions of donors' concerns about "budgetary anomalies".

In short, Fingers had elevated the code-word vocabulary of conference communiqués to an art form.

"What about a message of support?" he asked Hardwicke. "I can knock something up for you in a jiffy."

Fingers sucked his teeth while his fingers raced over the keypad.

"Got it! How about this: 'Kuwisha, land of promise . . .' That's not a bad start."

Hardwicke stuck his little finger in his ear, wriggled it vigorously, withdrew it with a squishing sound, and grunted his assent. "Go ahead."

Thirty minutes later the statement was ready.

"Needs a bit of polishing," said Fingers, "but you'll get the drift. The reference to Tanzania may be a bit close to the bone . . ."

Hardwicke read the statement, rubbed his hands with enthusiasm.

"Don't change a word. About time I had a go at Berksson . . ."

The election violence had left international aid donors in no doubt: only a coalition government could halt Kuwisha's drift toward anarchy, a prospect that threatened aid programmes across the country, and left at risk the donor targets for development spending.

"We politicians must put Kuwisha first," Nduka had told the news conference that marked the end of a three-day exchange with aid partners, under the sponsorship of the World Bank.

He looked into the cameras, rheumy eyes narrowing, a canny tortoise with the bite of a snake.

"In creating this new alliance of political parties, we will give the highest priority to the welfare of the citizens of Kuwisha and to the consolidation of peace, progress and unity. A slum eradication programme", he declared, "is an essential first step in the modernising of Kuwisha. It is evidence that the parties that make up the government I lead will overcome our differences and deliver to the people. It also marks the start of a new relationship with our friends from abroad . . . I appeal to the international community to be generous in their support for Kuwisha and to put their weight behind the new coalition. The long-suffering people of that slum they call Kireba deserve better – and this coalition will make its transformation our number one priority . . ."

The diplomatic corps, called to State House to attend the announcement, broadcast live, enthusiastically applauded.

"I wish to acknowledge the invaluable role of the United Nations Development Programme," said Nduka, lingering over each syllable of the organisation, and pausing between letters as he pronounced the letters that made up its acronym – "the U – N – D – P has been a loyal and reliable ally of Kuwisha. Their work in the past has shown that their strategy of meeting together, and resolving our problems, is productive, highly productive. I now invite our development partner to say a few words about the history of our association, and how we can take it forward."

As Anders Berksson, the long-serving UNDP resident representative, got to his feet, the British High Commissioner confided in his German colleague.

"Seems to me that the old man is looking to his legacy."

"When you Brits call an African president 'the old man'", muttered the ambassador, "and talk about his 'legacy', there is usually a defence contract in the offing."

The high commissioner's reply was lost in the applause that greeted Berksson.

"Friends of Kuwisha," he began, and Nduka knew this was the right man for the job. "One of Kuwisha's oldest, most steadfast supporters is unable to be with us in person today, but he is here in spirit. And it is my pleasure to present a truly inspirational message from Mr Hardwicke Hardwicke, president of the World Bank . . ."

Berksson cleared his throat and began reading the statement prepared by Fingers on Hardwicke Hardwick's behalf.

"I have fond memories of Kuwisha and its brave and resilient people, led with such distinction by President Nduka. Violence is no way to resolve differences. I urge cooperation with the international efforts to assist . . . The appointment of my old colleague Berksson, whose radical role in Tanzania transformed the economy, in particular the restructuring of the sisal sector, has made him uniquely well equipped to preside over constructive change in Kuwisha."

4

Digby Adams looked around the arrivals hall at Kuwisha International Airport in case Cecil Pearson had yet to come through. True, the journalist was on holiday. His successor, however, was away in Angola, covering a UN conference on culture and development. It was just possible that Cecil might be persuaded to do Dolly's story – particularly if it was offered as an exclusive. First Digby had to introduce him to Dolly. Clearly she was still shaking off the effects of the sedative, but he hoped that her charm would work its usual magic.

Then he remembered the journalist's boast about travelling light, hand luggage only, and guessed Pearson would probably be half way into the city by now . . .

There was no shortage of taxi drivers at the airport, and in a sea of welcoming faces, Digby chose the driver with the biggest smile.

"Aloysius," said Aloysius Hatende.

"Digby," said Digby, and the two shook hands.

He negotiated a fare, which, although high, had to take into account an unfortunate fact, about which it was only fair to warn Aloysius. If the journey to Heathrow had been any indicator, Dolly had a tendency to get severely car sick.

Aloysius shrugged. Car sickness he could tolerate and even sympathise with. It was the violent vomiting of passengers who had over-indulged in Tuskers that he couldn't understand. A waste of good beer!

He pocketed the extra 100 *ngwee* that Digby had offered.

Dolly safely ensconced, they set off for the office of WorldFeed.

*

If all went to plan, Digby and Dolly would meet David Podmore, the UKAid director in Kuwisha. A photo opportunity, followed by a briefing of the foreign press corps, would be chaired by Lucy Gomball, but with Digby answering the questions.

In one of his last acts before he left for Kuwisha, Digby had prepared the ground for the event, planting the story with the subtlety of his trade. He had phoned the foreign desks of several of the leading newspapers, urging them to ignore rumours that WorldFeed had appointed Mia Farrow as a "development ambassador" to Kuwisha.

"Absolutely not true," he said.

When pressed, he acknowledged that WorldFeed had indeed appointed an ambassador, code-named Dolly, but sought their cooperation.

"Look chaps, you know me. I have never lied to you and I don't intend to start now," he had told the news desks before he set off for Kuwisha. "Let me categorically rule out one name that's come up. Kate Moss is not, I repeat not, Dolly."

Alerted by their London offices, the foreign press corps in Kuwisha concluded that there was a strong chance that Angelina Jolie was the mysterious "Dolly" – and the prospect of seeing this celeb in the flesh was enough to ensure interest in the promised photo opportunity.

The journey into the city had been slow and tedious. Pearson was right in his advice to take carry-on baggage only. The wait at the luggage carousel could take half an hour – and in that time, traffic conditions could change. Unlike Pearson, who had managed to miss the worst of the hold-up, they were caught in the morning rush.

Although the Chinese contractors had completed their road-widening project, the highway was nevertheless clogged. Huge lorries, belching fumes, *matatus* with horns blaring, four-wheel drive vehicles, taxis in various stages of decrepitude, buses and cars, all competed for space.

The traffic lights had been switched off, their function taken over by policemen who manned makeshift road blocks, and whose job appeared to be to slow the flow and allow colleagues time to impose fines for offences that were largely imagined.

"Police," said Aloysius, shaking his head, "always eating."

His hand carried invisible food to his mouth in the symbol of corruption.

Digby looked on as the vehicles, with a bewildering range of acronyms emblazoned on their frames, crawled along, hooting their frustration. Most of the names were familiar to him and he felt proud to be joining their cause, a dedicated infantryman in Africa's battle against debt, disease and deprivation.

"Not a bad line," he thought to himself and took out his notebook.

"Infantryman in the battle against disease and deprivation . . ." he jotted down, with his local paper in mind. *"Our man in Africa experiences life on poverty's front line . . . foot soldier in the struggle against deprivation . . ."*

As he wrote, the four-wheel drives carrying the resident representatives of the high and the mighty of the aid industry rolled into the city, like a squadron of tanks: Danida and UNDP, Dfid and UKAid, UNDP and UNIDO, NorAid and Christian Aid, Oxfam and Save the Children, all part of a parade of international concern and compassion. The organisations they represented pursued every cause that involved or afflicted mankind in general and Kuwisha in particular.

Female genital mutilation, environmental degradation, child abuse, renewable energy, gender discrimination, intermediate technology, health care for nomads, promotion of the informal sector, the welfare of pastoralists, teaching illiterates: it seemed that not a concern was neglected and not an interest group unrepresented. Even obesity had joined the ranks, and PAD (Promoting an African Diet) was in the vanguard of change to the continent's eating habits.

Within the air-conditioned interior of their vehicles sat the men and women who did so much to help the frail economy of Kuwisha tick over. They were rich targets for the street vendors, who were making the most of this opportunity.

On a normal day the vendors would be sprinting alongside a customer's car as it gathered speed, handing over the purchase, delving for change, and dodging oncoming traffic. Today they were moving at a leisurely pace, up and down the marooned vehicles, whose occupants had become a captive market. From car to car they went, adroitly sidestepping the potholes that had reappeared after the first rains, moving back and forth, to and fro, as alert to a flicker of curiosity or interest as an auctioneer on a slow day at market, as assiduous and as persuasive in their patter as life assurance salesmen, while they good-humouredly touted their wares.

Festooned with fake mobile phones and battery-driven fans from Taiwan, apples from South Africa, screwdrivers from China, clocks and DVDs, the variety seemed endless.

Dolly looked around benignly. The sedative that she had taken before her journey must have been wearing off, yet she seemed unfazed by the cacophony that surrounded them.

"Not long now," said Digby and gave her a pat. It was over-familiar, and Dolly moved away. He regretted his gesture, for it was presumptuous. Worse than that, it may have had a bearing on what happened a few minutes later.

With their progress reduced to a walking pace, Aloysius pressed the door locks on his side of the car, and motioned to Digby to do the same.

"Thieves," he said, clearing his throat with a long rasping cough. "Bang-bang boys. Pretend that a car has hit them. When it stops, they steal. Very bad."

He wound down his window and expelled a gob of phlegm onto the verge, before closing it again.

A succession of supplicants knocked gently but persistently on the windscreen – blind old men led by young boys, women who held out their babies, and cripples, with the more fortunate perched on tricycles, while the rest pulled themselves along on what looked like tea-trays with wheels.

Suddenly Aloysius braked, and although they were barely moving, Digby was thrown forward by the jolt. It was the dreadful sound of steel on flesh that he recalled most vividly, along with the expression of pain on the face of a young boy as he was struck by the passenger side of the taxi.

5

As one man, the delegates rose to applaud the moving message from Hardwicke, which had been relayed with such feeling by Berksson.

The reference to Tanzania had been below the belt, and it was quite unnecessary, he felt, to remind the audience of his association with the disastrous nationalisation of Tanzania's sisal estates.

He put aside his irritation, and launched into his own address: "In a very real sense," he began, "we are all to blame for the tragedy that has threatened to tear Kuwisha apart over the past few weeks. And in the same very real sense, we are all citizens of Kuwisha."

"Speak for yourself," muttered the Japanese aid representative.

Unfortunately his remark was picked up by one of the microphones that relayed the proceedings to the national radio network. His new posting would be announced within days.

"We need to pull together at this demanding period in the country's history. We must move with the times," said Berksson. "It is essential", he went on, "to maintain the momentum! Let us forward development, and grow the foundations. This is a partnership of key stakeholders engaged in an ongoing consultative process which will lead to shared ownership of this great country, which is yet to deliver on its huge potential."

Nduka, who had listened impassively up to this point, grunted. Despite the promising start, Berksson was suspect. He would need to keep an eye on this impertinent diplomat whose reference to *potential* bordered on the offensive. Congo had *potential*, as did Sudan. Somalia had huge *potential*. A host of African countries had *potential* – a word used only to describe countries whose failures had become legendary and whose crises seemed endemic. Kuwisha might be in difficulties. The president was prepared to concede this. But *potential*? How dare the man use the word.

"Stakeholders . . . ownership . . . consultation . . . participation . . . accountability . . ."

Berksson was in full flight.

"A wound on our conscience, an affront to our humanity . . . a symbol of our compassion . . . "

While the UNDP chief continued to work the audience, Nduka pondered the next steps.

The riots had left many scores to settle, rewards to allocate, favours to repay, IOUs to honour, constituencies to reward or to punish . . .

A list! He had to draw up a list . . .

Kireba's problem, if problem was the right word, was its desirable location. Unlike many of the slums elsewhere in Africa, which were invariably located a safe distance from the towns they served, and designed as dormitories for cheap labour, Kireba was as close to the city's centre as it was possible to get.

This fact made it a tempting target for any commercial developer. But it also attracted the interest of a far more powerful force who sought to improve the lot of the half-million people crammed into a space the size of a dozen Wembley football stadia: the international aid agencies, impelled into participation by the need to leave a better world.

"Coordinated targets . . . strategic priorities . . . partnership of modalities . . ."

Berksson was still in full flood, and Nduka continued to speculate on the benefits of letting the donors turn the slum into what they called a "low income" housing estate.

A list! He needed to make a list of supporters who deserved a place in the new Kireba. It would not be free, of course – people who got something for nothing in his experience seldom appreciated their good fortune. A contribution to party funds would do the trick.

The older he got, the greater the pleasure of making a list. It could be a list of bright young men who had crossed his path and had subsequently been "disappeared"; or it could be a list of projects that donors might now be prepared to finance, projects that would testify to his success.

A new airport, perhaps, or a university, in his name; or a grand headquarters for the ruling party. A thought struck him. How about Nduka House, in the very heart of Kireba? That would teach those insolent slum dwellers a lesson they wouldn't forget.

Berksson was at last coming to the end and delegates were looking at their watches.

"This vision is within our reach! Together we can turn words into bricks, turn promises into schools, and turn our dreams into reality . . . And so tomorrow, let work begin. A minute lost is a life lost. The bulldozers will move in tomorrow!"

As Berksson ended his appeal, Nduka looked around for pencil and pad.

For a moment he forgot where he was. Thinking he was in his State House study he called out: "Boy! Boy! Bring me paper . . ."

Berksson was quick to comply.

News of the plan to demolish Kireba brought many immediate benefits. Hotel bookings soared. Short-term lettings of properties in Kuwisha's more salubrious suburbs boomed. And restaurants thrived as economists and sociologists, assorted consultants and multi-disciplinary experts poured into the country, determined to ensure that Kuwisha would have the benefit of their commitment to eradicate poverty. Specialists in the socio-economic consequences of urbanisation, proponents of privatisation of water supplies, advocates of a high-speed rail link from Kireba to the coast, lobbyists for a toll road on the same route, flocked to Kuwisha.

All the residents of Kireba were expected to do was to accept their good fortune, and respond to questionnaires seeking their opinion on crèches and clinics, on shopping malls and markets, not to mention their views on gender bias in the workplace, or the prevalence of ethnic dominance as a factor in job allocation – two subjects being investigated by post-graduate students from the London School of Economics.

For Charity Mupanga it meant that she had more customers than ever for her fried chicken necks, her avocado soup, her corn bread and her dough balls. Invariably the consultants' day started with a cup of coffee at Harrods and ended with an ice-cold Tusker, before they retreated to their hotels to write up their reports and compare their expenses, arguing over *per diems* and hardship allowances, complaining to each other about the rising costs of educating their children in Britain.

But among the visitors were a handful of men in brown suits who behaved strangely, as Furniver was the first to notice. While other delegations went to the trouble of actually venturing out and about, peering down the narrow footpaths of the slum – some, every now and then, some actually exchanging a few words with a resident – the "brown suits", as he called them, never ventured far from the bar at Harrods. They scribbled notes, but asked no questions, having nothing to do with the locals, but all the while taking a close interest in the rudimentary toilets . . .

"Just who are those chaps?" Furniver asked.

Charity shrugged.

"They will probably be working as locally hired experts for somebody . . ." she replied. "Why are you worried, Furniver?"

"Because they make too many visits to the toilets."

Charity's demeanour immediately changed from indifference to concern.

"I hope they washed their hands?"

"Not once."

"Not once?" she asked incredulously. "Not once even?"

"Nope. Didn't feel it as necessary, I suppose . . . All they did was to stand outside. Didn't actually use the toilets, not sure that I blame them . . . Kigali says they are from the city council."

Charity now looked really worried.

"That is not good, not good at all. Mayor Guchu must be up to mischief. Something is not right."

Furniver shrugged. One day the man would get his come-uppance. The longer he was in office, the richer he became, and the richer he became, the faster the collapse of city services. Rubbish festered on street corners, potholes went unrepaired, water and electricity supplies became more and more erratic, while city taxes soared. One day Guchu would be brought to book. But who would bell the cat?

6

To Pearson's surprise Lucy Gomball, the well-respected and widely lusted after resident representative of WorldFeed, was at the airport to meet him, although she hated early starts and emotional reunions.

"I thought I told you not to come," she said, emerging from behind the massed ranks of taxi drivers at the airport. "I thought we'd agreed."

Pearson took in her fair-haired, blue-jeaned, long-legged figure with relish.

She gave him a perfunctory kiss on his cheek and wriggled free when he attempted a substantial embrace.

"I said I'd spend a week in London during my home leave and we would have sorted things out then."

Lucy relented. The second kiss made his heart leap.

After all the agonising about coming to Kuwisha for a brief holiday break, it seemed he had made the right decision after all. He had been wrestling with questions about his future since his return to London. Should he attempt to pursue his relationship with Lucy Gomball, or should he drop any hopes that it could turn into a long-term – he was reluctant to use the word permanent – relationship?

Their last night at the end of his Kuwisha posting had been frustrating, and inconclusive. Lucy was laid low with a bout of malaria, and she had invited him to stay over in her home in Borrowdale. He had sat up most of the night wiping her forehead, bringing her tea and fruit juice, and dosing her every four hours. As dawn broke he fell asleep, still sitting on the side of her bed. A few hours later he was on the plane to London, where he had been offered the *FN*'s accountancy job.

So it was that when a two-week break came up, he decided he would fly to Kuwisha. No one would have been surprised if their relationship had not lasted. Not for nothing was Nairobi known for its low morals and high living, and the question, "Are you married or do you live in Nairobi?" had more than a grain of truth. And even if the wiles of horny hacks could be resisted in Kuwisha, there were other formidable hazards to overcome if a relationship was to survive this hothouse atmosphere.

It was only after they were half way into town that Cecil remembered Digby.

"Met a bloke who will be working for WorldFeed," he said. "He was on the same flight. Looked decent enough, but . . ."

"Damn!" said Lucy. "Must have been Digby, Digby Adams, that's it. I thought he was on the day flight. We're putting him up for the night. My driver is supposed to meet him. Didn't get a chance to read the email they sent. Apparently he's travelling with this woman called Dolly. Blast."

"Don't worry, we'll see him at Harrods," said Cecil and went on to tell Lucy about his encounter with Digby at Heathrow a few hours earlier.

"Why the 'but'?" asked Lucy.

"Treats women like animals. A shit, if you ask me. Amoral little shit."

"Talk about pot and kettle," said Lucy. "What about those African Union bonks you confessed to? Remember? About how you would turn up at one of those ghastly African Union summits that you knew would be so tedious, self-satisfied and balls-achingly boring, that only fools and Afro-optimists from Scandinavia believe anything will come of them."

"Don't remember," said Pearson.

"Oh yes you do. You told me how you'd look around at your fellow hacks – the hatchet-faced moanalot from the BBC, the AP woman with a ghastly laugh, the fat-arsed AFP stringer . . . and you'd think to yourself that you would need to be stuck in Goma for a month, and build up the appetite of a sex-mad hyena, to find any of them attractive."

"Rubbish," said Pearson.

"You told me that the first night you'd end up in bed with a World Bank report on Ethiopia. Then the next day, you felt a slight twinge in your twagger – only a slight one, mind – as you wondered whether the Norwegian press officer for Feed The Starving was a sleeper or a talker."

"Nonsense," said Pearson.

Lucy was merciless.

"Let me jog your memory. You also told me that women divide into two categories, those who talk afterwards and those who fall asleep afterwards."

Pearson grunted.

"On the third day of the summit something in you snapped, you said, your judgement was destroyed and lust triumphed. And on the evening of the final day, no doubt overwhelmed by relief that the bloody summit was nearly over, the worst happened."

"Meaning?" said Pearson.

"Meaning", said Lucy, "that the AU tedium had worked its malign magic and by that stage you'd discovered that the Norwegian is a talker who had extracted the most demanding amount of cock tax you ever had to pay – a ratio of an hour's talking for every five minutes of what Charity calls hanky hanky.

"You buggers have the sex drive of a randy baboon and the morals of a rabbit on Viagra. You go off on your trips and return to wives and girlfriends with limp dicks and piles of dirty washing. And you'll do it once too often. The trouble is,

Pearson, you're all easy lays. So don't give lectures about amoral aid workers – it doesn't suit you."

She kissed him on the cheek as she swerved to avoid an errant *matatu* and Pearson knew that he'd been forgiven for his AU folly, although he has still under Lucy's close surveillance.

"Anyway," said Pearson. "Whatever. I told Adams to come for tea at Harrods this morning. Bring Dolly, of course, introduce her and so on . . ."

Lucy's expression suddenly hardened.

"Bastard! Here I was", said Lucy, "thinking to myself that for once you behave decently with an NGO. Not because you needed a lift on their charter flight, or a ride in their car, or briefing that you dress up as your 'eye-witness' account, but just out of the goodness of your heart . . ."

"Don't get you."

"You just want to meet Dolly! That's the only reason you were so friendly. You just can't help it, can you? Led by your twagger!"

"So what's up on the aid front?" Pearson asked, breaking an awkward silence.

Lucy shrugged.

"Have a look at the papers. On the back seat."

Lucy narrowly missed an oncoming bus, packed with commuters, arms protruding through its windows like pieces of straw from a loosely packed bale.

Pearson reached behind him, and paged through the papers, while Lucy continued: "Full of Nduka's plans for Kireba. That and the warning that North East Province will soon be in a food deficit situation . . ."

"I assume that means they are hungry."

He started to read: "Millions of innocent civilians are at risk of starving in a humanitarian crisis unless the international community acts to avert this looming catastrophe . . ."

"Shit!" said Lucy. "I told them to cut that line out."

"They did – I made it up."

Lucy ignored the provocation.

"There's flooding in the central province. Land clashes in the south, scores killed; teachers threatening to go on strike in the west, drought in the east. As for Kireba, they all seem thrilled by the news of Nduka's scheme. Everyone claims they own their hovels, and demands compensation. Cement prices have gone out of sight – like cement itself. There's not a bag to be had. Overnight. Just like that. I checked on the way out to collect you. So," Lucy continued, "situation normal. Cock-ups all round."

"I bet WorldFeed is getting excited about it," said Pearson.

"Read for yourself," she said, "it's all there."

Pearson studied a statement, run on the front page of *The Nation*, issued by a US non-government organisation.

"Maize production this year will stand at 15 million bags, against a demand of 35 million bags . . ." he read out. "The poor output is blamed on Kuwisha's prolonged drought . . . Maize is the staple food for 96 per cent of the country's 40 million people . . . Farmers need to plant proper seeds, depending on the climate, as well as better storage and handling facilities, said a spokesman for the NGO that is heading a crisis committee of the biggest aid donors."

"You agreed to this? Including the bit about seeds?" asked Pearson. "And the papers say that WorldFeed is backing the Kireba project . . ."

"Don't get on your high horse, for God's sake," said Lucy, hooting as she passed an over-laden *matatu*, smoke trailing from its exhaust. "Told you, Pearson. Nothing has changed while you've been away. Facts the same. Two-thirds of Kuwisha is arid, yet the population has doubled in 25 years. Can you believe it?"

"We've been through this before," said Pearson. "No one worries if the buggers can't feed themselves. They've learnt that

41

the UN and the NGOs will make sure they don't starve to death. And you chaps still measure success by lives 'saved' and tonnes of food shipped in, most bought from US farmers. And now US agri-business want to sell Kuwisha its seeds."

"Don't bang on," said Lucy.

Pearson hadn't finished.

"So who announces the food 'crisis'? Not the president. Not a minister. But a bloody NGO! Poor bloody Kuwisha! You lot have cut off its balls."

Lucy shrugged.

"Show business. What do you think about the Kireba project?"

As Lucy raced with taxis and dodged motorbikes, she brought Pearson up to date with developments since the rioting.

"The really big news is Nduka's promise to transform Kireba. The UN and the World Bank will lead . . . and WorldFeed is on the steering committee."

"And you bought this; actually signed up with Nduka?"

"What do you expect us to do, Pearson? Sit on our collective arse and say it can't be done? That corruption makes it impossible? That project money will be milked? We're damned if we do, and damned if we don't. We are in Kuwisha to help, whatever you claim. Either we get stuck in, knowing the risk, and get into bed with Nduka and his pals, or we do bugger-all but say that sleaze makes life impossible for donors in Kuwisha. The first time we say this in public, we make the front pages. The next time it's old hat, boring, boring, boring, and what we say is on page 94 – and then what do we do? If we lose our first-hand, front-line experience, whatever we say is devalued. So yes, we opted to take part, knowing the risks."

"What does Charity say?"

"Comes up with a bloody local proverb . . . 'Good fruit cannot grow on a tree planted in bad soil.' Claims that Nduka's plan for Kireba will eat itself – whatever that means. And bangs on about the need for decent toilets. Except now she's as mad as a snake. She phoned me this morning saying that cement prices have soared since the announcement . . . No cement, no toilets. The truth is, everything we do seems an act of faith."

The rest of the journey passed in silence.

Lucy had indicated that "hanky hanky" was out of the question. She had to attend a press conference on nomads, followed by a briefing on the results of a survey on obesity and child abuse in Africa, and then a lunch with the Dutch ambassador.

"I'll try and rearrange, but it won't be easy. You could stay at Borrowdale," she offered, the green and pleasant suburb where WorldFeed was based. "But I've had to find room for that woman from Nomads. Barking mad, absolutely bonkers."

The prospect of having to be polite to her house guests was demanding; and the thought of being caught between the dogma of Promoting an African Diet and the zealotry of Spare A Seed For Nomads filled him with horror, and quelled his ardour.

Pearson had no hesitation in opting for a room at his favourite hotel, The Outspan.

"See you at Harrods," he said as they arrived, and was rewarded with a kiss on the cheek.

"Love ya," she called out as she drove off.

But Pearson was not sure whether the sentiment was directed at him, or at the concierge, who had allowed Lucy to drop him at reception. On balance, he reflected as he made his way to his room, it was more likely to be the concierge.

He looked at his watch: it was just seven. Time for a nap before heading for Charity's bar.

7

Charity usually set the alarm clock early, giving herself a delicious extra ten minutes in bed. She liked to ease herself into the world, a process that included counting her blessings. How fortunate she was, Charity reminded herself, to have a roof over her head that did not leak when it rained, to have blankets that kept her warm while she slept on a mattress without bed bugs, protected by a mosquito net that kept her safe from malaria. And as she shook off sleep, Charity took pleasure from looking round her white-washed room in the slum's only clinic, rented from its staff nurse, Cousin Mercy.

This morning, however, no sooner had the alarm gone off than she had been up and about, washing her face at the white enamel basin, which she had filled with water the night before.

Although the sun had yet to break the horizon, the heat was already building up. Only rain would bring relief; but with rain would come mud. The crude hole-in-the-ground latrines that dotted Kireba would overflow, and human waste would join the rest of the filth that made up the black stream that ran through the slum.

She was brushing her teeth with a stick when an unfamiliar rumble began. She cocked her head, paused and listened attentively. There was no mistaking it – a new unwelcome sound among the everyday noises that marked dawn in Kireba. It could be heard in the background, behind the call of returning night watchmen, the ring of bells on hawkers' bicycles, the rich variety of coughs that marked the end or the start of sleep, the rattle of pots and pans as breakfast was prepared, the low growl of the buses that packed the roads leading from the slum to the city, the strident calls of the *matatu* boys soliciting passengers.

The new intrusion was the deep grumble of the massive bulldozer signalling the start of a process that, if President Nduka was to be believed, would lead to the transformation of Kireba into an inspirational model of low-cost housing.

The enormous mechanical beast was to begin cutting a swathe through the blood-red earth, digging the trench that would carry huge water pipes that would serve the blocks of low-income flats which would replace the shacks and shanties that were home to half a million souls.

While Charity got dressed she compiled the day's menu in her head, before chalking it on the blackboard, propped against the steel side of one of the three shipping containers that made up the bar.

Perhaps this morning she would begin with a Coke and bun – which she termed a "bad sticky" – or fruit juice and cornbread, the "good sticky".

She had thought long and hard about selling sweet sodas. Water, filtered water, was cheap and it was far better for you, that was obvious. But even people who were poor had a right to waste their money on sugary sodas.

"People must be able to choose," she had told her old friend Mildred Kigali. "Choose in politics, choose in food."

"Good sticky – 20 ngwee
Bad sticky, same price," she wrote.

Charity paused, rubbed a dab of Vaseline into her cheeks, and prepared to face the world and the bulldozer. What would her late friend, Anna Nugilu, have done? Anna, who had been a rare woman politician in a business dominated by males, had died in a car crash, like Charity's dear husband. And like David's death, there were rumours that it had been more than an accident. If the intention had been to discourage opposition

45

to Nduka, it had succeeded. Certainly nobody put their head above the political parapet.

Meanwhile other matters were on Charity's mind, including a decision for too long put off. What should she do about her persistent suitor, Edward Furniver, that pink-faced overweight Englishman who was burrowing his way into her heart? To call him overweight was perhaps unfair. He weighed no more than a Kuwisha man of the same age. But a local carried the extra pounds proudly and efficiently, equally distributed between his belly and his *butumba*, the one providing a counterweight to the other.

Not so with Europeans: as their stomachs grew, bulging over their belts, their bottoms seemed to shrink, and become two miserable, scrawny flaps of flesh at the top of their shanks . . .

Sooner rather than later, she had to tell Furniver whether she believed they had a future to share.

She wished yet again that she could consult her father, the late Harrods Tangwenya and in particular her dear husband, David Mupanga, bishop of central Kuwisha. Although the raw pain of David's loss in the car accident some four years ago had eased, she missed his benign presence every day.

Charity tied a green apron around her waist and smoothed down her hair. It was still dark, too dark to make out the shape of Harrods International Bar (and Nightspot), even though the bar was barely fifty paces away. But she knew that in five minutes this would change. As the sun brought the early morning light, the shacks and shanties would emerge from the soft dawn that made the slum look almost attractive, and reveal the brutal reality of life in post-election Kireba.

For a while, the violent outcome of the December poll had catapulted Kireba and the East African state of Kuwisha into the international headlines, although foreign journalists based in the country were caught by surprise. This was not supposed to happen. How could Kuwisha, the African model of successful development, the reliable ally of the West, the region's safe base for the aid agencies; how could this country prove so rotten and so fragile?

Had not Kuwisha, under the authority of founding President Nduka, paid its dues to the all-powerful West, allowing Western warships access to Indian Ocean ports? Did not a million holiday-makers enjoy its golden beaches and glorious game parks every year? And did not the development organisations make progress in efforts to end poverty? And in a regional sea of privation and conflict, was Kuwisha not a reliable rear base for the international media?

But the foreign correspondents were nothing if not adaptable, postponing their New Year holiday plans, attending briefings by WorldFeed and other agencies, and taking Western diplomats to lunch, where together they pondered the strange ways of Africa.

The resulting insights soon rained down on unsuspecting readers: news stories and columns lamented the triumph of blood-lust, the supremacy of savagery, the sheer unpredictability of Africa; and described how rabbles were roused, condemned the firebrand politicians who fanned the flames of unrest; killings were senseless and brutal, and civil war and genocide were said to beckon, with the spectre of Rwanda ever in the background.

Charity had been lucky. She and Edward Furniver, who had been invited to her *shamba* on the strict condition that there would be no hanky hanky – "never before marriage" – had left Kireba before voting had begun. They had taken a *matatu* to her small-holding in the green hills, a two-hour drive from the city, where she cast her ballot.

But the peace she had left behind was illusory.

Within hours of the polling booths closing and the early results suggesting an opposition victory was probable, the onslaught orchestrated by the ruling party had begun. The devastation that followed changed the face and the nature of Kireba.

Harrods escaped the worst of the violence, partly because of its location on the edge of the slum, and partly because Cousin Mercy, who had taken refuge in the nearby clinic, had the presence of mind not only to lock the steel doors of all three shipping containers that made up the bar, but to set fire to some old tyres piled alongside. The resulting plume of black, oily smoke created the impression that the mob had already done their worst . . .

Other residents of Kireba were not as fortunate as Charity.

"The noise was dreadful," said Philimon Ogata who had remained behind, watching with horror from an old water pipe in which he had taken refuge. After the mob had passed, he had picked through the ashes of his Pass Port to Heaven Funeral Parlour, in the hope that he would find some of his tools, abandoned when he fled the advancing gang.

"It was like a train coming from down the track, getting louder and louder, as it got closer," he told Charity.

The sound had been distant at first: whistles that pierced the night, accompanied by the yelping of dogs; and then a crumple of collapsing sheets of corrugated iron, mixed with the cries of women, cut off in mid-shriek, creating a brief silence that was all the more chilling. All this blended in the liquidiser of chaos. But as the commotion drew closer there were other sounds that emerged – the calls of parents seeking their children, and the throbbing grunts that came from the bellies of the young men in the mob, under orders from local politicians, bearing flaming torches aloft and illuminating white teeth or capturing scenes of horror: a *panga* raised above a cowering figure, but so briefly that the consequences of the blow had to be imagined, for the sharp-edged tools were enveloped by dark as they descended on the cowering victims.

The gangs of youths, paid by the hour, chanted the ruling party's campaign slogan, *Kuwisha Kwanza* (Kuwisha First), as they led the pillaging. Decent people driven by desperation and despair did unspeakable things to other decent people, all clinging to a visceral sense of identity which dominated their lives, beginning with the village in which they had been born, spreading in a series of concentric circles to embrace clan, and district and province, all on a bedrock of tribal affiliation.

Then Kuwisha's plight slowly dropped down the world news agenda, until it was out of sight, allowing the foreign journalists to resume their tales about the horrors of Darfur, or Zimbabwe, or the Congo. Kuwisha's citizens were left to bewail their circumstances, while foreign non-government organisations rallied round and promised to repair the damage: houses and schools and clinics to be rebuilt; stalls and shops to be restocked; empty bellies to be filled. Children were recalled from school, and put to work for pittances. Only the clever and the fortunate went back to the classroom, carrying on their bony shoulders the hopes of their families and their siblings.

At the best of times, to send one child for education in a family of several children was akin to buying a ticket in Life's lottery, an achievement bought through sacrifice, and hard work. The outcome was awaited eagerly, though the benefits of schooling could take years to materialise.

But these were the worst of times.

For many, even this slim chance of climbing on the coat tails of a successful child was dashed by a plague called Aids. It left behind an army of orphans, who had nowhere to go but the streets of Kuwisha. This lost generation suffered twice: first as casualties, cannon fodder for the plague itself; then, even if they were spared, they found themselves deprived of their parents and grandparents, the former dead and the latter dying.

Bands of feral children roamed the cities, uncounted victims of the carnage in Kireba.

The sheds and plastic shelters and corrugated iron shanties which had been put to the torch could be rebuilt, and the black fire-torched gaps in the slum's alleys, like missing teeth, were filled. But many of the original residents did not return. Not necessarily because they were dead, though that was often the case. The living no longer trusted their neighbours, because they were from the south, or the east or the west – and the days when the Okot and the Ulu, the Kiyu and the Dere, could live as neighbours were over, perhaps forever.

8

"*Mo'ningi, mo'ningi . . .*"

The sound of the common *mo'ningi*, named after its familiar call, could be heard just outside Pearson's hotel room. How he had missed the cries that so often marked the start of his day in Kuwisha.

"*Mo'ningi, mo'ningi.*"

The cry of a shy visitor, traditionally associated with the start of the day, came again, but a little louder and a little closer. If he lay still, quite still, under his duvet, he might with any luck spot the *mo'ningi*'s traditional companions, notoriously shy and masters of the art of concealment.

"*Mo'ningi.*"

Again it came, with an interrogative note, as well as a touch of the diffident, almost apologetic tone that marked their cry. Pearson was tempted to turn over, and go back to sleep, but he knew he would regret it if, after coming all this way, he failed to make the most of the climate. After all, he could lie abed – should he choose – in grey, miserable London; to do so on another blue-skied African day was to be indifferent to one of the glories that made the continent so special.

How he had missed Africa!

He stirred, slowly, carefully, so as not to alarm the *mo'ningi*, and straightened a leg, opening his eyes, absorbing the traditional sounds of Africa awakening.

"*Mo'ningi.*"

The call was straightforward now, as if it was a signal to others who would follow in the *mo'ningi*'s footsteps, demonstrating that it was safe for them to come out. Pearson lay still.

He could not see the *mo'ningi*, or any of its companions. But they were there. Somewhere. All his experience of the continent and its many moods told him he was not alone.

How many times had he been proved right?

One was never truly alone in Kuwisha, no matter how desolate and remote it might seem. He recalled how in the north-east of the country – surely as bleak a region as could be found – he had been caught short on a long journey. After choosing a spot for its isolation, in a landscape that showed as much life as the surface of the moon, he responded to a call of nature, made urgent by a meal of dodgy goat stew and rancid milk.

He had parked his car on the side of the track, gone several unnecessary yards into the rocky terrain, lowered his trousers, and enjoyed the blessed relief – only to look up and see a herd boy watching with curiosity and sympathy.

What was more, when he had finished there was a man who turned out to be a teacher wanting a lift, waiting patiently by the car . . .

The *washingi*, low on nature's pecking order, notoriously shy, made a characteristic nervous foray, watched through the half-closed eye of Pearson, still concealed by the duvet.

Soon the *washingi* was joined by a *cleaningi*, and both engaged in their ritual dance-like movements, breaking out into their familiar songs.

Any second now, and the *teesuh* would knock on the door. Pearson gave himself the luxury of a five-minute lie-in, confident that the *teesuh* would wake him, with the sound of the gentle clink of cup and saucer he had got to know so well during his years in Africa.

It was in this environment that Pearson felt truly at home. And when his day ended, with the *stewardi* bringing him *drinksi*, life had nothing more satisfying to offer.

Every now and then, they would all gather round, at the end of the day, to entertain the *touristi*.

Who would believe that, without their traditional attire, one was watching the *mo'ningi*, who had set to one side her housekeeping duties, or the *washingi*, without the identifying bundle of clothes for the laundry, or the *teesuh*, hardly recognisable without his tray and tea cup, while the *stewardi*, a nocturnal creature, was a different man altogether when not bearing a gin and tonic, or any other type of *drinksi*. Pearson had seen them perform often, but never failed to be moved by their display.

Bowing and stooping, cheerful and cheering, they moved in unison, as they paraded in a time-honoured ritual. This was Africa in the raw, and Pearson felt privileged to be privy to it.

"Tea, suh."

Pearson must have drifted back to sleep, because when he next opened his eyes and looked around the hotel room, there was not a *mo'ningi*, or *washingi*, or *cleaningi* to be seen, although they had left behind traces of their presence. Clean towels, soap and shampoo. There were even tubes of shower gel, cotton buds and a shower cap.

He reached for the phone, and dialled room service. Outside, muffled by the plate-glass windows, and masked by the hum of the air conditioner, he could hear the rumble of early morning traffic. Room service rang back: there were no mushrooms for his breakfast omelette, and he would have to make do with honey rather than maple syrup with the waffles.

Pearson shrugged off his disappointment. He was home.

The mid-morning sun poured into the room.

He started to dial for a taxi to take him to Harrods. But then he wondered: was it really necessary to spend the day at the bar, whatever he had promised? Surely there were more pressing matters to attend to?

Pearson dialled a familiar number. Harrods could wait.

9

Digby's response to the accident on the way in from the airport had been immediate, instinctive and foolhardy. Before Aloysius could stop him, he had unbuckled his seat belt and opened the door of the now-stationary taxi. Just as he emerged, three things happened simultaneously.

The boy, who had been lying inert in front of the car, sprang up and ran off as Digby approached, swerving and jinking between the cars like a young gazelle; another boy, who had hitherto gone unnoticed, thrust an arm into the car and would have succeeded in making off with Digby's briefcase had not Aloysius intervened; and most distressing of all, Dolly took advantage of the distraction, left the car, and investigated the surroundings.

By the time Digby had registered her absence, she had crossed the road and seemed preoccupied by the sights, sounds and smells of Africa. A distraught Digby could only watch as his companion reached a spot on the edge of a sprawling collection of plastic shelters and corrugated iron shanties, where she faced the oncoming traffic calmly and with equanimity.

"Oh no! Come back! Dolly! Dolly!" cried Digby.

Looking back, he blamed himself. Had he stayed in the car, instead of following his instinct and dashing to the assistance of the boy who had been "hit" by the taxi, Dolly would still be safe.

Aloysius beckoned urgently from the car.

"Suh, suh, return to taxi. Please! They are bang-bang boys."

Although Digby had no idea what Aloysius was talking about, the concern in his voice was unmistakable.

For a few moments Digby was caught in two minds.

"Dolly! Dolly!"

His cries were in vain.

Dolly sauntered first to the traffic island, stopped briefly under the shade of a *msasa* tree, and then entered a maze of shacks and shanties.

Digby made a last despairing plea.

"Dolly, Dolly, come back."

His protective male instinct took over, and he was about to run after her when Aloysius intervened.

"Dangerous, very dangerous . . . Get back in the car. We are too close to that place, Kireba. Come, we will talk to Charity Mupanga and perhaps she will send one of her Mboya Boys to help find Dolly."

"Mboya Boys?" asked Digby, puzzled.

"The street boys who help Mrs Charity," explained Aloysius. "Some play football, and they are not bad boys. But others . . ." He shook his head. "They make much trouble."

"Oh God," said Digby. "I'll take help from anybody. I'll never get over this."

He took a handkerchief from his pocket and dabbed at his sweating face.

Aloysius remained baffled. His passenger's distress seemed disproportionate to the loss.

After all, Digby's briefcase was safe.

He would question Digby further – but first things first: to lose one passenger was regrettable; to lose Digby as well would invite the ridicule of his fellow drivers, and the Englishman was looking restless . . .

"Take me to Harrods," said Digby, and Aloysius was happy to comply.

A few minutes later the traffic eased, and the taxi pulled up alongside a densely packed slum, crammed into a space the size of a dozen football fields.

"Kireba," said Aloysius, and switched off the engine. "Harrods," he gestured. "Harrods International Bar (and Nightspot)."

It was said that if you sat at Harrods International Bar (and Nightspot) for long enough, most of Kireba's movers and shakers would eventually put in an appearance, such was its popularity.

For some customers, it was a club, a place to which they could direct mail – on the rare occasions they received a letter; to others it was an informal crèche; for many, it was a school where the illiterate could attend evening classes organised by the Ladies Sewing Circle; and for the street children of Kireba it was a precious sanctuary in a cruel and nasty world . . . but above all, Harrods was an eating house, where the food was good, nourishing and keenly priced.

One of the three containers, all formerly used on freight ships between Africa and Europe, now served as a kitchen, with a gas stove and charcoal braziers. It also housed a noisy fridge, run off an extended electricity cable, which was plugged in at the nearby clinic – indeed, Kireba's only clinic – run by Charity's cousin, Mercy.

A boy was sweeping out the second container which served as the indoor eating area. A hand-written sign advertised the next meeting of the Sewing Circle, as dull and boring a topic as Charity and Mildred could devise – thus guaranteed to keep men away, while their womenfolk discussed the pressing issues of the day.

The third container served as a bar, with crates of Tusker beer and sodas stored at the back and a wooden counter running its length.

The area between the two outer arms of the E had been covered in concrete, finished off with a red polish, and was shaded by a striped blue and red canvas awning, courtesy of an international soft drinks company. Under the awning were a couple of dozen white plastic tables and chairs, and a wooden trellis, covered with purple bougainvillea, provided additional shade.

Charity had chosen the location wisely. The bar stood at the point where the slum's muddy track, dubbed "Uhuru Avenue" by the locals, was crossed by the railway track, the dividing line between the city and Kireba, and Harrods provided a meeting place for two worlds.

Strictly speaking, the name of the bar was not Harrods, and had not been officially called Harrods for the past year. At the end of a nasty dispute, Charity had been obliged to rename it Tangwenya's International Bar (and Nightspot); a change forced on Charity by London lawyers who had forcefully pointed out that only the London *duka* they represented had the right to use the name "Harrods".

In vain, Charity, with the help of Edward Furniver, had pointed out that the bar had been named after her father, the late Harrods Tangwenya. She had gone to some lengths to explain to the lawyers in London how it was that her father had chosen the name "Harrods", rather than use his birth name, Mwaí Gichuru Tangwenya.

Did the lawyers not realise that their colonial kinfolk had a weakness, one which survived to this day? They could not speak the local language! Nor were they willing to learn. They could not even pronounce the names of the people, much to the astonishment of the citizens of Kuwisha, who invariably spoke three or four languages, plus English.

This posed serious problems for young people seeking a job. Unless you had a Christian name like Joseph or Charity, or adopted the name of commercial brand, like Willard, after the potato crisps, which could be remembered and pronounced by the British, you had little chance of success.

She told them how her father, just before his interview for a job as gardener at the British High Commission, had spotted a green bag marked "Harrods"; and had chosen that as his British name – and had got the job!

Alas, the hard-hearted men from London were indifferent to this remarkable achievement, by an extraordinary man, to whom Charity had paid tribute by calling her bar "Harrods". Instead they had insisted that this was unacceptable, and after a combination of faxes and misunderstandings, the bar had become – officially, at least – "Tangwenya's".

Not that it made any practical difference: regular customers continued to call it "Harrods", and new customers soon found themselves doing the same.

Digby got out of the car and surveyed the scene while Aloysius locked the taxi, double-checking each door. He then joined him standing alongside the cab, and sniffed the air.

It seemed thick with a variety of smells, ranging from the aroma of roasting maize to those that had a more fundamental origin.

Digby followed suit. "Fruity," he said, "rather fruity."

Aloysius was reluctant to contradict him, but nevertheless, his passenger was wrong, plain wrong. It was the unmistakable smell of shit. For a few seconds Aloysius wondered whether he should say as much, and then decided to compromise.

"It is very bad fruit, suh."

A rumble of thunder suggested the weather was about to change.

Aloysius sniffed the air: "Smell – rain is coming."

He pointed to bundles of white clouds in the blue sky, gathering on the horizon. If he was right, by afternoon they would turn grey, and then purple-black, as full with rain as a tick engorged with blood. With any luck, as the day darkened, thunder would roll and jagged shafts of lightning would pierce the heavens, and plump drops would bring relief from the heat.

Digby consulted the business card Pearson had given him the night before. He was in the right place, there was no doubt about that. He braced himself to acknowledge failure and seek Charity Mupanga's help. What an ignominious start to his visit to Africa. It was not supposed to have begun like this . . .

"Harrods. We have to walk now."

Aloysius was getting impatient. What was more, he was getting hungry, and he could smell something frying, chicken he guessed. He licked his lips.

"It's not far, but be careful."

Aloysius gestured, as if making a point.

"There, Harrods. And the lady you can see, by the bowls where they are washing, talking to an old woman, that is the owner, Mrs Charity Mupanga and the old woman is her friend Mildred Kigali. And that white man, over there, by the market ladies, writing things in his notebook, that is Furniver, her very good *friend* . . ." – he gave Digby a meaningful look – "who runs the Kireba bank. Her street boys are Titus Ntoto and Cyrus Rutere. She lets them sleep in the bar."

He shook his head disapprovingly. If he had anything to do with it, he would round up all street boys and dump them in the country, hundreds of miles away. But they had their uses. He conceded that.

"Maybe they can help you find Dolly. Let us go and meet Mrs Charity."

Trailed by Aloysius, Digby made his way cautiously across the rubbish-strewn wasteland that lay between him and the bar.

Progress was painfully slow. Every now and then he paused, and looked around, checked the card that Pearson had given him, and looked up at the sprawl of hovels spread out before him, an expression of bemusement on his face.

He re-read the scrawled message:

Charity,
I'm back! On holiday.

Please give Digby a dough ball.
See you at Harrods.
Best, Cecil

Digby stepped gingerly over a black, filthy rivulet that ran diagonally across the slum. He continued the hazardous journey across the intervening wasteland, regularly used by residents to dump their "flying toilets" – plastic bags into which they were obliged to evacuate given the absence of regular toilet facilities.

As Digby tried to take in the sights, his attention wandered, and his foot encountered a plastic bag that made a squelching noise.

"Take care, suh, take care, toilet, flying toilet."

Aloysius' warning came too late. Digby's foot had squeezed the bag like a tube of toothpaste. He looked down at the sludge that emerged, jerking his head back as a dreadful smell reached his nostrils.

"It is shit, suh."

Digby refused to be fazed. This, after all, was Africa.

He nudged a bulging plastic bag, one of many that had been dumped in a pile, with the toe of his shoe.

"Be careful," said Aloysius. "That is what we call a flying toilet. It is full of waste matter."

"Flying toilet? What a jolly good name."

The bar was straight ahead, and both men looked forward to slaking their thirst on a hot day.

"Try the mango juice, or passion fruit juice, with a handful of roasted peanuts," Pearson had told Digby when he handed over the card at Heathrow. "Or an ice cold Tusker beer. If you order two, you get a free helping of roasted potato skins. Just ask for 'bitings'."

These options had been set out on a blackboard, outside the bar, where a woman whom Digby assumed was Charity

Mupanga was chalking up the rest of the menu for the new day, tailor-made for the pockets as well as the palates of her varied clientele.

By now Digby and Aloysius were close enough to make out, beneath the grime of smoke and dust, the vague outline of the bar's name.

The first word was impossible to read, obscured as it was by soot, left behind when the slum had been put to the torch during the election rioting; but the rest emerged as "International Bar" and then continued around the corner. Clearly the signwriter had miscalculated the space available, and after getting as far as "Bar", had added the two last words "and Nightspot". But for reasons best known to himself, he had placed them in brackets. And while it seemed a trifle odd to new patrons, habitués accepted the display without a second glance.

One day, soon, Charity promised herself, she would get the sign repainted.

A boy of indeterminate age, with stick-like legs and a bulging belly, glue tube hanging from his neck, looked up, registered the presence of a stranger, and returned to his task of peeling potatoes. A second boy squatted next to one of the containers, using a nail brush to scrub his hands.

Aloysius, whose stomach was now rumbling, gave a broad hint.

"The pig's feet, suh, are very good, especially at breakfast. Boiled or baked. Myself, I prefer them baked because the skin gets crisp and they are most tasty. But if you only have little money you can buy chicken necks, the cheapest and the best in town. Or perhaps", he said, failing to elicit a response from Digby, "you would prefer one of those maize cobs."

He pointed at a brazier where a couple of youngsters were roasting cobs of tender green maize, the kernels turning yellow-brown after a few minutes.

"But the best", said Aloysius, licking his lips, "is the soup of avocados, made with some lemon and some sauce from a recipe that came from the late Bishop Mupanga's mother." At this point Aloysius crossed himself elaborately.

"If you are very, very poor you can buy for a few *ngwee*, a good serving of maize-meal, with groundnut relish."

"What's relish?" asked Digby.

"Like gravy, suh."

As the two men drew closer to Charity, apron wrapped around her stout frame, they could hear her humming to herself as she went about her tasks. A skinny lad assisted her in stacking the dishes.

"Fine," said Charity Mupanga, complimenting the boy on whatever task he had performed. "Fine. Take a dough ball."

Digby watched, fascinated, as the boy, with the concentration of a diamond cutter confronted by a particularly challenging rough gem, studied the four dough balls. Sitting in a pool of syrup, they were set out on a plate on the wooden kitchen table.

"He has washed his hands," observed Aloysius proudly. "Everyone in that kitchen has washed their hands, so you can eat without your stomach giving trouble afterwards. Never do they touch dough balls or any food with hands that have been unwashed. Never."

The lad bit his lower lip, and scowled in concentration. Finally he made up his mind, and carefully lifted with a kitchen spoon the dough ball he had selected, placed it on a piece of newspaper, and spooned over it an extra dollop of the syrup – vanilla-flavoured, judging by the smell.

The boy scampered off, clutching the carefully wrapped dough ball. Meanwhile, the white man in his late forties, wearing a blue long-sleeved shirt, wandered apparently aimlessly between the nearby rows of market traders, who sat on their haunches with their goods laid out before them. He was making notes, it seemed, and occasionally his voice carried to Digby and Aloysius – queries about price and quantity of the produce on display. Onions were cut into quarters, single tomatoes into halves, next to small pyramids of salt, or sugar. Every now and then he would pause over a bar of washing soap or a mound of detergent, and scribble in the notebook he was carrying . . .

"I do not know why he does that," said Aloysius. "But if you ask him, perhaps he will tell you."

A Prince Buster song, a favourite of the street boys, thumped away:

Enjoy yourself,
It's later than you think!
Enjoy yourself,
While you still in the pink!

But the noise did not seem to bother the customers making calls from a makeshift phone booth not far from the bar.

Every now and then, clients got up from the tables, or emerged from the cool interior of the bar, to use the rudimentary long-drop toilet, marked "For customers ONLY", washing their hands afterwards in a bowl of water, soap provided.

"Mrs Mupanga will talk about toilets for sure," said Aloysius. "She talks often about toilets. She told me that the plans for these new Zimbabwe machines, clever toilets that know how to kill flies, might arrive today. Or tomorrow. Come, you must have some tea."

Charity, who by now had spotted the pair, thought about calling out, and telling the visitor to take what might seem the long way round, but was a route that would save his shoes. She decided against it. She had nothing against foreigners. However, the young man could find out for himself, she thought.

She turned to the blackboard, and began humming a tune. The notes seemed familiar to Digby, and after a moment or two he recognised a hymn, one that took him back to school days and church services.

What a friend we have in Jesus . . .

On impulse, he joined in:

> *. . . all our sins and griefs to bear!*
> *What a privilege to carry everything to God in prayer!*
> *O what peace we often forfeit, O what needless pain we bear,*
> *All because we do not carry everything to God in prayer.*

Charity put down the plates she was carrying, and turned to face him, hands on her hips, head cocked to one side.

"Good morning, madam," he called out. "My name is Digby, Digby Adams, regional director for communications, at WorldFeed. Cecil Pearson said you make the best dough balls in Kuwisha."

Charity gave a brief nod of acknowledgment.

"You have a good voice. Let me hear you sing more!" she urged.

Digby obliged, faltering at first, and then louder. Without prompting, Aloysius joined in, as did a dozen or so customers waiting for tea, with an unselfconscious grace and harmony.

> *Are we weak and heavy laden, cumbered with a load of care?*
> *Precious Saviour, still our refuge, take it to the Lord in prayer.*
> *Do your friends despise, forsake you? Take it to the Lord in prayer!*
> *In His arms He will take and shield you; you will find a solace there.*

"That is good," said Charity, clapping her hands. "For an Englishman you sing well, very well. We must thank the Lord above for your voice. Tea?"

These people, they get younger every day, she thought. Another one, sent from England . . . at least he could sing.

"Sit. I will bring your tea to your table. Sit."

Digby obeyed, but first gestured towards Aloysius, indicating that he should be included in the invitation.

"The boy has good manners," Charity said in Swahili.

She recognised Aloysius as a regular customer.

"Tea, Mr Hatende?"

"Yes, please, mama. Tea with condensed milk, double helping, since the boy is paying."

Aloysius took out the stub of a cigarette that he had picked up and re-packed at the airport that morning, applied the flame from a red plastic lighter marked Kuwisha Airways, and sucked his first drag of the day deep into his lungs.

"Yes, the boy has good manners. Unlike many white people, he does not call me 'bwana', or 'my friend'. And he lets me read his newspaper, and he told the paper boy to keep the change. Although that is foolish. They spend it on girls. And he sits next to me, in the front of the car, not like a boss, who sits in the back."

Aloysius took a sip from the tin mug of tea Charity had set down beside him, added a spoon of sugar, gave it a stir, and returned the spoon to Charity.

He took another drag, and slowly expelled the smoke.

Charity's nostrils twitched as the sour-sweet scent of Mtoko Gold – Kuwisha's best bhang – drifted into the warm air. She was about to rebuke him, but decided against it. If she allowed street boys to poison themselves with changa and glue, how could she tell a man old enough to be her father that he could not smoke bhang?

"Yes, the young man is polite enough," he continued in Swahili. "But he is very unhappy. I met him at the airport, this morning."

He cleared his throat, and was about to spit, when he caught Charity's warning look.

"Yes, he is from London. He brought a present from the people of England. But he has lost it."

Charity turned to Digby. "What can I do for you, young man? What have you lost?"

Seldom had Digby Adams felt so inadequate, never had he felt such a fool, as he heard himself say:

"Good morning, Mrs Mupanga. My name is Digby Adams. I have lost my goat. She is called Dolly. Please, will you help me find her?"

10

"Your goat? Lost your goat?" asked Charity. She tried to keep a straight face. "That is very serious."

As she questioned Digby, her tone changed from polite concern to growing incredulity, while Aloysius listened intently, occasionally interjecting with a comment or question of his own.

He was the first to broach a delicate matter, one which he'd been wanting to raise almost from the moment that he had met the Englishman.

"How much did you pay for your Dolly?"

"She cost £20. But it's not the price, it's the principle. Dolly was the first. And I have lost her. What do I tell her family?"

Aloysius and Charity were both lost for words.

Twenty pounds for a goat? Exorbitant! And what was this about a goat and its family? Aloysius decided that he should tread carefully. He gave Charity a meaningful look.

It was Charity's turn.

"Aloysius tells me that your goat has, er, um, a family in England?"

"All our goats have families. Families who pay for them to come to Africa. But Dolly's family was the first. From Oxford. They bought Dolly for £20, and have given her to the people of Kuwisha, as a present."

Aloysius and Charity digested this extraordinary information.

"Too much."

Aloysius broke the silence: "In Kuwisha, a goat costs very little. Your friends in Oxford are being cheated."

"Ah," said Digby. "What you have failed to take into account is the cost of vaccination, vet fees and so on. A WorldFeed goat is a happy goat, as our slogan puts it."

There were several more questions to come, for neither Charity nor Aloysius was clear about a link between goats, Kuwisha and families in England.

"Why?" asked Aloysius.

"Why what?"

"Why this goat? We have goats in Kuwisha, plenty goats."

If there was any subject that Digby was qualified to expound on it was goats. Indeed, he had written a thesis on the subject as part of his course in development studies at the University of South-West London: *Life and Livestock: Goat-gift as a Paradigm of Aid to Africa*.

Goats, he explained, were at the cutting edge of current development strategy. Gone were the days when aid agencies put their resources – Digby never used the word "money" – into development programmes, or into balance of payments support.

Aloysius coughed politely, a noise that Digby took to mean assent.

Charity looked on, non-plussed.

"Absolutely," he said, "absolutely. Seems hard to credit, but it's true. The beauty of giving a goat is that it goes to those most in need, has an immediate benefit, and then there is the demonstration effect like the hook and line, and finally the multiplier effect – the blighters breed like, well, like rabbits. There is more to it than this, of course. Not didactic, or patronising, the stakeholders are committed, and empowered. We keep paperworkn to a minimum, and for a donation of a few pounds you are the proud owner of a goat. We prefer the donors not to visit their goats, although, should they wish to, we wouldn't stop them. But everyone who gives a goat has a certificate of ownership."

Charity looked thoughtful.

"So . . ." she paused, making an effort to choose her words with care, "people in England buy goats, but they cannot keep them. Is this because their children are all at school, not like the children in Kuwisha, and no one is at home to look after them? Why then buy a goat in the first place?"

Charity spoke slowly and carefully, doing her best to summarise Digby's position on goats.

"And they give their goats to Kuwisha people?"

"Absolutely," said Digby, relieved that the general drift had been grasped.

Aloysius could not resist another question. He ignored Charity, who had moved behind Digby to ensure that she could come between this crazy white man and her street boys, who were working away in the kitchen.

"And you sell the goats to the people in Kuwisha?"

"No," said Digby. "As I said, we give the goats away."

Aloysius was astonished.

"Who gets these goats for nothing?"

"The poor people in Kuwisha."

Aloysius launched into a paroxysm of coughing, cleared his throat and before Charity could stop him, propelled the contents towards a mound of rubbish that was several feet away.

"Goats!" he said, angrily. "Eating, always eating, everything. Today there are too many goats – in my village, when I was a boy, total goats was 277. Exact. Today more than 700. These people in England . . . they must love goats too much."

Charity put her finger over her lips.

"The boy has been questioned for long enough," she said in Swahili. "It is time we let him rest. He is not well. Confused. He has no hat. And he has been in the sun for a long time – too long. This young Englishman must sit down . . . the sun can make for foolish talk."

"My boys will help you find your goat," she reassured Digby, though adding in Swahili, "I would not be surprised if they'd eaten her already."

Just then Charity's mobile rang.

"So you are back in Kuwisha, Pearson. Why are you not here, at Harrods?"

Digby could hear a tinny exchange from the receiver. Whatever was said it clearly did not impress Charity.

"He is here," she said to the caller. "He has lost his friend Dolly. Let him tell you. Digby, speak to Pearson . . ."

"What do you mean, you have lost Dolly?"

Digby launched into an explanation, but Pearson cut him short.

"If Charity is on the case, I'm sure she'll be found. But to be on the safe side, you probably should let the High Commission know. DBS. Distressed British Subject."

"Isn't that expecting too much, taking it a bit far?" said Digby. "I'm fond of Dolly, but I really don't think . . ."

Pearson had had enough.

"Look, I'll see you at Harrods tomorrow. The *FN* want me to tweak the introduction to the special report on accountancy. Gotta dash. Someone at the door."

He put the phone down.

"Callous sod . . . Now then. What will it be? Toasted cheese sandwich or mushroom omelette?"

"I hope that is not all you're offering," said Lucy.

Digby handed the phone back to Charity, sat down at the table and realised that he, just like Aloysius, was hungry. But it was not without trepidation that he took a bite of a chicken neck that Charity had placed on a white enamel plate in front of him. The first mouthful was enough.

"I say!" he exclaimed. "This is rather good."

"Just as well," said a voice behind him. "Saved your bacon! Anyone who enjoys her chicken necks can't be all bad – at least that's Charity Mupanga's view of the world."

The speaker held out his hand.

"Edward Furniver. Been pottering around the market, checking on prices for my prices index. The size of the washing soap is a third smaller than it was last month," he said. "And the poor blighters are now selling onions by the quarter . . . Things are getting harder and harder."

"Digby Adams," said Digby, looking towards the kitchen in the hope of another serving of chicken necks.

The two chatted about the merits of chicken necks with or without the piri piri sauce that was available for 5 *ngwee*, before Digby's curiosity got the better of him.

"Don't want to pry or anything," said Digby, "but I didn't entirely understand the index you said you were working on . . ."

Furniver needed no excuse.

His inspiration, he told Digby, had come from the beer index, a simple but ingenious way of determining whether an African currency was undervalued, overvalued, or about right. All one did was to put the cost – in the domestic currency – of a litre of the locally manufactured beer in one column, and in a second column put the price in US dollars, converted at the official rate of exchange.

Thus if a Tusker cost 10 *ngwee* a litre, or 50 US cents at the official rate, it was roughly on a par with the price of a similar quantity of beer produced by its regional neighbours and, moving further afield, the UK or the United States. If, however, the weakening of the *ngwee* continued, it would show up in the index.

"Let me show you," he said.

Furniver took out his laptop from its case, and prepared to enter the stats he had collected during the week. Before he started to peck with two fingers at the keyboard, he reached down to his battered brown briefcase at his feet, and extracted the monthly digest of statistics and a thick, well-thumbed volume entitled *Africa: Development Data, Published by the UN on Behalf of the World Bank.*

"Wonderful read," said Furniver. "As long as you take their figures with a pinch of salt."

It was, said Furniver, his development "bible", packed with statistics that ranged from sorghum production in Sierra Leone to maize in Malawi, infant mortality in Congo, and the population of Nigeria.

"So what is it that you do, exactly?" asked Digby.

"Collect the prices, sizes and sales of everything from salt to cigarette sticks, and the size of soaps and so on . . . smaller they are, harder the times. Plan to give a paper to the next meeting of the Kuwisha Economics Society."

"And you," said Furniver. "What do you do, Mr Adams?"

"Let me give you my card," said Digby.

It was easier said than done. What with his safari jacket and trousers, he had a dozen or more compartments to look through. His search ended in a pocket located just below his knee, and with a small cry of triumph, he came up with his card.

Furniver examined it.

"Aha! In the public relations business, I see . . ."

Digby chuckled.

"Not as such. PR went out ages ago. More sophisticated these days. More a matter of profile consultant, image improver."

Furniver took another look at the card, stiffened, and was about to say something when Digby interjected.

"Do you have a pen?" Digby asked. "Slight mistake on the card. They left out the 'senior' in my title . . . Small thing, I know, but you might want to correct it . . . I also help out with DanAid."

Furniver positively quivered with excitement.

"I know this sounds odd, but would you mind correcting the card yourself? Just to be sure . . ."

He looked over the younger man's shoulder, clearly fascinated, as Digby used the pen to amend the card, which now read:

Digby Adams
Senior International Profile Co-ordinator & Consultant
Cross-cutting Media Expert & Specialist
WorldFeed
(East Africa)

Furniver's voice seemed to rise a pitch and his hand trembled slightly as he took the card from Digby.

"And you're not employed by the UN?" he asked.

"No."

Furniver looked at the card again.

"A six-pointer, by God! A six-pointer!"

"Pardon?" said Digby.

"Sorry, old boy . . . Talking to myself. Have you given out your card to anyone else – here, in Kuwisha, I mean?"

"No, you have the very first. Why do you ask?"

Furniver gave a little hop of excitement.

"You've made an old man very happy. Not a word to the others, there's a good chap. All will be explained. A six-pointer! Never thought I'd see the day!"

"Charity!" he called. "Where are the cards? Show them to young Adams here . . . We really must squeeze in a round."

Charity produced a bundle of what at first sight appeared to be a stack of small playing cards. On closer inspection they turned out to be well-worn business cards, which she handed to Furniver.

"There is no time now for your games," said Charity sternly.

"Not even for a couple of rounds before lunch?" pleaded Furniver, shuffling the cards. "At least let me explain the rules to our visitor . . ."

11

Like most games devised to pass time at Harrods, this one was simple, childish and hugely enjoyable, especially if accompanied by a Tusker or two.

It was called "Experts", and had been thought up by Pearson during his stint as the *FN*'s Africa correspondent, while sitting in the ante-room to the office of the Nigerian minister for aid and development planning.

With the exception of Pearson, the other visitors were all supplicants for favours – a delegation of middle-aged men, including bankers, a man on his own who looked like a South African, and an east European. They had settled down for a long wait. Most were snoring gently, having first undergone the ritual of handing out the all-important, indispensable business card.

Pearson shuffled through the half dozen he had been given, and added them to the 20 or so cards he had accumulated in just the couple of days he had been away. But while he was putting the cards in alphabetical order, he came across a dozen or so that dated back to his last visit, about a year earlier. Pearson was struck by an evident change in the information on the cards.

"I call it title inflation," he had told the others on his return, when explaining the principles of the game he had devised. "Experts and consultants are now two a penny. Just like my business – it's no longer good enough to be a plain journalist. You've got to be an 'investigative journalist', or a 'columnist', or an editor of some department or region or subject; failing that, an 'executive editor' or at the very least, an 'editor at large'. As a last resort, they'll make you an 'associate editor'. So it is with the people who work for the aid donors. Plain old experts, advisors and consultants – they've all but disappeared. Now you find 'Expert Advisor' or 'Advisory Expert', or a 'Consultancy Advisor' or an 'Expert Institutional Specialist'. Just the other day, I was talking to a 'Senior Expert Advisor and Consultant'. So when I went through my collection of business cards, an idea struck me. How many experts do you think come to work in Africa every year? About 100,000. Imagine all the titles in that lot . . .

"You have a point system, of course. One point for an expert, one for a consultant, and so on. There is one important rule. You can claim any title you like in the cards in your hand, but if another player demands proof, you either produce the card with the title, or admit you were bluffing and fold. Yes, you are entitled to bluff, and claim that the card you had presented face-down on the table was worth more than – or less than – its value. Oh, and another rule: any player may include in his or her hand a new business card which has come their way – provided the point total is declared. The card can be challenged on any ground – that the title does not exist; that the points claimed are too many; or even that the card is blank. Oh yes . . . Any card connected with the UN is automatically disqualified, on the grounds that it would only encourage the buggers."

The opening hands were dealt from a pack of business cards kept on the bar counter at Harrods. Players were allowed to return one of the initial five cards into the pack, in return for another card, issued face down from the pack by the dealer. The opening move in the game was a declaration: "I am a consultant" – though seldom did anyone challenge that claim. Consultants, after all, were as common as fleas on a dog and hardly a day went by when Lucy, Charity, Pearson or Furniver did not have one of their cards pressed into their hands. Challenges became more frequent, however, as the game progressed, and after two successful challenges against them, a player had to retire.

The rejoinder to the opening challenge – "I am a consultant" – was "I am an expert", and got the game under way. As the titles became longer and grander, so the stakes rose – usually expressed in bottles of Tusker.

Cards were dealt from a stack that was regularly replenished by visitors to the bar, most of whom were unaware that they were contributing to the game.

Players could either go for broke, using the one card; more often, they would back up what they hoped was the winning claim with what they called a "full head" – four cards from different sources but with the same rank – i.e. Consultant, or Expert, Expert Consultant and so on.

In the time since Pearson had first devised the game, the all-round winner had been:

Africa against Obesity and Child Abuse
Senior Gender Specialist, Expert Consultant.

"So those are the rules. Simple, really," Furniver told a bemused Digby. "Best learnt by actually playing. Sure there is no time for a round of Experts?"

Charity was not amused.

"There are more important things, Furniver, than playing cards. Our visitor has lost his goat. She's called Dolly. And she comes from London, England. Mr Digby," she continued, "I'm going to introduce you to two of my boys who can look for this Dolly – but I think it will cost you many dough balls."

Digby's request for help finding his goat did not go down well with the boys.

"*Mzungus*," muttered Ntoto, and joined Rutere in kicking a tennis ball against the steel side of one of the Harrods containers.

Charity intervened.

"Ntoto, you will not have to do it for nothing. You will do it for dough balls, surely."

The interest of the two boys immediately picked up. The ball play stopped.

"We are listening now," said Ntoto.

"First, Mr Adams," said Charity, "you must describe your goat Dolly to these boys. Boys, listen carefully to what he says. Now, please, describe Dolly."

"She's sort of, well, goatish, really," stammered Digby, "pongs a bit, to be honest, loves chocolate . . . mustard colour, sandy I suppose, with a brown patch . . ."

Charity raised an eyebrow.

The boys looked at him with contempt.

"There are many brown goats with a patch in Kuwisha," said Rutere. "Every herd boy knows every goat in his flock, and they have names for the patches, even. Some are shaped like the *msasa* tree, some like the cloud before rain. To say you have a goat with a brown patch is like telling someone . . ." He paused. "Like telling somebody that you live in a house in London with a door, and think this is enough for them to find you."

Aloysius intervened. "I will tell them about the goat," he said to Digby. And, breaking into Swahili, he addressed Ntoto: "And don't give me any of your cheeky nonsense, you tick on a hyena's arse, or you'll get a sound thrashing."

Ntoto was about to say something equally rude, but then he remembered, much to his embarrassment, that Aloysius' taxi had been the target of one of their pranks, which had seemed entertaining enough at the time. But Aloysius had not forgotten the noxious smell that came from his taxi's driving wheel for weeks. It was never a good thing to have a fight with the Mboya Boys who had no compunction about using flying toilets as their weapon.

"Now tell them, Mr Digby," said Aloysius, reverting to English, "how much you will pay them."

The negotiations that followed were complex and protracted. Charity listened with growing admiration as Digby revealed a tougher, more subtle side to his nature. When the deal was concluded, Digby jotted down the details in his notebook.

"That is well done," she said. "I myself thought it would cost maybe six dough balls."

Ntoto and Rutere, each cramming a sugared dough ball into their mouths, headed off to the city centre – if anyone could find Dolly, or tell the boys who had eaten her, it was the cripples.

"I don't like *mzungus*," said Ntoto.

"Worse than Guchu?" asked Rutere. "Never!"

Ntoto had the last word.

"I myself would give . . ."

He paused, wanting to be certain, absolutely certain, that he really meant it.

"Yes, for sure, I would give my last dough ball to a boy who made Guchu squeal."

Rutere nodded solemnly. Ntoto was right.

"More chicken necks?" Charity asked Digby.

"That was jolly good . . . Wouldn't mind."

"Would you like a plate? Fresh! I make the best chicken necks in Kuwisha."

Digby nodded, grateful.

"For two, please."

Charity bustled off to the kitchen.

"I have a question, Aloysius," he said, examining the menu. "I understand that times are hard, but what baffles me is why a Coke and a sticky bun is so popular. Why don't poor people eat sensibly?"

"Sticky buns? Who is wanting sticky buns? Dough balls only," said Charity, returning from the kitchen.

"I was wondering why people who are poor, really hard up, don't spend their money on proper food."

He pointed to the menu which announced: *Good Sticky for Today*.

"Very good value," said Charity. "A maize cob roasted over the fire, shredded cabbage salad with vegetable oil and lemon juice dressing, chopped carrot and a cup of milky tea or glass of fruit juice," she added with satisfaction.

But just below was the option: *Bad Sticky for Today* – Cola and iced bun.

"Choice," Charity explained. "People want to choose between decent food and rubbish food. Otherwise they are like animals . . ."

Yet another aid worker, Charity thought, as she went to prepare a new batch of chicken necks in the kitchen. Another foreigner who was embarking on his disaster tour, seeking to tick off the aid industry's "big five" in the same manner as conventional tourists looked for the lion, leopard, elephant, rhino and buffalo. A visit to an Aids orphanage, to a UN feeding centre, to a donor funded school, to a low-cost housing project, and to a borehole . . . Visit Kireba and you could see all five in an hour.

Locals had learned to live with the attentions of foreign journalists, visiting pop stars, politicians and aid workers, who were also to be seen more and more frequently in Kuwisha, an increasingly fashionable destination.

Charity had lost count of the number of callers who ended their tour with a drink at the bar. Their behaviour reminded her of the only time she had visited a game park in Kuwisha, persuaded to do so by Furniver. At sundown she had sat on a game-viewing platform, overlooking a watering hole.

"These people who come to Kireba, they are like the tourists on safari," she had told Furniver. "They sit in their buses, or on their verandas, safe, and watch the animals as they come to drink water. These people who come to Harrods, they are the same, looking, looking at the animals of Kireba."

She snorted derisively.

"I hear them, Furniver. I hear them talking. They come and look at us in Kireba, as if we are animals in a game reserve. They talk, talk, talk to each other . . . 'I say, I've spotted a charcoal burner, just behind that coffin maker. And look! Just over there! An Aids orphan, being looked after by a very kind nurse.' "

And then, amused by her own vivid image, she could not help laughing, and Furniver joined in.

12

Were it not for the passion it provoked, together with a desire for revenge, the feud between Titus Ntoto and Mayor Willifred Guchu would have been amusing. It went back to that morning when a flash flood swept Ntoto and Rutere out of one of the same pipes that were now about to be laid in the earth, and which they had made their home. The onrush of water had left them half drowned on the banks of what was supposed to be a river but in fact was closer to being a sewer that ran through the slum and emptied its contents in the dam.

Ntoto, half buried in a muddy, oozing, stinking wasteland, ended up in the clutches of the man he feared and hated above all others – Mayor Guchu. Normally Guchu, widely seen as President Nduka's business partner, steered clear of Kireba, but the World Bank president was due to visit a pilot housing project the next day, and Guchu was anxious to ensure that all went smoothly.

Accompanying Guchu on that dreadful day had been his security officer, Sergeant Sokoto, who had enthusiastically administered a thorough beating to Ntoto. At one stage the mayor himself had joined in, and Ntoto had never forgotten the relish with which Guchu had whipped him. And when Ntoto told Rutere what had happened, the anger and humiliation brought tears to his eyes, and in front of his friend he made a solemn vow.

"One day I will make that Guchu squeal."

More than a year had passed since the boy's humiliation at the mayor's hands and Ntoto had yet to deliver on his threat.

"Wait until the *nshima* (porridge) is cold before you put the poison in," was an excuse that was starting to wear thin.

"If the other boys", warned Cyrus Rutere, "think you are afraid, they will not be afraid of you." As he said this, he seemed to become an old man, reflecting on the ways of the world, wise beyond his years.

His suggestion, however, of throwing a flying toilet though the window of the Rolls was dangerous, notwithstanding its superficial appeal.

Ntoto had no doubt. The mess would be cleaned up, not by the mayor or his officials, but by street boys forced to help, who would then blame Ntoto for their unpleasant experience.

"Enough nonsense, Rutere, or I will give you to *mungiki* – and you know what *mungiki* do to boys who are not circumcised."

Even the mention of *mungiki* made Rutere shudder with apprehension. The rival gang not only had a reputation for ruthless treatment of their enemies, including on-the-spot circumcision with the crudest of implements; if press reports were to be believed, they had made participation in obscene oathing ceremonies a condition of membership.

Rutere was about to protest, then saw the look on his friend's face, and thought the better of it. The hard, cold and ruthless expression belied his fourteen years, and for just a moment, Rutere felt sorry for the mayor – though only for the briefest of moments.

Digby wiped his mouth on his shirt sleeve and took a long draught of Tusker. Those chicken necks had been really, really good, and the world now seemed a better place – indeed, if only Rutere and Ntoto could find Dolly, he would call himself a happy man.

"Another Tusker? Thirsty work, those chicken necks, especially on a hot day," asked Furniver, who had reappeared, notebook in hand.

"Read my mind, would love one. How did you end up in Kireba, if you don't mind me asking, doing . . . well, whatever it is that you do?"

"How did I end up here? Luck, pure luck . . ." was Furniver's usual glib response to any question about how a wealthy London banker had come to make his home in an East African slum, running a micro lending business.

But for those who persisted, and provided he was in a good mood, he told a story which began on a miserable, rain-swept summer day in London . . .

For all his success in the City, Furniver told Digby, he had tired of the remorseless greed of his profession, had quarrelled with his wife and had been irritated by his son. He still found it painful to recall the evening he turned up at his home in Notting Hill, late as usual, to be confronted by a wife who told him that their marriage had reached an end. His son David also had news for him. He had decided to pursue his law degree and had dropped plans for a gap year in Africa.

Father and son had quarrelled and David had thrown a letter on the floor, in a gesture of defiance and an assertion of adolescent independence. It was an invitation for an interview with Water Africa, which, if successful, would have led to him spending nine months in Kuwisha helping to build a water plant in Kireba.

At the end of the sad and rancorous evening, Furniver had picked up the letter, stuck it in his pocket and had forgotten all about it until the next day when, driving into the office, he reached for his wallet and discovered the envelope.

"So I just took a chance," he said to Digby, "and went to the interview that David had arranged. The panel looked somewhat surprised to see me when I said I was there on behalf of my son – not to explain his absence, but to take his place. It was a rather odd experience, but had a happy ending."

Digby listened attentively as Furniver gave his account of what happened next . . .

"So you want to do a gap year, Mr Furniver?"

"Yes."

"In East Africa?"

"Absolutely. I'd like to take my son's place."

"Gap years are usually taken by, well, people between about 18 and 25."

"You're not discriminating against me on the grounds of age, are you?"

"Of course not, it's just that it's . . . well, a bit unusual."

"Ten minutes later they had warmed to me," Furniver told Digby, "and a week later I was off to Kuwisha to start what I hoped would be my brilliant gap year. And so within a month or so of arriving here, I had my feet under the table at Harrods wondering what the hell I was doing in the water business. One morning I helped Charity negotiate a loan that went towards buying a much-needed second-hand fridge. And from there on everything fell into place. I realised that cheap money was as important as clean water and, while I knew not a sausage about clean water, I knew a helluva lot about managing money. So I moved in to what's been home for the past three years or so."

He gestured towards the Kireba Co-operative Bank's offices, one of the handful of brick and mortar buildings in the slum, which included a one-bedroom flat on the upper floor.

He had opted to live there against the unanimous advice of Kuwisha's expatriates, who had warned him that it would be a dangerous act of folly. The expat ladies had, during the first few months of his stay, tried to persuade him to move to the safer, "low density" enclaves of civilisation, and resorted to appeals to the baser appetites of a fifty-something bachelor, making regular gifts of home-made cakes and jams.

Their husbands made clear that they regarded him as mad, a view shared by Kuwisha's remaining white settlers. Furniver had declined all offers of alternative accommodation, and to the general surprise of expatriates and settlers alike, he had come to no harm. His flat had remained unburgled, and he had yet to be mugged. Neither fact was unconnected with the discreet presence and protection of members of the Mboya Boys United Football Club, a polite name for the local gang of street children, led by Titus Ntoto; and in particular members of the under-15 football team, whose ubiquitous presence Furniver had come to take for granted.

Much against his egalitarian instincts, Furniver had agreed to employ a steward. Try as he did, he could not get used to being greeted first thing in the morning and last thing at night by a small and elderly man invariably dressed in spotless whites, his wrinkled brown knees peeping out between his long socks and his even longer shorts. Didymus Kigali made himself indispensable.

"Seems you are well known at Harrods," said Digby.

"Become my open-air office," explained Furniver.

The power supply was erratic, and although he had installed a stand-by generator, it only produced enough power to keep the all-important computer running.

However, Furniver had turned the electricity black-outs to his social advantage. The relaxed atmosphere of Harrods bar was a better place to do business than the office of the society. To see the man from whom you needed a loan sitting at a table, casually dressed, sipping a mango juice and nibbling on a handful of groundnuts, was a far less intimidating prospect for potential clients who would never have dreamt of crossing the threshold of a commercial bank.

"Tell me about your work," said Furniver, an invitation he regretted as soon as he saw Digby's eyes light up with enthusiasm.

"It has a dual thingie," said Digby earnestly, "functioning at two levels. One is a sort of play on words, like a pun, sort of, you know. The other is showing that outside help – and outsiders *can* help – on a practical basis can have a positive and constructive impact. In a very real sense. It's been a controversial issue. When the WorldFeed executive committee got to hear about it, the proverbial hit the fan. Luckily I was able to show that the vegetarian faction in WorldFeed – a nasty bunch, mark my words . . . Unless there is a purge of those blighters, they'll take over . . . where was I? Oh yes, they had made a balls-up of their figures. The protein co-efficient is never as high as they claim. Anybody who has done first year in development studies knows that."

What on earth was the boy on about, Furniver wondered, though was too polite to say as much.

"Going a bit fast for me . . ."

If Digby heard him, he gave no sign.

"All about stakeholders and the need to guarantee ownership of Africa's transition."

Digby lingered over the last words in the sentence, suggesting that they had a special significance.

Furniver decided to be obtuse.

"Confess I'm stumped . . ."

"Guaranteeing Ownership of Africa's Transition. Goat! Got it? One of the lobby groups that WorldFeed sponsors. As I said, works at two levels – intellectual and practical. Hence Dolly. We have made quite a breakthrough."

"In a very real sense, I hope," said Furniver. "Coffee?"

"Wish I'd come out here on my gap year," said Digby, washing down his last dough ball with a mouthful of Furniver's coffee made from beans collected on Charity's *shamba*.

Given that only a few minutes earlier the banker had seemed enthusiastic about the idea, the intensity of the response took Digby by surprise.

"Rot," said Furniver. "Utter rot. Waste of time."

He took another sip of his coffee and thrust the weekend edition of *The Guardian* in front of Digby's nose.

"Do you know," he said, "that I came across one ad for a gap year which talked about helping Africa, and ended with the phrase 'no experience necessary'? The gap year business has been a growth industry for years," he continued. "Their parents not only pay for the air ticket out here, they also fund the charity their children leave behind, but as soon as their children return, the good cause collapses, the clinic or whatever. It's a case of visiting far-off lands, meeting interesting people and patronising them, turning Africa into an adventure playground for middle-class youth from Europe."

Once launched he was unstoppable.

"Don't believe me?" he asked. "Well, just you have a look at the internet. Scores of websites showing young white people in charge of black people. Invariably the gap year bods hold positions of authority – administering medicine, writing on a blackboard, supervising a building project, in charge of a classroom . . . While all the time smiling black faces respond to white folks' wisdom."

It was seldom that Furniver got going like this but when he did, it was with passion and anger.

"Something is wrong," he said. "You can spend a thousand pounds for two weeks in Ghana under some 'media programme', run by an organisation that tells you that by the second day you can be broadcasting to a grateful nation. Anyone would think that Africa is populated by cretins, grateful for anybody with 'O' levels from Europe. Something is wrong," he said again.

For Furniver this was the equivalent of a speech and as he realised he'd got carried away by the subject he coughed apologetically.

"Time for a round of Experts?" he asked hopefully.

13

Digby opted for an early night, and accepted Furniver's offer of a lift to the WorldFeed headquarters where Lucy had offered him a bed.

"See you tomorrow at Harrods," said Furniver. "Pearson and Lucy will be there. And believe me, you can learn about life by sitting on your bum and looking at the world around you. It's called the gap hour, when you think and look around you. Far more important than a gap year. See you tomorrow," he called out as the taxi left the grounds.

"Next stop, the Thumaiga Club," he told the driver.

If the truth was told, he rather enjoyed the Club, bastion of privilege and order, and in particular the outspoken sentiments of its Oldest Member, who remained resolute and defiant in his unceasing battle against the follies of post-independence life.

A few evenings earlier, Furniver had been shown into the cool, dark, fusty room that was called the Club Library, frozen at a period in the past, perhaps just before Kuwisha became independent, when far more weighty matters than keeping the library up to date were on the minds of the committee.

"The member sends his apologies, suh. The night did not pass well for him. He asks you to wait. Tea, suh?"

Furniver thanked Boniface Rugiru, declined tea, and looked around.

Dornford Yates reigned supreme in that long-gone world, where members were urged to write down the title of their latest borrowing, and the date on which they borrowed it, in a notebook attached to a reading desk by a piece of string.

He came across some of his favourite reading – a series called the East Africa Year Book, and paged through the advertisements of a world long gone. The Union Castle Line, Imperial typewriters, the *Illustrated London News* – "the greatest illustrated newspaper in the world".

The book's statistics made him pause. In the mid-fifties Kuwisha had as many as 30,000 Europeans, and some 5 million Africans. Today the number of whites had halved and many of those worked for the UN and NGOs, while the African population had boomed: over 40 million – eight times that number of half a century ago.

The 1950s were a golden age for the East African traveller, an era of river boats on the Nile, flights to Sudan, picnics at Pakwach, steamers on Lake Victoria. Most were destinations that were now described as war-torn or shell-shocked, reached by pot-holed roads fast reverting to an encroaching jungle and made impassable by landmines laid by rebels and dissidents. Hotels that once provided hot showers, cold beers and clean sheets had long since become ruins.

Someone had made a desultory start to rearranging the library and clearing out unwanted novels, magazines and tracts. *All books in this box 20 ngwee.*

Furniver looked through them, and one in particular caught his eye. Young Rutere would find it useful. He dropped a note into the honesty box, and saw that the notice was dated a decade ago.

The bats were swooping low over the swimming pool, and the brief, in-between light of dusk was rapidly turning into velvet African darkness when Rugiru ushered him into the presence of the Oldest Member.

Although he had misgivings about patronising an institution that was a refuge for the country's elite, it had an abiding appeal, for it was an obvious sanctuary for a newly arrived white man in Africa. Furniver's membership of his London club included reciprocal terms for Kuwisha's centre of privilege, defended by its now overwhelming black membership as vigorously as it had ever been during the years of colonial rule.

For his first few nights in Kuwisha, Furniver had taken a room there, and the man he came to call the Oldest Member had been one of the few at the Club to welcome him with anything like genuine warmth, offering to nominate him should he wish to become a full member.

The exchanges had led to something that became friendship and for all the conservative views expressed by the old chap, who had been a district commissioner when the country was ruled by the British, Furniver came to enjoy their sessions.

Once a week, usually on a Wednesday, he dropped in for a gin and tonic and a natter with the OM, crusty and cantankerous though he was. Had his outspoken views been uttered by anyone else, they would have attracted the attention of the country's special branch.

There was much speculation about the reasons for this apparent immunity. Some members recalled a rumour that he had known the Ngwazi in the war years before independence; others suggested that at heart the OM was a "liberal", whatever the impressions to the contrary. All members, however, had come to accept the old boy as a fixture, rather like the contents of the musty Club library, with its first editions, comfortable leather armchairs and out-of-date club announcements on a green-baized notice board with a pencil stub hanging from a string.

The OM spotted the approaching Furniver.

"Mr Rugiru!" he roared. "Gin and tonic for my friend, and more cashew nuts, if you please! And don't forget fresh lemon."

Pleasantries with his guest exchanged, the OM got down to business.

"Going to get on my soapbox and have one of my whaddyacallems? Rants, that's it, when I let off steam."

He winked at Furniver.

"Always feel better afterwards."

When the old boy was on form, the passionate outbursts and tirades, delivered in staccato form and pace, were a stimulating mixture of prejudice, shrewd insights and lessons drawn from decades of experience as a district officer in pre-independence Kuwisha.

On this particular evening, the Oldest Member began with a salvo against members of Africa's post-independence generation – the "born-frees", as they were known.

"Got everything on a plate," declared the OM.

"On a plate," said Furniver emphatically, nodding as if in enthusiastic agreement, while allowing himself to drift away and think about how he might persuade Charity Mupanga to give her hand in marriage.

"On a plate," he said again.

He recalled her smile – not to mention her splendid teeth, revealed to their best effect when eating corn off a fresh-roasted cob . . .

"One year," said the OM, getting into his stride, "the indigenous were bending their backs under the burden of the colonial yoke, the next year they were running the show, their bums in the butter. And their sons and daughters, the so-called 'born-bloody-frees', joined their parents and put their own snouts in the trough."

"Snouts," said Furniver, nodding his head.

What was more, Charity's sense of humour was tuned to his own . . .

"Soon it all went wrong."

The OM popped a couple of cashews into his mouth.

"Went wrong, absolutely, wrong," said Furniver.

As for her dancing . . .

"Take Boniface, for example. Had he been born a couple of years earlier, he would have got a job in the civil service, when the Brits pulled out."

Boniface Rugiru didn't look up from the glasses he was polishing at the bar. It was not the first time he had heard the OM let off steam.

"Hips," said Furniver.

The way she moved her hips . . .

"For God's sake, Edward, stop thinking about that woman. Time you made an honest man of yourself."

Furniver was jolted back to the real world.

"Word of advice. Do it. Clearly a sensible woman. Way she handled your *jipu*."

A cloud crossed the OM's face.

"Many a marriage would have been saved in the bad old days had a district officer been able to have their *jipus* dealt with. One lad had the thing on his wotsit, buggered around with it, got an abscess, and damn near cost him the family jewels. Wife left him. Poor show. Gather Charity and her cousin, wotshername, Mercy, did a damn good job on you."

The fly known as the *jipu* had a propensity to lay its eggs in laundry hung out to dry, all too often preferring underpants; and when an egg, thriving in warm sweaty crevices, became a maggot, the itch that signalled its presence was as irritating as it was embarrassing.

For a few moments, both men seemed lost in memories that were too painful or too personal to reveal.

"Patronage," said the OM, breaking the silence. "Curse of the continent."

He tossed a handful of cashew nuts into his mouth, and Furniver prepared to take evasive action. The combination of dentures that didn't quite fit, a subject that provoked a passionate response, and a handful of cashews almost invariably led to the listener being enveloped in a formidable spray of partly chewed nuts.

"Corruption."

The OM looked defiantly at Furniver, as if challenging him to contradict an assertion of a self-evident and universal truth.

"Patronage!" he continued. "Just a polite way of saying corruption. Destroys the whole country. See it everywhere."

He prodded the pile of newspapers that lay on the table, full of reports about looming hunger and imminent famine in north-east Kuwisha, and claims that business men and politicians were making millions out of food imports on which they had avoided paying tax but priced as if they had – thus doubling their profit.

North East Province was in "a food deficit situation" according to the UN World Food Programme, which was appealing to international donors to rally round. The OM stabbed the offending article with a nicotine-stained forefinger.

"There! Read it for yourself."

Furniver put on his specs, and obeyed. But by the end of the account, he was no wiser.

"Usual weasel phrases by the WFP," he said hopefully, but pretty sure that he had missed the offending point.

The OM stayed silent, and Furniver tried again.

"Can't let the blighters starve . . ."

His voice trailed off, knowing that the OM was perfectly capable of calling for such drastic action.

"Let the blighters starve, you say? Steady on! Still, good to hear you calling for no-nonsense measures. Let the blighters starve!"

The OM shook his head, like a parent unsure whether their child's precocity should be reined in or rewarded.

"Don't suppose you can help it. Chip off the old block."

Furniver groaned inwardly, and looked around the bar to see who was in earshot. Boniface continued polishing the glasses. About a dozen members sat gossiping, in various stages of inebriation.

One of them looked his way, a former justice minister who had strong views on the benefits of capital punishment. The

Oxford-educated lawyer caught Furniver's eye and gave him the thumbs-up.

Furniver's reputation for being to the right of the most conservative of settlers owed much to the OM. God knows how the misunderstanding had arisen. The OM had also got it into his head that Furniver was related to a notorious colleague from his colonial days, called Miles "Flogger" Moreland, now living in retirement on the coast, and whose willingness to use his *sjambok*, a rhino hide whip which never left his side, was legendary.

Sometimes Furniver wondered whether he was not the butt of a perverse game, the nature and purpose of which was known only to his tormentor. He had once tried to suggest as much, and was greeted with a look of such glacial incomprehension from the OM's pale blue eyes that he had felt obliged to beat a confused retreat.

"You get carried away," his host had remonstrated. "Bit too enthusiastic for the old days and its ways. Best kept under your hat."

The OM, whose voice carried across the Club room at the best of times, repeated his advice with a roar that could be heard at the swimming pool.

Furniver took another sip of his drink, and waited for his host to get to the point.

"How's Flogger? Still living on the coast, is he?"

The Oldest Member did not wait for a reply. Instead he stabbed the newspaper, covered in underlinings, exclamation marks and scribbled notes.

"Now, that one, read that ad."

Furniver took a closer look.

The UN Development Programme and WorldFeed were seeking a "regional transport expert co-ordinator" to operate in North East Province. The successful applicant would be expected to liaise closely with government agencies and oversee a communications strategy, in which the applicant displayed an ability to implement a comprehensive "knowledge management process".

Furniver read it carefully, but still found it hard to grasp what the OM was banging on about.

"Absolutely," he said.

"Thank God for that! Thought the penny would never drop! More cashews, Mr Rugiru, and bring on the gin and tonic. Now let me tell you about the North East . . ."

Furniver went for a pee. It was going to be one of those nights.

14

In his office in the suburban enclave which housed all the UN agencies, Anders Berksson was working late, studying the grim findings of the latest economic review of Kuwisha, which showed that 60 per cent of its people were living on $2 a day. To Berksson's dismay, the report had already reached Head Office, and had triggered a predictable response.

In such a promising environment, HQ had noted, there could be no excuse whatsoever for the fact that the UN Development Programme was facing a humiliating prospect. An agency that should be playing a leading role in Kuwisha's struggle to overcome poverty was failing to reach its budget target, let alone exceed it by a respectable amount. Unless it raised its game, UNDP would actually underspend in the current year by as much as 3 per cent.

A knock on the door interrupted Berksson's depressing reading. His deputy, an Argentinean econometrician, widely regarded as one of the most talented employees in the organisation, had come to offer some solace.

"Don't blame yourself," he argued. "You could not have done more."

He ticked off Berksson's achievements: "Let's begin with education."

Children of UN employees, he pointed out, now had a choice: to attend the local international school or to go abroad.

"Or take security," he continued.

The growing problem of law and order in Kuwisha had led to a doubling of security patrols for UN workers and their families.

"And health," he went on.

Health insurance had been extended, and treatment could now be obtained in Europe.

"The fact is, the spending problem is structural. We live in a society where graft has been institutionalised. How can we possibly exceed our budget targets under these circumstances? Every project has to be reviewed, and the outcome, as likely as not, is cancellation, suspension or further review – usually at the pre-implementation stage."

Berksson nodded.

"I tried telling that to headquarters and it didn't get me very far."

He had listed the problems they had faced over the years, including past attempts to bring water to Kireba – at least 80 per cent of the projects had failed, despite UNDP's best efforts.

The two men stood at the window, taking in the lights of the city.

"Good luck! You really deserve it."

The deputy handed over the latest assessment of spending in the financial year ending that month, and bade farewell. He was due to present his paper to a conference in Abuja: *Discretionary Funding in Times of Austerity: The Kireba Experience.*

This time, Berksson pledged, it would be different.

True, the news on the economic front was grim. The agency's spending was down nearly 4 per cent, if the last quarter's figures were taken on an annualised basis. And there was worse to come.

The latest analysis suggested that over the four years that Berksson had been in charge, spending had fallen nearly 5 per cent.

"God knows I did my best," he muttered to himself.

The new highway scheme had been cancelled, he pointed out, when it was discovered that the fruit processing project it was intended to serve happened to be located a few miles from President Nduka's birthplace. That, coupled with the consultant's report that questioned the viability of growing fruit in an area that was near-desert, was enough to put the scheme on ice.

Then there was the proposed harbour extension! A victim of a cement scam. As for the new tourist resort on the coast, it had been unfortunately set back by the disclosure that most of the Cabinet had title deeds for land located in the centre of the planned development.

It would not be easy to rally the development agencies behind the Kireba project, but Berksson was determined to put his heart into the president's scheme.

"Bring me paper," he growled. "Bring me paper."

It was time to call in a couple of IOUs from that Mauritius freebie, Commonwealth Finance ministers on global warming. Or was it the Maldives? Didn't matter. How did the proverb go? Something about drums and drummers, pipers and tunes . . .

He searched his mobile for names and numbers.

Adams, that was it. Digby Adams. How had his DanAid colleague described the boy?

"A tosser, but a tosser with talent."

The same description could apply to Japer, Jasper Japer, the acclaimed host of the previous year's NoseAid appeal, and columnist with the leading London tabloid, the *Clarion*. Didn't matter. He needed the talents of both of them.

Berksson buzzed his secretary. Within a few minutes, she put him through.

The bats were still wheeling and swooping above the Thumaiga Club pool when Furniver returned from the Gents, determined to stand up for himself.

"Somebody has to do the job and feed the people," he said, risking the wrath of his friend. "Even if that ad is gobbledygook and they pay their staff too much. Talking to Lucy the other day, and she reckons that a million people are at risk in the province . . ."

"Balls," said the OM, thumping the newspaper that lay on the table between them. "Absolute balls! Who is counting? Got a soft spot for the girl. Lot of guts, But how does she know? Millions! What she means is that an awful lot of people are hungry in North East Province. But no one knows how many live there, let alone how many of them are hungry. The last census was a bloody fiasco. Sending Kiyus to count Liyus simply doesn't work. Both believe they are the biggest tribe, neither will take second place.

"Apart from the fact they can't stand each other, outcome affects the army. Ethnic balance, they call it. The number of Kiyus and the number of Liyus are supposed to reflect the population make-up. That's the law. The last count was during the bad old days when we were in charge, and even then it was dodgy. Give me one, just one, statistic you can trust," demanded the Oldest Member.

He shook the paper like a dog with a rat. According to a front-page report, more than 5 million people had died in the war in the Congo.

"Five million? Can you believe it? Truth is, we really haven't a clue. When we say a million, we mean a lot. When we say 5 million, we mean a helluva lot. And when we talk about genocide, we mean that a helluva of a lot are dying, in an especially nasty way, in a very short time."

The OM took a long draught of his gin and tonic.

"When it comes to most African statistics, one should pause for thought and add a bucket of salt. There's an outfit that claims 4 million African children under age five die every year of preventable illness. Could be less, could be a lot more."

He shook his head and toyed with a handful of cashew nuts.

"Gone off my feed," the OM explained.

Furniver felt obliged to come to the defence of the aid agencies.

"NoseAid raised 5 million quid for mosquito nets. Isn't that a good thing? Millions at risk and so on . . ."

The comment just fuelled the OM's wrath.

"Why aren't the governments leading the way? Buying the nets themselves. Anyway, how do you know that a million people die from malaria each year? Could be twice that, could be half that. The truth is, we don't know. And how could we?"

The OM paused long enough to take a swig of his G and T.

"When we gave these chaps independence . . ."

He started again.

"When they won 'the war of liberation', as we must now say, the stats departments were the first to be run down. Then when it became clear that the place was going down the tube, the IMF and the World Bank demanded figures before they could help out with loans. Fair enough . . . by the way, how's your cost of living wheeze going?"

For several weeks Furniver had been preparing his own economic index, based on prices and sizes of market goods, and had put his ideas to the OM. Tonight, however, he was more interested in what the OM was saying.

"Fine," Furniver replied, "just fine . . ."

"Bit hush hush, is it? Understand why. Damn sure it will show that most of the local stats are made up."

He held a finger to his lips.

"Hush hush! Say no more. Lips sealed, tight as a monkey's arse . . . Where was I? Oh yes . . . That's when guesses and thumb sucks came in. It suited both donors and the government, IMF and World Bank – they pretended to monitor the terms of their loans, and our chaps pretended to meet the conditions, but spent the cash on homes in London. Result: complete cock-up. The fact is", snorted the OM, "there is barely an African statistic that is not the product of a statistician's thumb suck, a politician's self-interest, UN guesswork or an NGO's wishful thinking."

The Oldest Member coughed again.

"Here endeth the first lesson. Don't trust the stats. More to say, but feeling a bit off colour."

That night Digby Adams fell into his bed at the WorldFeed house, exhausted. And although he slept soundly, his dreams were vivid and colourful.

Chicken necks had come to life, walking across the table tops at Harrods on stunted bandy legs, and singing hymns. Small boys pelted them with dough balls and flying toilets that whizzed through the air, bursting on impact and releasing thousands of business cards that settled like confetti as he and Dolly pranced and danced to a band of Tuskers, each bottle blowing a trumpet.

But when he awoke the next morning, his spirit was high, his enthusiasm undiminished and to his amazement and delight, his safari suit, socks and pants had been washed, ironed and returned neatly folded, awaiting him alongside a tray of tea.

Africa, he decided, was where he belonged and where he was needed.

It was only when he had poured a second cup that he saw the message, written on a scrap of paper attached to the day's papers:

"Mister Digby, Please call Mister Berksson, urgent, at UNDP."

Digby rang from the old Bakelite phone that was in the hallway, and was put through to Berksson immediately. Ten minutes later the two men had agreed to a proposal that would change the face of Kireba.

15

"Furniver, have you noticed anything strange about my rats?" asked Charity.

He thought carefully.

If anybody was behaving a trifle strangely, surely it was Charity, what with her growing concern about the men in brown suits, an extraordinary interest in toilets and her preoccupation with the flavouring of yesterday's avocado soup. Furthermore, what Furniver called her time of the month was fast approaching – the stock-taking exercise that Charity loathed. He had no intention, however, of saying any of this – but there was no safe answer.

A breath of criticism, real or imagined, about her rats, as she called Ntoto and Rutere, and Charity would be down on him like a ton of bricks; but if he had nothing to offer he would get terrible stick, for it would be seen as evidence of his indifference to their welfare.

"Apart from the fact that Rutere is picking his nose more often, I can't say I have."

He took a sip of his coffee and paged through the manual he had bought the previous evening.

Charity began spluttering in fury.

Uh-uh, thought Furniver. Here it comes!

"How can you call Rutere a nose-picker?"

Charity drew herself up, puffed out her chest:

"Rutere is not nose-picking. If you look, you will see that his finger does not go inside the nose hole. Never," said Charity. "Never. Since he first came, that Rutere, and asked to work in the kitchen, he has been the boy who always washes his hands.

Always! I put him in charge of all the kitchen *totos*, in charge of hand washing. A very important job. Now tell me, Edward Furniver, would I, Charity Tangwenya Mupanga, owner and manager of the best bar in Kireba, the best place to water your mouth, official, put a boy who is a nose-picker in charge?"

She wagged her index finger to underline her point, and her voice rose as the enormity of the accusation struck her anew: "Edward Furniver, I ask you, would I put him in charge of hand washing for kitchen *totos*?"

In the three years Furniver had come to know, admire, respect and love the formidable woman before him, he had learnt one enduring lesson. When she called him Edward Furniver, it was time to abandon all positions, however sincerely held, and to beat a retreat.

This time his retreat was neither fast enough or far enough.

"All I can say is thank God you make them wash their hands before working in the kitchen . . ."

Furniver got no further.

"No more nonsense, Furniver. Using his finger is Rutere's way of showing that he is thinking. He is a clever boy. He is not foolish. Edward Furniver, how can you say he is nose-picking when you yourself said that he is the cleverest boy not to have gone to St Joseph's school. Tell me! Now you call him stupid! Shame!"

Although Furniver had got used to Charity's flights of fury, he still made the mistake of trying to defend himself.

"I never said the boy is stupid. I just wish that when he thinks, his finger is kept well clear of his nostril."

Like a storm that had blown itself out, Charity's burst of anger abruptly ended.

"Furniver, you are right. Rutere is doing too much thinking these days. He is too young to have all these thoughts in his head."

Charity sucked air through her teeth in a way that indicated concern.

One day, thought Furniver, one day I will ask her how she does that. The mechanics were easy. Anyone could suck air through their teeth, whether through front teeth or side teeth. The great mystery was how to achieve the impression created by the sound, which conveyed irritation or contempt, concern or satisfaction, and subtle gradations of the same.

Just like his house steward, Didymus Kigali and his repertoire of coughs – the interrogative, the placatory, the apologetic – the sound of clicks made with tongue and teeth, sounds of air sucked in, or expelled, they all extended the capacity to express oneself, almost as if one spoke another language.

"Furniver! Furniver!" she said sharply, seeing him start to drift off. "It is more than a problem of nose-picking. Yesterday, even, there were no words when they shared a dough ball. It is not right. Best friends are fighting, always fighting. How can young boys, teen boys even, say polite things all the time? Saying thank you, and please, and begging pardon?"

She knew she was right to be worried; for if the riots had strained the friendship of Ntoto and Rutere, could any friendship not built on tribal identity, survive the stress and strain of politics in Kuwisha?

The squall had passed and Furniver knew that it would be a good time to change the subject.

"Found Rutere under my taxi the other day", he said as if nothing had happened, "checking the brake wotsits . . . The next day he was back again, this time under the bonnet, like a rat down a drain, tinkering away, as happy as a pig in the proverbial."

Charity grunted non-committedly, wondering what was going to come next.

"I thought I'd give him this."

He held up the battered old manual.

"Found it in the sale box last night, in the library, at the Club."

He handed it to Charity for inspection.

She read out the title: *Maintaining Your Car: A Do-It-Yourself Guide.*

"With any luck the boy might become a decent mechanic," said Furniver. "The only way out of Kireba is to learn a skill or a trade and there will always be a need for mechanics. And judging by the number of old bangers that are kept on the road, there must be some pretty smart garage chaps in Kuwisha."

"Furniver," said Charity, "you are dreaming again . . . and this is one of your dreams that I like very much. Rutere is a lucky boy to have this fine book."

They handed it over to Rutere when he turned up for kitchen duty. A scowling Ntoto could not resist making derogatory comments about his friend's ambition. Rutere, however, ignored the jibes.

"One day," he said, "I will be in charge of your car engine, Mr Furniver, suh. And I will keep it in the very best condition."

"Jolly good," said Furniver, feeling somewhat embarrassed. "Now get lost, Rutere, I'm trying to work."

Ntoto and Rutere, the latter clutching the manual, took their breakfast of *ugali* and relish to their favourite perch in the eucalyptus trees, where they were able to monitor the comings and goings of visitors, whether aid workers, UN officials, or members of Guchu's staff on reporting missions to their boss.

"That bulldozer, it is like an animal, every night taken back to its compound," observed Rutere.

As he spoke, the mayor's vintage Rolls Royce, polished and gleaming, drew up on a rise overlooking the slum, like a predator surveying the land before a potential kill.

"Guchu's car," said Rutere. "He loves it more than his women . . . They call it Guchu's best friend."

Ntoto studied the Rolls, barely a hundred paces from where they were concealed, its paintwork aglow, silver door handles shining. With the boys looking on, watching his every move, the plump, besuited figure of Mayor Guchu himself emerged from the car. Hands on hips, he surveyed the slum that spread out before him. There was something odd, distasteful, almost sexual in what happened next.

Guchu caressed the bonnet of the car, sliding his hand along its jet black surface like a farmer stroking his prize cow. As Ntoto watched, saying not a word, a look came into his eyes that Rutere recognised, one of frustration and fury combined. Long experience told Cyrus that this was not a time to question his friend. When Ntoto was in one of these moods, it was best to concentrate on finding ways to bring him out of it.

"Let's go fishing, Ntoto . . ."

Titus Ntoto was as happy as a street boy could get, paddling and splashing in the muddy shallows of the dam which had once been the home of the Kuwisha Sailing Club. He watched as Rutere made his way over some stepping stones towards him. In one hand he held the car maintenance instruction manual; in the other a fishing hook made out of a bent pin, cork and line of string.

"This way, Rutere!" he called out.

The boys spread themselves out on the bank, put the makeshift tackle together, and watched the cork for any sign of a fish that might have taken the bait. Ntoto picked up the manual.

"Be careful with that," said Rutere. "That is very, very important information. It tells you how cars work, and how you must look after them, and not let bad things happen to them."

Ntoto, whose ability to read did not match that of Rutere, struggled with the table of contents.

"How to make sure your battery does not go flat . . . how to make sure your brakes always work . . . how to make sure your steering is always reliable . . . When I grow up, Rutere, I will pay boys to look after my car," scoffed Ntoto. "I don't need a book like this." He made as if to throw it in the water, much to Rutere's alarm.

Ntoto read on: "Always check your tyre pressure. Always make sure your tyres have a good tread . . .

"What is this nonsense, Rutere? It is useless."

He was about to toss it at Rutere's feet when a section must have caught his eye. But this time he read it to himself, his lips moving as he formed the words. And as he read, his face changed, lit up by whatever it was he had discovered.

He changed his tune: "Phauw, Rutere, this is a very interesting book indeed . . ."

It must have been a good half hour later that Ntoto made the announcement that Rutere feared might never happen.

"I am now ready to make Guchu squeal. First, Rutere, we must collect sugar. At least three kilos."

"And where do we get this sugar?" Rutere asked. "It is very expensive."

Ntoto shrugged. "Where do you think, Rutere? From the kitchen at Harrods. We steal it."

Rutere was shocked, as much by the matter-of-fact indifference displayed by his friend at the prospect of stealing from their protector, as by the hard and tough expression on his face.

"End of this playing nonsense," said Ntoto. "It is time to do business with Guchu."

16

Getting the key to the padlock of the shipping container that held the stores turned out to be easy, far easier than Ntoto and Rutere had expected. But what impressed and disturbed Rutere was not only his friend's cunning and guile, but evidence of a streak of gratuitous cruelty.

Mildred Kigali's back had been turned, and it was simple for Ntoto to seize the opportunity to extract the key from the padlock that secured the container in which valuable items, including sugar, were stored.

The timing could not have been better. Didymus Kigali had summoned his wife for lunch. Mildred had responded like the old-fashioned spouse she was to the call from an old-fashioned husband, who expected immediate compliance. A second after the call came, Ntoto slipped the key into his trousers.

"Phauw!"

Mildred looked at the padlock with an expression of mild surprise, for she had no recollection of taking the key. She patted the pockets of her apron. Nothing. She was about to ask Ntoto, who had busied himself washing his hands, when Didymus called yet again, a note of impatience in his voice.

"I'm coming," Mildred responded.

With a couple of backward glances, just in case the key had dropped to the ground, she set off on the short journey to Edward Furniver's flat, above the offices of the bank.

What happened next made Rutere uneasy. Other street boys would have stolen the key, and that would be that. But Ntoto displayed truly exceptional cunning . . .

Mildred's journey to the flat required some concentration. For a few perilous steps one had to keep to the stepping stones that had been installed by the Mboya Boys under Furniver's directions. One misstep and you could end up in the evil-smelling mire that only polite people called mud. Mildred was half way across when Ntoto called out.

"The key, Mrs Mildred, you have dropped the key."

Mildred, who denied that she was going deaf, may or may not have heard . . . But as it transpired, the object of Ntoto's call was not Mildred but Charity, who was busy serving customers.

On her return, Mildred had searched her pockets, and looked on the ground, and it was at this point that Ntoto intervened.

"Mama, you dropped the key on your way to Mr Kigali. I called to tell you when you were crossing."

"Yes, Mildred," confirmed Charity, "I heard Ntoto call."

Mildred shrugged.

Perhaps she *had* dropped the key . . . But the prospect of sieving through the filth was not one that appealed to her. And it would cost a fortune in dough balls to get a street boy to do it. Better get a new key cut . . .

Then came the gesture that infuriated Mildred, a gesture that was quite unnecessary in Rutere's opinion. Knowing that the old lady was watching, Ntoto made circular movements with his forefinger, held against his head, while rolling his eyes and winking at Rutere.

If looks could kill, Ntoto would have been a dead boy . . .

Equipped with the key, it was a simple matter to carry out the opening raid on the sugar.

"How much do we need?" asked Rutere.

Rutere was shocked by the amount that Ntoto said they had to steal.

"At least three kilos," repeated Ntoto.

"More if we want to make *changa*."

*

What the boy had not reckoned on, however, was that Charity was preparing to check the stocks earlier than usual, and the missing sugar was immediately spotted.

Charity was not sure what irritated her most: that almost certainly the boys were stealing her sugar, although she could not prove it; or her response to the problem. She was reacting just like a white madam, angered by a thieving houseboy who watered the gin and put tea in the whisky. Much to her chagrin, she had concluded there was nothing for it but to consult Results Mudenge.

"I feel very foolish," she confessed to Mudenge when she went for a consultation at his Klean Blood Klinic. Results raised his eyebrows and initially said nothing. Years of experience had taught him that the most effective way of getting information from a client with troubles was to stay silent, look sceptical, and wait for the customer to elaborate.

"I am sure the street boys are stealing sugar," Charity concluded, "and I don't know how to stop them. But I do not want to be always watching, and using colonial tricks to catch houseboys."

Mudenge shrugged and broke his silence.

"Dogs bark, goats have ticks, street boys steal. That is the nature of street boys – they cannot help stealing. The only way is to deal with them as the settlers did. I know that the white madams were cheeky – but sometimes they were also clever. And they spent a lot of time finding ways to discover who was stealing their sugar. We can learn from them."

Charity looked miserable.

"But Mr Mudenge, I heard that the madams used poison. How can it be right to poison small boys' stomachs, even street boys, for stealing sugar?"

"As I said to you, Mrs Mupanga, the settler madams were clever."

He lowered his voice.

"Let me tell you a secret . . ."

"Phauw!" said Charity when Mudenge had finished, and laughed. "Very clever," she said. "So you will help me, Mr Mudenge?"

"Of course. And you pay on results only. But I believe, Mrs Mupanga, my *muti* will work . . ."

The time had come to put Mudenge's *muti* – a combination of wisdom, herbs and old bones – to the test. The stealing had to be nipped in the bud . . .

Titus and Cyrus had been expecting a reaction from Charity and, although faster than they had anticipated, her summons to attend an investigation into the missing sugar had come as no surprise.

On Mudenge's instructions Charity had drawn up a notice, worded exactly as he suggested.

"WARNING," it said in bright red letters across the top of the page. "*Notice to street boys*," it continued. "*There is a very important meeting today, 3 pm sharp, for all Mboya Boys to discuss SUGAR that has gone missing. ALL street boys to attend. Dough balls suspended until further notice.*"

Within minutes of it being pinned to the blackboard, which also carried the menu for the day, the street boys had gathered around, chattering like chickens facing the dinner pot.

Later that day, they assembled at the entrance to Harrods, nervous as birds, and smelling like dogs. Most had bottles of glue, their heavy-lidded eyes and dilated pupils testifying to their regular sniffing, their threadbare grubby clothes stained by the mud and squalor that was Kireba.

Charity stepped up, wiping her hands on her green apron.

"Mr Mudenge is coming in a minute. We know the boys who are guilty. Mr Mudenge has already used *muti* to find out. Do they want to be brave, behave like men, and step forward for their punishment?"

Rutere nudged Ntoto.

"Do they want to be foolish . . . like women?"

Ntoto suppressed a giggle. No one moved and the group looked on, anxiously awaiting the next development.

Results Mudenge arrived on cue, stood in front of the blackboard and told the boys to gather round. With a flourish, he removed a cloth that was covering an object on the tray that he held. It revealed a brown packet which was marked, in black capital letters, front and back, POISON.

With the boys looking on, fascinated, Mudenge dipped a teaspoon into the bag, held it up as if judging the quantity and quality, and sprinkled what looked to be a white powder over the sugar bin held by Charity Mupanga. He then stirred in the powder until it was thoroughly mixed.

Charity watched with growing alarm.

"Mr Mudenge. Are you sure you have not given too much?"

"It is the right dose, Mrs Mupanga. It is enough to kill a mouse but let a street boy stay alive, although feeling very, very unwell. It is the right dose."

"It looks very strong to me," said Mildred, who had interrupted her work on the vegetables to watch the proceedings. "But I am not sure whether it is strong enough for street boys who steal."

She looked at Ntoto.

A shudder of apprehension ran through the ranks of the assembled street children. Many of them had no doubt that Mildred was a witch; and all of them, including Ntoto and Rutere, had a healthy respect for her sharp tongue and firm hand.

"No boys ready to behave like men?" asked Charity.

Her mood was not helped by some gratuitous advice from Ntoto and Rutere.

"I think," said Rutere, running his finger round his nostril, "that Cephas, who is a circumcised street boy, has been the one stealing the sugar. Boys who are circumcised are usually thieves."

Ntoto could not resist chipping in. "I myself think that *mungiki* are stealing the sugar. Or perhaps it is a *tokolosh*," he said, referring to that creature with the mysterious ability to take the shape of a donkey or a goat and which was often accused of mischievous deeds. "But Rutere is right. You should first look for Cephas. He is a circumcised boy and you never can trust those people."

Charity was about to remonstrate. The politics of the foreskin had become more and more powerful since the riots.

"A cold Tusker over here," called out a customer and she went back to the bar, leaving the boys to continue their talk in private.

"Sometimes", said Ntoto, "she must think we are stupid, Rutere. I think she and Mr Mudenge are using the trick of settler madams."

Rutere nodded. "A very old trick," he said, but added: "You still have not told me, Ntoto, why we are stealing sugar?"

"Wait," said Ntoto. "Be patient. But we must look out for Mr Mudenge. He is very, very clever."

That night the boys raided the sugar once again.

Rutere looked suspiciously at the fine white powder that had been sprinkled over the top of the container.

"I bet it is flour," said Rutere, "I am certain sure she would not use poison. Mudenge maybe. Mrs Mildred, yes, but Mrs Charity . . ."

The two boys examined the sugar carefully, and blew away a fine white dust. There was definitely contamination of the sugar. Ntoto licked his index finger, plunged it into the bin, and withdrew it, coated with a white powder.

Rutere tried to stop him, but it was too late. Ntoto licked his finger clean. A few seconds later he collapsed, holding his stomach, clearly in agony.

"Rutere," he moaned, and Cyrus knelt next to his friend.

"Doctor," Ntoto pleaded, "call doctor," before lapsing into unconsciousness.

17

It was unusual for Furniver to visit the OM on successive days, but signs that the old boy's health was uncertain had alarmed him. The Sportsman cigarettes were given only a token puff or two before being discarded; the cashew intake was dropping; and the gin and tonics becoming stronger, and increasing in frequency.

The evening began in the time-honoured manner, with the OM bellowing his order at Boniface: "The usual, please Mr Rugiru, and something for our guest."

Then followed the OM reminiscing about pre-independence days, when he won a reputation as the toughest district officer in the country. But when Furniver encouraged him to comment on current events, the OM could not contain himself. Indeed, he was so angry that he nearly forgot to order a second gin and tonic for his guest.

"Sorry, old boy. Distracted. Been reading the bloody Overseas papers again."

Despite his anger – or perhaps because of it – he still managed to imbue the word with the status of a capital letter, along with half a dozen others – such as Continent, Overseas, Abroad and Foreigners.

He tapped the offending article in *The Guardian*, a paper he claimed to dislike but read assiduously. "Know the enemy, what?" he would say to Furniver.

"Their Africa chap writes about the locals who were born after Kuwisha got independence. Says they are called the 'born free' generation."

He took a long draught of his G and T and ordered another round.

"The bloody feckless generation, if you ask me. Just look about you . . . Don't forget the lemon," he called after Rugiru. "Make sure the glass is cold and don't be stingy with the nuts . . ."

"Every time, without failing," Boniface Rugiru complained to his deputy as he made up the order. The ambitious young man who had his eye on Rugiru's job, said nothing, while Rugiru engaged in a jolly good moan.

"When did I forget he wants his glass chilled? Never. When do I forget that the gin must be kept in the freezer? Never. And the tonic must be near to freezing? Never. And the lemons – fresh every day from the garden. Never. And cashew nuts, do I ever give a stingy? Never."

Rugiru emptied a packet of cashews into a large wooden bowl.

"Never! That old man . . ."

He shook his head.

Boniface took the drinks to where the OM sat with Furniver.

From their table, they could see the trunk of a palm tree, stretching beyond the roof, illuminated by a light in the courtyard.

"Seventy years old and in its prime," said the OM, who went on to point out that the rings on the bark indicated its age. "Apply much the same principle in Africa."

"What d'you mean?"

"You must have seen it yourself," said the OM. "Africa shows its age like the rings on a tree trunk."

"Don't get you," said Furniver.

"Straightforward, really," said the OM.

He adjusted his thin, lanky frame in his favourite wicker chair.

"Remember me telling you about back to the future? Days when there were more places to fly to in the region than there are today?"

Furniver nodded.

"Absolutely. Matter of fact, I was looking at the old East Africa guides from the '50s, splendid collection in the library."

The OM's eyes lit up: "Morning at the Murchison, picnic at Pakwach, sandwiches in Sudan, that sort of thing . . . ending the day in a decent hotel. Those were the days, the good old bad old days, before independence."

But more than travel destinations that were no longer on departure boards, and timetables long abandoned, were on the OM's mind.

It turned out that over the weekend the former district commissioner had made a nostalgic drive back into his past, and it had been an uncomfortable experience.

"There are landmarks all around. Like rings on that palm tree. Saturday. Drove to my old office, near Somabula, down a pot-holed memory lane. Wished I hadn't. You could date the decline. My office, barely standing. Rose garden? Might never have been there. Independence in '63. Rot starts. Country club – now a drinking den. The last dairy farm, few miles on – closed. Patel's shut down in '66, when Indians lost their trading licences. Dam – used to sail there, provided water for the whole district – now silted up. Clinic – run out of drugs . . . all rings on Africa's post-independence trunk."

He sighed, paused for half a minute and recovered his strength with a sip of his gin and tonic.

"They claim that Kuwisha had 6 per cent growth last year. It's no more than office-wallah thumb suck. Fact is, no way of telling, what with stats department so bloody useless. In my day we counted the number of new tin roofs. Do you know what? Last Saturday I drove for about four hours up-country, and not one new roof. Plenty of mobile cafés or whatever they call them, selling bloody phone cards. And you can watch Arsenal play Chelsea on satellite television. But new roofs? Not one. Six per cent growth? Bottom talk, that's all it is – bottom talk."

He insisted it was his round, and summoned Boniface Rugiru.

"Boniface! More firewater, please, and don't be so stingy with the nuts. Another one for the road? No? Then excuse me, young man. I have to have a natter with Boniface . . ."

Rutere was not amused. "A stupid trick," he called Ntoto's fake collapse, "very stupid," he said.

In a rare concession to Rutere, Ntoto reluctantly agreed. "It was very stupid," he said. "I am sorry."

Cyrus could hardly believe his ears. Titus Odhiambo Ntoto had said sorry! He decided to press home the chance to question his friend.

"Please, Ntoto," he said. "What is happening? What is the plan for Guchu?"

Ntoto decided that it was time to tell Rutere – or at least to reveal part of the scheme.

"I have bought a job as a pump boy. That is the first thing to do."

As Ntoto expected, it brought a scornful and sceptical reaction from his friend, who shook his head in disbelief.

"How", he asked incredulously, "does becoming a pump boy help us to get revenge on Mayor Guchu? First you steal sugar, now you become a pump boy?" He shook his head, baffled.

Buying and selling a job for a day or so was far from unusual. The seller would value their job at, say, 100 *ngwee* a day, and would offer to "sell" it for 75 per cent of that rate. The purchaser would hope that by working hard, and earning tips, they could not only recover their outlay but make a small profit.

But it was something that no self-respecting Mboya Boy would contemplate, let alone someone like Ntoto, who had a reputation for cold-eyed brutal thuggery. Rutere tried to learn more, but he was unsuccessful.

"Think, Rutere. You can work it out. You have all the information that I have given you."

Rutere made the mistake of teasing his friend. He held his nose between finger and thumb, and wafted away the air in front with an open palm.

"Pump boys smell of petrol. It is a useless job."

Ntoto hit back.

"And what is a good job for street boys?" he asked. "I expect you want to work as a waiter, serving coffee . . . I know, Rutere, you want to be a *Java*!"

Cyrus was outraged. Indeed, had the insult come from anyone else, he would be honour bound to challenge him to a fight. *Java*, indeed. He let rip, pointing out that it was him, the cleverest boy never to have gone to St Joseph's School for boys, who had told Ntoto about Tom Odhiambo Mboya, the assassinated trade unionist they admired so much they named their football team after him.

To call Rutere a *Java*, even in jest, was intolerable.

Fortunately for both boys, Charity intervened.

"Noise! Stop that noise! This minute! You two stop making noise, right away."

What was happening to those boys?

"Ntoto, what are you saying to Rutere?"

"He called me a bad name," said Rutere. "A very bad name."

After some patient coaxing by Charity, and a firm rejection of his request for a dough ball – "half, even" – as a reward for disclosing the name, Rutere finally agreed to tell Charity.

Rutere whispered in her ear.

"Phauw!" she exclaimed, "Phauw!"

The strong reaction gratified Rutere.

"Yes, mama, he called me a *Java*."

Charity was mystified, but decided not to ask what a *Java* was. Instead she hoped that she could work it out for herself.

"Is this true, Ntoto? Did you call your friend Rutere this *Java* thing? A *Java*?"

Java made no sense to her, except as a source of coffee, and the name of a popular chain of coffee shops that catered not only to expatriates and tourists, but to a growing group of Kuwishans that appreciated the taste of properly roasted beans, and enjoyed the socially mobile, middle-class ambience of the cafés.

"He called me a *Java*," repeated Rutere.

"Hah! But why should he call you this bad name?" asked Charity. "And why should I care that boys who steal sugar should call each other bad names?"

"But mama," said Rutere, "it is a very bad thing he said. He said I was behaving like a *mzungu*, that I wanted to become a *mzungu*, a black *mzungu*, and drink coffee in Javas." Ntoto looked on, smirking.

Then she understood. *Java* was the derogatory term for a black man with aspirations to live as a white man. To be accused of being a *Java* was as offensive a charge as any in the boys' vocabulary of abuse.

Furniver intervened.

"Did I hear someone say 'coffee' . . . ?"

He listened patiently to Rutere's version of the insult, leaning towards the boy so as to hear him better. Like Charity, his response was involuntary, his head recoiling.

"Phauw!"

Ntoto's breath was truly awful.

Rutere accepted Ntoto's apology.

"It is duck's water off my back," said Cyrus magnanimously. The two trotted off.

"Phauw," said Furniver. "That Rutere boy! His breath is really appalling. Could kill pigeons at six paces."

"Tell me, Ntoto," Rutere persisted. "Why you have bought this pump boy job? I may be clever, but I don't understand."

Ntoto relented.

"It is the only way," he replied, "that I can get close to Guchu. And you know, Rutere, that if you are not part of a big man, you cannot get a job. A pump boy, even, comes from the same tribe as the owner of the petrol station. Or the owner is his relative. Or the owner is doing a big man, like Guchu, a favour."

"That is correct," said Rutere.

"So think, Rutere. Think!"

Cyrus ran his fingers through his curls, and was briefly distracted by the discovery of a nit that had been proving especially irritating. He cracked it between his fingernails, and flicked the remains away.

"The pump boy is circumcised," continued Ntoto. "I myself saw this when swimming in the Malubuzi River during the floods last year."

Rutere remembered the event, which had triggered a long and sometimes heated debate about differences between the circumcised and the uncircumcised communities. The one side argued that it shouldn't affect ability or potential; the other side believed that the operation marked a gulf between the two groups that could never be bridged.

Rutere, still not any the wiser, asked Ntoto to continue.

"Well . . ." said Ntoto. "The owner is a Luya man, and Luya men are never circumcised. This means that the pump boy, who is circumcised, got his job because his relative is an important man, who, in the language of Kuwisha, must surely drive a big desk, and wanted a favour from the owner. And the big man who fills his car at the station, right full to top, same day every week, is our old friend Mr Guchu . . ."

It was slowly becoming clearer to Rutere what his friend had in mind. As he digested the information and its implications, his eyes opened wide in appreciation of Ntoto's sheer cunning, mixed with fear at the retaliation they risked from the mayor.

He looked at his friend with renewed respect. He had one final question but it could wait.

"Well, Mr Mudenge . . ."

The flour trick had not worked, Charity complained the next morning, as Mudenge sipped his breakfast glass of mango juice.

"There is no doubt," said Mudenge, "these thieves are very clever. But there is no question, Mrs Mupanga, that if I don't succeed your money will be returned. I have one more trick, but it is the very best *muti* that I will be using. Let us see what happens."

He rubbed the corner of his eye, resisting the temptation to take it out and give it a good wipe with his handkerchief. Mudenge had lost his left eye when still in his teens, the result of a chip of granite that had flown off the stone he had been preparing for the foundations of the family house. The injured eye had been replaced by a glass one, which Mudenge every now and then took out from the socket, polished with his handkerchief, and slipped back.

"Rest assured, Mrs Mupanga, no results, no pay."

18

It was soon after the announcement that Kireba was to be rede-
veloped that Philimon Ogata, looking as happy as a butcher's
dog, turned up at the bar and made an expansive gesture.

"Tuskers on me," he announced. "One each," he added,
looking round. "Dough balls for the boys."

Charity, who was tending the bar, looked sceptical. While
Ogata was not a mean man, he was not a well-off man either.
He made good money out of the funeral business, but three of
his sons were still at high school, and his parents, blessed with
a long life, relied on him.

Ogata slapped 100 *ngwee* on the counter.

"Deposit! And more where that came from," he said, tapping
a brown envelope that Charity could see bulged with cash.

It did not take her long to work out the source of Ogata's
wealth.

"So, Mr Ogata, you have been sleeping with lawyers. Be
careful! Lawyers are very cunning. You may think you can beat
them, and then, poof, you have no money. Indeed, you will
have to repay money that you think is yours. Tell me what
happened."

Ogata's tale was a familiar one.

It began, he said, with the visit of a well-known lawyer,
Dr Strong Kapundu. After an exchange of pleasantries, they got
down to business.

"How long have you lived at number 79 Uhuru Lane?" asked
Kapundu.

It was not an easy question to answer. If the truth were
made known to the City Council, it could prove an expensive

business. He had not paid local taxes for many years. Ogata, who had in fact been living in Kireba for nigh on 30 years, decided to take a gamble.

"I've lived here for 15 years," he said.

"Very good," said Kapundu and went on to ask a series of other questions.

Had the terms of the lease changed? Had the owner changed?

Ogata thought carefully once again. The owner was a Luya company, whose main objectives were to buy land for its members and extract as much money as possible in as short a time as possible from its non-Luya tenants. The last thing Ogata wanted was trouble with landlords.

He decided to stick to his relatively honest approach. He named the company but his concern was apparent to the lawyer.

"Don't worry," said Kapundu. "Don't worry."

He produced a calculator, pressed several buttons, and showed the result to Ogata.

"This," he said, "is how much you will get if you sign these papers."

It was a small fortune but Ogata remained wary.

"And if I do not sign?"

Kapundu shrugged.

"Do you need the money?"

"Of course," said Ogata.

Kapundu shrugged again: "Why should one beat a horse to make it drink if it is already thirsty?"

"So I signed," said Ogata. "And here is the money."

Who could blame him?

As word spread about Nduka's project, residents of Kireba took advantage of the situation. You did not need to own the hovel in which you lived, or the land on which it was built, to benefit from a compensation scheme – at least, that was the claim of lawyers who, in the words of Charity, were "cleverer than lawyers from London, even".

All that was necessary was to make a plausible claim that you had lived on the land for five years – or three years, or ten years, depending on the lawyer. This gave you the right, according to the law of the land, to compensation from the property developer.

"But remember," she said to Ogata or anyone else who asked her advice: "The judge has sold himself to the man who offers the most money."

Just then her mobile went off.

Pearson and Lucy were on their way and Digby would follow.

Anders Berksson looked out at the audience of a specially convened meeting. It was time to rally the troops. Morale in the development agencies was suffering. Cement delays and land compensation claims, not to mention the fact that the road lobby and the rail lobby were in a state of open war, had combined to make the timetable of the Kireba project look like wishful thinking. Indeed, the assessment of the operating environment had changed from "challenging" to "demanding". Any more setbacks and it would be termed "hostile".

The audience was packed with front-line fighters in the battle for change, veterans of the struggle for the soul of Kuwisha. In an inspiring display of unity and common purpose, UNICEF and UNHCR, WFP, HABITAT, UNESCO and UNEP sat shoulder to shoulder with representatives from WorldFeed, DanAid, ScanHelp, GOAT and HARE. Between them they accounted for a substantial chunk of Kuwisha's foreign exchange earnings, not far behind tea, coffee and tourism.

"Time is running out," Berksson told his anxious assembly.

"Unless we put our weight behind the president's proposal for Kireba, we face the real prospect of a cut in our spending allocations next year. We all know what this means . . ."

As long as he headed UNDP, he told the gathering, the battle against poverty would be ceaselessly and untiringly waged.

"So let us reject the isolated piecemeal planning of the past. Let us make a clear shift away from the over-preoccupation with foreign exchange problems external to the region. Let us make a decisive move towards the integrated development of the urban resources, institutional mechanisms and technological capacities required to assess and utilise the natural resources and raw material endowments of the region. Let us expand local markets, enlarge the range of complementarities and strengthen the links between industry and other sectors of the economy. Time is running out," Berksson repeated, "but help is at hand, from friends in high places."

He paused for effect.

"I am sure you will join me in sending a warm Kuwisha welcome to one of our distinguished goodwill ambassadors for NoseAid, who has promised to support us . . . let me be first to bring wonderful news . . . the famous columnist for the *Clarion*, the fearless campaigner for rhinos and true friend of the people . . . Mr Jasper Japer!"

For some in the audience, the name rang no bells. But the spontaneous gasp of appreciation and round of applause that came from the rest of the gathering warmed Berksson's heart.

19

Sitting at Harrods, drinking good coffee made from beans grown and roasted on Charity's *shamba*, or enjoying a glass of freshly squeezed juice or a cup of tea or an ice-cold Tusker, Pearson felt as though he'd never been away. And when he returned from inspecting the site for the VIP toilets his benign view of the world included Titus Ntoto and Cyrus Rutere, both of whom he privately described as "devious little shits". Charity had given him a hug and Mildred Kigali, no admirer of journalists, acknowledged his presence.

And above all there was Lucy, blonde and blue-eyed and exuding an unquenchable enthusiasm . . .

"Great plans for the toilets," she called from the kitchen where the blueprints had been laid out for public inspection. "God help those bloody flies."

"What ho!" said Furniver heartily, grasping his hand warmly and clapping him on the back. "Welcome back."

Just then there was the sound of disgust.

"Sis," said Lucy. She was scraping away at something disgusting that clung to the sole of her shoe, picked up during the short walk from the local taxi rank to the bar.

"Nice T-shirt," said Furniver. "By the way, where did you get to yesterday?"

Lucy blushed.

"Something came up."

"I bet it did," said Furniver, glancing at Pearson.

Lucy ignored him.

"Managed to put off lunch with the ambassador, and sorting out *The Times* and the *Telegraph* was easier than I'd thought.

Got them to settle their differences and come on the weekend trip to Kigali. All I had to do was to point out that they could pay their fare in local currency, and after that it was like feeding lumps of sugar to a horse."

While Charity went back to chalking the menu on the blackboard, now bearing the slogan, "Best Place To Water Your Mouth", the others exchanged views on the state of Kuwisha.

"It really has changed, you know, Pearson," said Lucy.

"I thought you said nothing had changed?"

"I was talking about the fundamentals – population, land, drought and government cock-ups," said Lucy. "But the country has still changed."

"Everybody tells me that," said Pearson, "usually followed by theories as to what the Chinese are up to."

Furniver took up the issue. "The country is changing. You'll see. Twenty-four-hour supermarkets, mobile phones and the property boom – that's the positive side. But the dark side is getting darker. Hit squads knock off human rights activists, and this coalition government has its head in the sand, its snout in the trough and its bum in the butter. You'll see," he said. "You'll see . . ."

In surroundings that were so familiar, it was all but inevitable that old arguments and old disputes would be aired afresh.

In this latest skirmish between the camps of the Afro-pessimists and the Afro-optimists, neither was able to convince the other of the merits of their argument.

"Of course," said Furniver, "I gather that things used to be terrible in Africa. The 1980s and 1990s in particular were grim. We had all those proxy wars waged by Washington and Moscow. Today for the first time in donkeys' years, there are no wars in Africa. True, there are nasty things going on in Sudan and Somalia, Nigeria and Congo. But there is no full-scale war. And it's also possible to make money out of an African investment. If you'd invested $100 into Blakeney Management seven years ago, it would be worth nearly $1000 today. Beat that!"

Pearson had been making a valiant effort not to interrupt, but failed.

"No wars, you say? Okay, I grant you, no all-out wars. But let me throw in a few more names of countries where things are, shall we say, difficult. Sudan, Sierra Leone, Zimbabwe, Kenya . . . A spot of fighting in Nigeria, a few problems in Uganda and Malawi. There are more refugees in Africa than ever before, there is more poverty, however you measure it. And, yes, investors may have done well by putting their money into African banks, mobile phones, breweries and properties, but I've yet to see a successful portfolio that's built on actually making things, such as bicycles or water pumps or solar heating panels."

It was Furniver's turn.

"You need to look at your history, my boy. It took Britain a hundred years to quadruple its economy. Germany, France and the US took half that time. Japan did it in 25 years, then Singapore, South Korea followed and now we're looking at China and India who are making even faster progress. Today, whether you hacks like it or not – and for some reason, most of you don't – Africa leads the growth table. Just take a look at this."

Furniver pointed to a graph in an article from the *FN* which he had cut out and kept. It showed Ethiopia and Rwanda keeping pace with China, India and Vietnam.

"Well?" he said. "What have you got to say for yourself?"

"It's crazy to compare them. Ethiopia and Rwanda, China and India? Talk about minnows and whales."

Furniver made a final effort.

"What about private capital flows?" he asked. "I don't want to get too technical but the flows to Africa have risen from a few billion a year to over 30 billion annually while the amount to developing Asia and Central and East Europe is negative."

He pushed the document under Pearson's nose.

"As the chap says, from the sickly sister of the world family to an empowered *über*-babe of a continent today."

"Believe that," said Pearson sourly, "and you'll believe anything. Just you wait. Remittances from Africans living abroad are going to fall even further . . ." He shook his head. "Just you wait."

"What does the OM have to say about the North East Province?" asked Lucy. "By the way, how is the old bugger?"

"Not too fit, I fear," replied Furniver.

Furniver recounted not only the OM's observations about conditions in the province and the number affected, but his views on the role of WorldFeed and other foreign aid agencies.

"At the end of the day, the OM said you chaps do more harm than good. All in all pretty depressing, I don't mind telling you," he concluded.

Lucy's reaction surprised him. He'd expected her to mount a vigorous case in defence of the aid agencies. Instead she looked thoughtful.

"Isn't there something in what he said?"

"Well, the world has certainly changed – is changing," said Furniver. "If he's right, you chaps at WorldFeed will soon have to fold your tents and bugger off – leave the locals to it."

"Already starting to happen," said Lucy. "Had a message from HQ this morning. WorldFeed income fallen 20 per cent since the credit crunch. They're looking for volunteers – redundancy packages. I'm thinking of putting my name in."

Furniver was visibly taken aback. "Thought you liked your job?"

"I do," said Lucy. "But maybe the time of the NGO is coming to an end. The funds are going to dry up. Our high street WorldFeed shops are doing okay, but otherwise . . . we'll become what we started as – an outfit offering first aid, fast. That will always be needed. But as for our hopes that we could change Africa . . ."

She shrugged.

"After 40 years of trying, there's not much to show for it. The need for help is still there. In fact, it's greater than ever. Remittances from abroad have dropped. Still falling. Stands to reason. Fewer jobs, less money to spare. Perhaps it's a blessing in disguise. As I say, after 40 years bashing away, time we all took stock – foreigners and locals."

She looked at Charity, now back from the kitchen. But if she was expecting Charity to comment she was to be disappointed. The manager had other things on her mind.

"Good news! I've had good news, Lucy. Those toilets, the Zimbabwe toilets, the plans have arrived and the holes are being dug. All we need now is cement – whenever it is on sale, at a good price," she added sourly. "Come and look at the holes. We are making progress. But we cannot stand here talking all day. Talk, talk, talk. Always talking, not enough doing."

Furniver coughed diffidently: "By the way, Pearson, Lucy said you had a World Bank report on Ethiopia from the last AU summit. Would you mind if I had a look at it?"

Pearson resisted the temptation to discuss the fall in property prices in London, but he could not stop himself from teasing Furniver about his elaborate coffee-making ritual.

"Far from being the elitist gesture you suggest, it is my daily attempt to improve understanding between the races," Furniver replied, mock-pompously. "Until not so long ago the country that grows some of the world's finest coffee, managed to turn it into the world's least palatable drink. Hotels and restaurants seemed to vie with each other to produce a noxious, foul-smelling brew, which was drunk almost exclusively by foreign visitors and white locals.

"This created a division between Kuwisha and the rest of the world. The people of Kuwisha, quite understandably, believed their visitors were bonkers. Anyone who drank the brew called coffee must be odd. Then along with mobile phones, and deregulation and privatisation came a breakthrough. Coffee shops in Kuwisha began selling good palatable coffee. And the people began to realise what they were missing."

"Okay, okay, I take your point. The coffee is better, and Africa is changing," said Pearson. "But not in the way that you've made out. And not for the better."

Furniver kept his counsel and took a sip from his mug.

"Quite astonishing," Pearson continued. "Driving in from the airport. Everything is changing, from the billboards to new buildings, the traffic and the ads for mortgages. All that seems to have happened in the time I've been away. And yes, I do miss the Africa I got to know. It was all about IMF agreements and World Bank loans, civil wars and rigged elections, aid flows and gap-year teenage volunteers from Europe."

Furniver could not resist repeating Lucy's dig.

"Fact is, old boy, you took a perverse pleasure in that old Africa, and I suspect you have mixed feelings about the new Africa."

Pearson ignored the intervention.

"Of course the place is changing. Of course it is," said Pearson. "Can't miss it. But is it closing the gap? When I was at school, the gap was simple, easy to remedy. I had books, blackboards, chalk and teachers. And there were 30 of us to a class. Today's schools in the West have computers. Schools in Kuwisha still don't have decent classrooms, let alone computers. And that's the gap that counts. As I say, it's getting wider. At best it's staying the same. Take the airport. Duty free shops are better stocked, the toilets are clean, and the coffee is tolerable."

He took a sip of passion fruit juice, and smacked his lips. Cold, with a tangy almost sour undertaste.

"But what does that tell us? Then the journey into town. Double or even treble the time it used to take. I reckon you could calculate annual GDP growth, using a base rate of 2 per cent. So if the trip takes twice as long, except on Sundays of course, growth is 4 per cent, and if it's three times . . ."

"Yes, we get the picture," said Lucy impatiently.

Pearson ignored her.

"On the way, look at the billboards – banks, estate agents, airlines and satellite TV. Average is 40 ads for every minute of the journey. If it's 50, the economy is overheating. Then when you check in at the hotel – and you have to book to be certain of a room – look out for the nationality of your fellow guests . . ."

"A point for every South African," interjected Furniver, who decided to enter into the spirit of Pearson's analysis.

"Wrong! Deduct a point."

"Don't get it," said Furniver. "You'll have to explain."

"South Africans were in the first wave. Mainly white, it was the only way to escape the glass ceiling at home. But that was years ago – by now they've bought their own places. No, it's not South Africans. It's Lebanese, and Central and East Europeans, Italians and, of course, Chinese."

"You accept that the economy is in better shape?"

"Up to a point. After all, the country had gone though a recession. So we are talking about 6 per cent annual growth from what the World Bank calls 'a low base' – i.e. the place was on the bones of its arse."

"Something must have been going right," interjected Furniver.

"The world economy was going right," said Pearson. "This meant that everyone from Kuwisha who was working abroad, and God knows there are hundreds of thousands, could send more money home. It's called expatriate remittances. Along with UN money and aid money and foreign investments."

"Well, at least that's a positive development," said Furniver.

"Ah, but much of it is going into oil and mining, telecoms. Banks and breweries. Long way to go before you can talk about a recovery. Just you wait," said Pearson darkly, "the bubble has burst. As for your lot, Lucy. You say I'm out of date, have been away too long. Well, you've been here too long, so long that you've reached the point of no return. Either you believe you and WorldFeed have made a difference, or you've wasted the best years of your life."

"Fact is," he continued, "Kuwisha is like one of those canaries miners used to take down the pits. Any methane gas and the poor bloody canary would fall off its perch, quicker than you could say 'dead parrot', and the miners would head for the exit. In the aid world, watch Kuwisha. Forty years after independence, and billions of aid dollars, the most tangible thing is that the population has doubled in 25 years.

"You and your aid friends see what's happening around you as evidence of an economic recovery. I see it as the last kick of a dying canary."

"I'm off," said Lucy, "Promised to be at that DanAid lunch . . . Bloody hell! I've stood in it again."

20

When Furniver called in at the Club the next day to check on the OM's health, he was glad to see a tray with a bowl of ice and a fresh gin and tonic that awaited mixing. More encouraging was the fact that the box of Sportsman's cigarettes was next to the G and T and the OM was taking a deep draw on one of the filterless sticks. The member spooned ice cubes into his glass, measured out the gin, tipped in the tonic and settled into his armchair. Yesterday's paper was by his chair, and the stories and ads that had provoked him had been marked in angry red ink.

Clearly the situation in the north-east was still on his mind.

"I didn't expect to see you this early," he said to Furniver. "I suppose Lucy is still getting hot and bothered by reports on the state of the North East Province?"

Furniver nodded.

"You tell Lucy that North East Province always was what she calls a 'food deficit' part of the world. Served there as a young district officer. Those days, no bloody NGOs. These days, you trip over them wherever you go. Over here and overpaid. A chap who works for the UNDP can expect a starting whack of a top civil servant. About 50,000 *ngwee* a year. Work out the dollar rate for yourself. But how a whippersnapper from Scandinavia, in Africa for the first time, can justify their fat monthly pay packet beats me. Doesn't end there, of course. Benefits galore. Medical cover, tax breaks, children's education. Not to mention the foreign exchange fiddles. Import their bloody cars free of duty, sell on the open market when their tour is up after three years – and remit at the official rate. Makes a fortune."

The OM popped a handful of cashews into his mouth.

"Take a look at the ad in today's paper. Never mention the salary for the bods who spend a few days a month in the province. And for good reason. They earn a small bloody fortune. Instead, just talk about 'salaries commensurate with experience' or some such piffle. If they put the salaries in black and white, people would start to ask questions."

He paused.

"Where was I? Oh yes. Fact of life. If you got hungry, you either moved or starved. Population stayed much the same. Today, you stay, 'cos you're sure to get fed. Move and you'll be in trouble.

"But the point is, who does the feeding – and helps out with the health clinics and books for the primary schools? Outsiders. Foreigners. Get my drift?"

The sun broke into the shady veranda where the pair was sitting and warmed Furniver's shoulders. He was paying the price of a Tusker too many the night before, and found it all too easy to slip into a state of drowsy relaxation. Furniver clutched his G and T and allowed his thoughts to turn to Charity.

"Drift," the OM said firmly. "It's called the social contract. Chap pays his taxes, does his military service, tries to obey the law, and so on. In return the government provides the basic services – roads, schools, clinics, so on. And the buggers in parliament don't do their job, we can vote 'em out. Fair summary?"

Furniver nodded.

"Summary . . ."

"But what if the government doesn't deliver? Nor do you have any choice in a one-party state. What if the chaps in the north-east, who by the way are not fools, come to realise that although there is a 'food deficit' every year, they won't starve?"

The OM prodded Furniver with a bony forefinger.

"Why? 'Cos WorldFeed and Oxfam and their UN chums will chip in. All managed by foreigners. Tens of thousands of the buggers come out each year, all catching the gravy train that chuffs its way around Africa. The foreigners get off and at every station locals get on, heading for Europe.

"Want evidence? Look at the death notices in the local papers. Signed by every surviving family member, relative or whatnot. Half of them are graduates living in London or Washington."

He snorted.

"So what has happened to the bloody social contract? If you are starving, the UN will feed you; if the mozzies are killing your kids, Bill Gates will provide a mosquito net; if your road needs rebuilding, UKAid or DanAid will help; if no water, then WaterAid will dig a few wells; if the railway is falling apart" – he tapped that day's paper, with its ads for UN posts – "then WorldFeed will bring in a foreigner to coordinate and help out."

The OM's face was getting redder.

"And if you don't want to pay your country's debt, a Harvard economist briefed by DebtAid will come up with a raft of reasons not to do so – but that's another story . . ."

He took a further sip of his gin and tonic.

"What is more, these aid thingies don't work . . . Goats to Africa, I ask you.

"So if the state can't deliver, why be loyal? Why pay your taxes? Instead you look to big-man politics – to your relative, to your clan, to the ethnic leaders or the regional boss. Result? The state breaks down, and patronage, corruption, takes over. I could live with the donors' do-good arrogance if their aid worked. I could overlook the fact that the goat population is as big a threat to the environment of Africa as global warming."

The OM paused.

"OK, nearly as big . . . but at the end of the day, the best you can say about aid is that it does not save lives – it just delays the deaths of a few, and contributes to the deaths of a hell of a lot more."

"Absolutely," said Furniver.

The OM beamed.

"Knew we'd see things the same way. Let me call a *matatu*. Nearly lunchtime. Boniface! Bring Mr Furniver one for the road!"

Boniface Rugiru watched anxiously as the OM pottered around the Club gardens, stopping every now and then to sniff the roses or to examine a badly trimmed lawn edge with a critical eye. The steward had concealed himself behind the veranda trellis, knowing that any display of concern would not be tolerated. The OM was not fooled. As he headed back to his favourite arm chair, he called out.

"I see you, Rugiru. Your shoes give you away. Size of an elephant!"

Back on the Club veranda, he called for his G and T.

"You and I need to have a word. Sit down, Mr Rugiru."

For the first time in his 45 years of service at the Thumaiga Club, Boniface sat in a member's chair, knowing instinctively that this was no time to let convention come between him and a man he considered his friend.

"Suh," he said, and braced himself.

"Mr Rugiru, I have been making plans for my departure, and I want you to handle the show."

Rugiru frowned. Arrangements for members' home leave were usually handled by the Club secretary.

"Suh," he replied non-committedly.

"I've had a decent innings, and I want to finish with a six. I'll run through a few things, the opening and suchlike, leave the rest to you."

The OM gave a convulsive cough, and lit another Sportsman.

"Better get a pen and paper, don't want anything left out."

Rugiru hesitated.

"For cricket scores?"

The OM coughed again, and brought his handkerchief to his lips.

"Not bloody likely!"

Although the day had been hot, the night was chill, and they moved into the Members' Lounge. Rugiru threw another log on the fire. The two men sat companionably, looking into the flames, each lost to old memories.

Rugiru and the OM had grown up together on the same farm. At 12, the OM had been packed off to boarding school, and the relationship between the two boys had changed fundamentally. But something of the old friendship remained. Indeed, it was said in the club that Rugiru owed his job to the OM, which some members saw as evidence of a liberal heart – though none dared say as much in his hearing.

"Right," said the OM. "Let's get down to business. But first I need another G and T, Mr Rugiru, and a bowl of cashew nuts. And I mean a bowl, not a handful. You dish out those bloody nuts as if you expect me to sign a chitty for each and every one."

The truth was, the OM's appetite for nuts was much diminished, a sure sign that something was amiss with his health.

Rugiru raised an eyebrow, nodded at the deputy bar steward, a sociology graduate on whom the OM kept a sharp eye.

As the OM had explained to the Club secretary: "In the bad old days Rugiru and his pals would water the gin and cadge from the kitchen. Seldom got any worse. True, fiddling with the gin was hanging offence in my book, but we knew where we stood. Today, the buggers are after your job and my membership . . ."

Rugiru waited for his instructions.

"Anyway, Boniface, whatever, I need to put my affairs in order. At my age. Getting on. Want to plan a decent send-off. Not one of these wishy-washy weepy ceremonies that happen every day. But something rather special. I've jotted down a few thoughts and I want to go over them with you – because you are going to be the one who will run the whole show."

The deputy steward arrived with the drinks.

"More ice, suh," said Rugiru, concealing his alarm.

He rose to his feet. He was starting to feel uncomfortable. Rules of the Club, which went back to the early days of British colonial rule, were maintained with a ruthless rigour by post-independence committees. Near the top of a list of rules of conduct was a ban on any fraternising or undue familiarity with the staff.

"I said sit down, Mr Rugiru."

The alarmed bar steward took up the note book and pen, which his deputy had left with the drinks, and proceeded to take down the OM's last will and testament.

"I, David Artemis Carruthers Smeldon, being of sound mind, hereby set out the order of service for my cremation . . ."

It was clear the OM had given it much thought, for it included everything from an insistence on the time pips of the BBC and the playing of "Lillibullero" to open and close the service, and a selection of guerrilla marching songs, to a request that extracts from the last sermon of the late Bishop David Mupanga be read at the conclusion of proceedings.

"Why 'Lillibullero'? You may well ask, Mr Rugiru. It reminds me that Northern Ireland gave me hope for Africa. All the tribalism on the continent couldn't match the Irish for their sheer venomous pigheadedness. Gave me hope. Showed that bigotry is universal. And whenever I heard that tune, with its words, I wanted to cheer. Now the blighters have made up, Africa is much harder to defend. Yes, I know. You have the Muslims and the Balkans, but most Brits know little about these places and care less, too far from home. But Northern Ireland was in the Brits' back yard and of course English colonialism caused the whole bloody problem at the start."

He trailed off.

*

140

Rugiru listened patiently to the OM's many gripes, every now and then indicating with a cough or a modest grunt that he had taken on board the points that were being made. But when the member had a go at the BBC, Rugiru's loyalties were strained.

The news about and from Africa seemed trivial and confusing, complained the OM. Countries bickered, and people quarrelled, as an increasingly irritated world looked on.

The World Service of the BBC was part of the family, but increasingly he seemed to regard it in the same light as an uncle who had disgraced himself, who had wandered off the straight and narrow.

"Listen, listen!" he used to say, gesturing at the radio. "Can you credit it? Can you bloody well credit it? Haven't a clue what the bugger is saying. Does it make sense to you, Rugiru?"

Boniface had to admit that some of the local contributors spoke a heavily accented English that was difficult to penetrate, and try as he might he could not make out just what was being said or discussed.

"Rebels based in the north . . . Urban protests . . . the national football team, the golden hooves . . . black warriors . . . robbers killed by police . . . New Africa . . . Sustained growth."

One day it seemed that there had been a police mutiny in the western region of Gambia, the next day it might be Zambia, and in both cases the minister in charge had vehemently denied that members of the army had been called in to arrest the mutineers. More than that, complained the OM, the content was parochial at a time when the news should be international.

"In the real world, Israel is invading Lebanon, oil is selling for more than $100 a barrel and a Saudi arms deal will keep 5,000 British workers in jobs for life.

"The buggers at the BBC insist on treating Africa like a bloody retard, like the village idiot. The worst thing . . ."

As the OM thumped the table in front of him, the cashew nuts shook and the newly ordered gin and tonic spilt.

"Damn and blast."

He took out a handkerchief and wiped the table dry.

"The worst thing", he continued, "is the way they handle floods and whatnot."

There had been unseasonable rains across the continent, from Ghana on the west coast, to Uganda in the east, and floods had destroyed crops and cost hundreds of lives.

"So, when did the BBC decide it was a disaster? Not when the local johnnies said so. Oh no. They weren't good enough. It only became a disaster when the aid agencies decided it was time to appeal for help. I ask you, isn't there something wrong when the NGOs make these decisions? So much for this new information technology. We know more and understand less."

Rugiru coughed.

The OM seemed to be talking to himself.

"Another G and T, if you don't mind. We've got business to get through."

Rugiru went to the bar to collect the order himself and frowned disapprovingly at his young deputy, who stood nonchalantly cleaning his nails.

"You are too good to that old man. I heard him ask you to make arrangements for home leave . . . All he wants to do is to watch cricket. That is not your job."

Rugiru ignored him. He returned to where the OM was sitting on the veranda, opposite his favourite rose bush.

"Suh."

"A piece of advice, Mr Rugiru. Watch that deputy of yours like a hawk. Like a hawk. He is a cheeky native. I heard every word. Not deaf, you know."

"Suh."

"And the bugger is watering the gin. I have seen him. Puts in an extra couple of cubes of ice and in this way gets an extra couple of tots out of every bottle."

"Suh."

"Now then, Mr Rugiru, a few more thoughts about my last show. My will is pretty straightforward. It's lodged at Muite's practice. Bright lawyer," he continued. "One of the best. You'll see I've left a few bob for the clinic. Apart from the service, could you lay on refreshments; tea, sandwiches, that sort of thing? And make sure dough balls are on the house, especially for the street boys. Give them half a dozen each. And I want to be cremated and I expect you to scatter my ashes."

He leant over, and muttered in Rugiru's ear: "For God's sake don't tell Bunty but I'd like them to be sprinkled on the rose bushes at State House."

Rugiru did his best to keep pace with the OM's instructions. Mrs Benton's agreement could be taken for granted. She and the OM had long been good friends . . . And more than good friends, if you believed the gossip.

"But I'm getting ahead of myself. This is how it should kick off . . ."

For the next ten minutes Rugiru made notes.

"Now, read them back."

"Do you think that Didymus will put in a few words for me?"

Both men knew it was asking a lot of Didymus Kigali, steward to Edward Furniver and a senior elder in the Church of the Blessed Lamb.

To get Kigali to deliver one of his famous sermons, or "admonitions" as they were known by members of Kuwisha's fastest growing sect, was one thing. To ask him to deliver it in a cathedral, rather than in the open air, in which the Blessed Lambs conducted all their services, was another.

"Last item," said the Oldest Member. "You know my radio?"

"Suh," said Rugiru, hope rising in his breast.

Did he know that radio? He knew that radio like an old friend.

"Well, the BBC is so bloody awful these days I've decided to have it cremated at the same time and join my ashes. BBC's had its day . . ."

The OM was starting to mumble now and Rugiru knew that the end of his journey was not far off.

21

It was the boys' last sugar raid. All had been straightforward up to now, but distinct recollections of his late grandmother's warnings all those years ago had lodged in Rutere's mind.

It was well known that *tokolosh* roamed the land after midnight; and if not *tokolosh*, there were *mungiki* to look out for, not to mention various ghosts and ancestral spirits.

Ntoto inserted the key into the padlock of the container and the boys let themselves into its dark and gloomy interior.

Rutere lit a candle.

He spotted it first, squatting, vigilant and malevolent, atop the counter where it had a panoramic view that included the sugar container. The boys froze and lowered themselves behind the bar counter, out of its sight.

"If we stay low on our stomachs we can go out," Rutere whispered nervously.

Ntoto motioned him to stay still and keep silent. He pulled down a tea towel from the counter and, clutching the cloth in his hand, advanced from behind the object.

Rutere, looking through a crack in the bar counter, held his breath and watched with concern.

The next morning Charity went to inspect the sugar. The lid to the container had been left off by the thieves and in front of it was something the size of a pigeon egg, covered by a tea towel. Charity gingerly lifted it up and recoiled.

Mudenge's glass eye looked up at her, all-seeing, never sleeping, always watching, but blinded for the night by a clever thief.

*

The phone call for Lucy came a moment before Charity had urged her to inspect the sites of the Zimbabwe toilets.

"Six, six of the best. Very modern," she said proudly. "But this cement business . . ." she added, shaking her head. "A problem, a big problem. Shortages . . ."

Lucy called for silence.

"Bad line . . . but good news – I think."

"Sorry, Berk, can hear you now . . . No . . . No! . . . Really? . . . Really! . . . When? No! . . . Really? . . . That's great. Great!"

"Good news, I gather?" said Furniver.

"Brilliant news," she replied.

Lucy broke into one of the jigs with which she welcomed a big story or a huge disaster, and did a blue-jeaned, pink-toed dance around the table, suntanned arm punching the air.

"Best news I've had since Mercy confirmed the cholera cases in Kireba during the last floods. Thanks, Berk, for letting me know." She switched off the phone.

"Listen, chaps, NoseAid has backed the Kireba project! And guess who is coming to Kuwisha, to present a documentary, filmed here, in Kireba, about that boy, Mlambo, who lost his job as kitchen *toto* at State House?"

"Let me guess," said Pearson sourly. "George Clooney?"

"Have you been reading my emails?" demanded Lucy. But nothing Pearson could say could dampen her enthusiasm or spoil her pleasure.

"It's not just George Clooney," she crowed. "It's Madonna! And thanks to Digby, we have this brilliant idea.

"Tell them, Digby!"

Digby blushed with pride.

"I suppose we all remember that NoseAid song," he began. "It was one of the best moments of my life, watching that. Remember how they closed the show?"

Who could forget it? Led by Ferdinand Mlambo, the former Kireba street-boy, the entire cast of pop stars, celebs, wannabes and has-beens, models and newsreaders, sang a rousing finale to the NoseAid marathon fundfest.

"There will be a television link-up," said Digby. "And BBC and KTV will share ownership. The idea occurred to me . . ."

He checked himself.

"But rather sort it out before talking about it."

"Sing, Digby, sing 'Together' for us!" cried Lucy.

Digby obliged:

Together, together we stand
United, all children demand,
Forgive the debt that we owe,
So we all can grow,
And each build a home
Let every goat roam . . .

"Not sure about the goat business, otherwise you've got a winner," Pearson conceded.

"Jasper Japer arrives soon", said Digby, "to help with production. We have not a minute to spare."

Giving credit for a great idea was one thing; but tolerating an opinionated columnist was another, and Pearson could not help responding bluntly.

"Japer's a wanker," he said. "He's a total tosser."

"Couldn't agree more," said Digby. "But no Japer, no deal. Tied to a deal with his paper. The *Clarion* have agreed to launch their latest appeal, Toys for African Tots, in Kuwisha. And there's this brilliant idea: the final round of 'Peel 'Em Off for Africa' will take place in Kireba."

The page three starlet Phoebe Unsworth would fly to Kuwisha and appear covered from head to toe – "From tits to fanny more like it," said Furniver – in stamps worth £500 each. For every £500 contributed by *Clarion* readers to TAT, Phoebe would remove a stamp, until only the last few remained, strategically placed, of course.

The winner – whose name would be chosen from the list of donors – would be flown to Kuwisha.

"What's the prize?" asked Furniver instantly.

Digby looked at him pityingly.

"The winner gets to remove the last of the stamps, of course."

And Japer had agreed to be the MC, Digby added.

"There is more to come. But you'll have to wait. All depends on whether Nduka gives the go-ahead."

But despite their entreaties, Digby would say no more.

The cement shortage continued, and it was only when an old customer of the Kireba bank came to seek a loan that Furniver realised just what was happening and why.

Ezekiel Mapondera had submitted a breakdown of costs for a hen run he proposed to build. Furniver ran his eye over the figures.

"Some mistake, Mr Mapondera. You have cement at 200 *ngwee* a bag."

"No mistake, Mr Furniver," Ezekiel said proudly. "That is the price I negotiated and I have it in writing, but good for 72 hours only."

"Hang on a mo," said Furniver, burrowing in his brief case to find the notebook that had the data for his index.

"You did well there. I assume your dealer is circumcised?"

Mapondera looked at Furniver pityingly.

"Of course. Otherwise I could not trust him. Anyway, I will collect the cement with the loan. Repayment, 20 eggs a month, yes?"

It had been 25 eggs in fact, but Furniver was not going to argue.

"This Kireba housing business," said Mapondera. "Smells of fish. One day, Nduka tells us that he loves Kireba people.

Next day, cement sales stop. They said there was a hold-up at the port."

He cleared his throat and spat his contempt onto the floor, rubbing it in with the sole of his shoe.

"Myself, I blame the Asians."

He perked up.

"Anyway, I have it in writing. I will collect myself."

Ezekiel had not finished.

"I hear that Mrs Charity has had to delay the new toilets?"

Furniver nodded.

"We couldn't find cement anywhere – not unless we paid the earth."

Ezekiel nodded sympathetically.

"Greetings to Mrs Charity. I might be able to help her. But I will let you know."

Furniver shook the old man's hand and saw him to the door of the office.

"Any help on the cement front would be much appreciated," he said. "But you get your hen run finished first."

Ezekiel tipped his hat to Furniver, muttering as he went: "That Mupanga woman . . . First-class toilet person, first class . . ."

22

The end, when it came, had been mercifully quick. One moment Boniface Rugiru looked up to check that his friend was not in need of a top-up, the next moment he saw the Oldest Member apparently asleep. Only that evening the bar steward had urged the OM to have an early night, and had received an uncharacteristically quiet response.

"Don't fuss, Rugiru. No fuss."

Minutes later his final journey had begun.

It was fitting that the news about the Oldest Member's passing was delivered to Harrods by Rugiru, who had ridden in from the Thumaiga Club to Kireba on his bicycle.

"The *bwana* is now air force," he said simply. "We deliver him into the embrace of the Lord on Wednesday."

Digby, who had arrived just before Rugiru's announcement, whispered to Pearson, "Air force?"

"Not working, out of action – goes back to the guerrilla war. Rhodesians bombed a training camp just outside the city, and the Kuwisha Air Force stayed on the ground. Hence 'air force' – anything or anybody who has thrown in the towel."

"Sounds a bit disrespectful . . ."

"Depends who says it, what circumstances," said Pearson.

A wail from the kitchen indicated that Mildred had been given the news, and her keening attracted the attention of Charity who went to comfort her.

When she emerged, Rugiru called Charity aside.

"He has left money for medicine for the clinic and he has given his clothes to people in Kireba. He has left money for the

Mboya Boys' football team to buy boots. He has also . . ." Rugiru paused. "He has also asked me to organise dough balls for the boys. As many as six. Each."

"You must tell the rats yourself. They will not believe me. This is the first time anybody has given them anything in their will. My goodness!"

Charity summoned the boys and Rugiru gave them the news. It was received with suspicion by Ntoto.

"How much?" he asked.

"How much what?" said Boniface.

"How much is he charging for dough balls?"

"They are free. No charge. They are free."

"Why?"

Rugiru shrugged. How should he know? If it had been up to him, they wouldn't get a single dough ball, let alone free ones, but he set aside the unChristian thoughts.

"Six? Each?"

Rugiru nodded.

Ntoto went into a huddle with Rutere and a couple of other boys. After much whispering, he emerged with an announcement.

"We will be happy to eat the dough balls. But first we will go to the funeral service of the old man to pay respect."

Rugiru's eyes opened wide. This was something he had not anticipated and would add to the considerable difficulties and challenges of running the service. He had already realised that news of the OM's generosity would spread through Kireba as quickly as cholera in a refugee camp and he was prepared for a packed service. But street boys were another matter. However, he was left with no choice: the street boys insisted. They would attend the service.

Rugiru looked around for Furniver. The banker was deep in discussion with a bank member, doubtless discussing the terms of a loan. There was no need for words. Together they walked back to Harrods where Charity pulled two ice-cold Tuskers from the depths of the bar's fridge, ceremoniously opened them, and placed the bottles before the two men.

"He played good cricket," she said simply. "He played good cricket."

23

President Nduka sat immobile behind his oak desk, lost in thought.

The project for Kireba was, just as he had expected, running into problems. That was what happened when you left a project in the hands of ministers not up to the job. It was also what happened, he admitted to himself, when you got old . . .

Cement, water, land rights, power supplies. The list of hold-ups and cost overruns seemed endless, and everyone wanted a little something. Greed, how he hated greed!

Then he took out the rose from the vase on his desk – the thorns had been carefully removed by the duty *toto*. He shook off the drops of water, and attached the flower to the lapel of his pin-stripe suit.

His diary for the day had begun with a meeting with the Chinese trade minister, which he had deliberately allowed to overrun by 20 minutes. The British High Commissioner, who had arrived to discuss the role of UKAid in the redevelopment of Kireba, had no choice but to cool his heels in the ante-room that ran off the ornate ballroom, where the air conditioning had broken down.

That would teach him – though it might not stop the white man delivering another lecture about the importance of good governance and transparency. It really was quite tiresome.

Soon he would have to leave for the funeral service.

He liked to prepare for these occasions. In the early days of independent Kuwisha he had had a hand in the demise of more than one political opponent, as well as several members of the ruling party. He used to find their funerals most productive events. They gave him time to think, and from the pulpit he delivered some fine eulogies in honour of the men and women he had dispatched. But now in his seventies, he spent more and more of his waking hours in conversations with these very same ghosts from his past.

The time for him to join these ghosts was not far off. The Sitholes, the Chisizas, the Mboyas, the Oukos – all had been clever men. They were Africa's lost generation, their talent unfulfilled.

When a funeral service that he attended was particularly tedious, he would pass the time selecting a Cabinet from the ranks of the "disappeared" – the men who had died in unexplained road accidents, or victims of "accidental shootings", or whose health had mysteriously and rapidly deteriorated. True, they would get up to tricks in the Cabinet, but they couldn't help it. That, after all, was why they had been disappeared.

Nduka examined with distaste the papers on his desk, dealing with the redevelopment of Kireba. Provided the World Bank and other aid agencies made the funds available, the first phase of the Kireba project would create up to 500 flats.

To the president's irritation, the World Bank was insisting on holding a donors' conference to draw up the blueprint and to raise the money from the donor community.

They had become so predictable, he thought to himself: *Kireba – Meeting the Challenges, Achieving Potential*, read the title of the main paper.

That word *potential* again . . .

At least the vexed question of whether to renew the contract with the upholstery firm in Surrey was easy. Or was it Sussex? He needed them to help refurbish his home on the coast. It had been on his mind. He had postponed any renewal until after the World Bank auditors had been to Kuwisha, poking their noses into presidential business.

It just took one example of what the bank called "unautho-rised off-budget spending", and their forensic auditors could follow a paper trail of spending that went who knows where? Sure as eggs, the trail would lead to the entertainment budget, which in turn would put investigators on the path of hospitality arrangements for the foreign officials responsible for the order of Mirage jets.

And the British press would sniff around.

After the audit and not before, he decided.

There was no reason, however, he had to deny himself a bit of fun. He decided to send an official invitation to the couple who ran the upholstery firm to attend the independence day celebrations that year. How they would squeal when the recep-tion committee at the airport took them not to a five-star hotel but to jail.

"After, not before . . ."

He would give orders about their reception to Mboga, the senior steward.

"After, not before . . ."

He liked the sound of the words. They emerged with a rasp, a huskiness, authoritative, with an air of menace. He said again: "After, not before," and took a sip of the hot water, laced with honey and lemon, which the new kitchen *toto* had just placed on the table beside his mahogany desk.

The *toto*, who was standing to bare-footed attention, dressed in khaki, trousers and singlet, but no pockets, looked terrified.

He was still on probation.

Only when the old man in front of him, with rheumy eyes and a sharp tongue, gave his approval would the boy become senior kitchen *toto* – official. And then, and only then, would he be entitled to put aside the drab khaki and replace it with a sparkling all-white outfit, a shirt with pockets, starched shorts, complete with belt, knee-length socks and plimsolls, also white.

How the youngster longed for that day; how he craved the uniform that would give him status.

He stared straight ahead, as he'd been instructed. Never should he look the Ngwazi in the eyes. He sensed, however, the president looking at him, with his cold, malevolent glare.

The fact was Nduka missed the *toto's* predecessor, Mlambo . . . Ferdinand Mlambo. Now there was a bright boy! Devious and treacherous, yes, deceitful and cunning, yes. But clever, the boy was clever. And he knew his football. Oh yes. He knew his football.

"Mboga!"

"Mboga!" he called again.

The senior house steward failed to appear.

The *toto* coughed.

"Suh, Mr Mboga, suh, Mr Mboga is retired, suh."

Nduka fixed the boy with his sinister, piercing look.

"Boy, only talk to me when you answer my questions. Be very careful, boy. I think you may be cheeky. A cheeky native – now that is very, very dangerous. If I think you are a cheeky native . . ." He didn't finish his sentence. "Go! You piece of nothing! Tell the driver I am ready."

The lad scuttled off, the sound of his bare feet slapping the polished wooden parquet and echoing down the long passage. Nduka savoured the silence that ensued, broken only by the distant cries of the State House peacocks. Critics unkindly compared the birds' harsh cackle to the president's laugh.

It all came back to Nduka now.

Mlambo's part in the stupid plot to discredit the president, dreamt up by that British journalist, Pearson, had cost the boy his job as the youngest kitchen *toto* on record.

Nduka made a noise in the back of his throat, as if clearing it. Yes, it came back to him. He should have followed his instincts and had the boy killed. Instead he had taken the advice of Mboga, State House steward and Central Intelligence Organisation senior officer.

The boy had made a fool of Mboga, who became mad. What happened next? Yes . . . the boy had been helped by British diplomats to fly to London. That Mlambo. He knew his football. And what was more, he missed him. Getting soft. He should have disappeared him.

A buzzer sounded on his desk. The car was ready to leave for the chapel.

Nduka's knees creaked as he got up from his desk. The security detail saluted as he left his office. He would consider the case of Mlambo later. First the Ngwazi had to say goodbye to an old adversary.

Nduka looked again at the project title. *Potential*! Why could it not be something simple, straightforward? *The Kireba Project*. That was enough. That said it all.

Soon he would have to join the Cabinet of the disappeared. The shadow cabinet. Nduka chuckled. He liked that. The shadow cabinet.

24

"All aboard! All aboard!" declared Furniver. "We leave for the chapel in five minutes. For goodness sake, get a move on, Ntoto."

"I'm coming later," said Ntoto.

Rutere extended his hand.

"Good luck, Ntoto."

The streetboys looked at the bus Furniver had arranged to take mourners to the funeral service with deep suspicion, reluctant to enter such a confined place in case it was a trap. One by one they got as far as the door, looked inside, scratched their crotches thoughtfully, but refused to enter.

"Like herding cats," said Furniver, exasperated.

Only when Charity, acting on a suggestion from Mudenge, gave way to her own increasing exasperation, did they respond.

"Get on the bus, NOW, or dough balls will be cancelled."

One boy broke ranks and the rest followed onto the bus.

Furniver and Ogata stood on either side of the bus entrance.

The last of the boys was about to get on when Furniver held him back.

"Absolutely not. Not a chance."

With much reluctance, the boy surrendered his plastic bag, which he had attempted to smuggle on under his T-shirt.

Mildred Kigali looked on, regretting the fact that she had not been able to convince Furniver that the boys should also be required to surrender their glue bottles.

"That's a step too far," said Furniver. "Let's just be thankful that there are no flying toilets."

Philimon Ogata was having second thoughts about attending the service.

Business at the Pass Port to Heaven Funeral Parlour was booming, he told Charity, though in truth he wanted to give in to the temptation to embrace an ice-cold Tusker.

"Fine," said Charity.

She chalked on the blackboard: "Sales of liquor suspended until after the service for the late OM – out of respect."

Clarence "Results" Mudenge joined Ogata on the bus but not without apprehension about what lay ahead.

Like Ogata, for the first time in his life, Mudenge was going to a white man's service and he felt far from comfortable. There were dozens of small courtesies he wanted to observe, but was uncertain about the cultural conventions.

Would anyone be addressing the ancestors, for example, and explaining why it was that their son would be burnt, his ashes retrieved and then scattered?

He found it hard to conceal his distaste for the European way. Ogata agreed with him.

"These white people are very, very superstitious, and very arrogant. They seem sure that God is a Christian."

Mudenge crossed himself and checked his pockets. The empty bottle, with a cork stopper, was there. It would take just a few seconds to fill from the basin of holy water he was told was kept at the back of the cathedral.

He, like Ogata, yearned for a glass of Tusker. But much as he might want a beer, he knew the consequences. It had been five years, almost to the day, since he had abandoned the demon that was drink, at the end of a binge that had begun with a sip of cold beer and concluded with him sprawled, yet again, in the foetid filth called "mud" in Kireba.

A glass of mango juice, however, with a hint of ginger and crushed mint . . . He closed his eyes and wondered if there would be time . . .

"All aboard," cried Furniver. "Last call!"

"Digby, you sit with me."

Digby, flattered to have been invited, scribbled in his notebook: "How appropriate that my first invitation should be to a funeral . . ."

The party set off.

The journey to the chapel would take at least 30 minutes, longer if the traffic was bad, as it almost certainly would be.

"How about a game of Experts?" asked Furniver, setting up a cardboard box between the seats that would serve as a table. There was a murmur of approval and he began dealing.

As the rules of the game required, he displayed the card that he would be introducing to the pack, exercising the right to have first use of it himself.

The first exchanges in the game were unremarkable, and the stakes were modest. Furniver changed all that.

"You will have to pay to see this one! I claim a six-pointer."

Digby watched, fascinated. That was his card, he was sure. Why all the excitement? Charity and Lucy both whistled in astonishment. If Furniver was bluffing it would cost him dearly – quite possibly a penalty Tusker. But if he really was justified in claiming a six-point business card it would be unprecedented in the history of the game.

Charity was the first to move. She knew her man and he would not be bluffing when the stakes were so high. She dropped out and Lucy followed suit, which left Pearson and Furniver the only two players in the game. Pearson looked at Furniver and detected what he thought was uncertainty in his adversary's eyes.

"See you for three Tuskers. *Cross-cutting Sectoral Advisor* I can just about believe. But a senior consultant as well?" said Pearson.

Furniver's expression didn't change.

"I get these buggers on my doorstep every day, but this one is special, I assure you."

"Pay or fold, pay or fold," cried an onlooker, carried away by the tension.

"Let me get this clear," said Pearson. "You claim that you have, on the same card, an individual, an individual who claims to be a senior international profile coordinator, consultant, cross-cutting media expert *and* a gender specialist . . . but who doesn't work for the UN?"

"Absolutely."

"I don't believe it," said Pearson.

"You know what to do," replied Furniver.

The street boys who had been assigned seats in the back of the bus crept forward, sensing the excitement.

Six Tusker bottle caps were on the table, representing the six bottles of beer that were at stake, the equivalent of a week's income in Kireba.

The onlookers began to chant: "Pay or fold, pay or fold."

"Hush, hush," said Charity.

Contestants were allowed five minutes, maximum, to decide their next move. And while the two men studied the other's face, side bets were laid.

"Okay, show," said Pearson.

Furniver turned over the card in front of him.

Digby Adams
Senior International Profile Co-ordinator & Consultant
Cross-cutting Media Expert & Specialist
WorldFeed
(East Africa)

"Beat that!" said Furniver, triumphantly.

To his credit, Pearson acknowledged his defeat like a man. Those who had been making side bets settled up, and the business card itself was reverentially passed around, evoking calls of astonishment and incredulity.

Pearson was about to ask Furniver if he could keep the card as a souvenir, when he looked more closely at the details. He was right. Although it had been in small letters, obscured by a smudge, it was unmistakable. On the back were the handwritten words: "DanAid advisor."

Pearson cried out. "Furniver has broken rule number five!"

He passed the card round, and invited onlookers to check for themselves.

"I happen to know for a fact that a film on aid and gender issues, in which WorldFeed is playing a consultancy role, is funded by DanAid. And as a WorldFeed profile consultant, Digby will be involved."

Digby confirmed the claim.

Lucy?

"It's true. Match forfeited. It's not your fault," she said to Digby, who had been looking on mystified. "You had nothing to do with it. Edward, you should have checked. You know the rule – Scandinavian aid workers, useless bunch . . . Any link, and a point is deducted."

"Fair enough," said Furniver, "fair enough. Worth a try."

"Want to play in the next round, Digby?" asked Furniver. "There's a good 20 minutes to go till we get there."

As a newcomer to Kuwisha, and a first-time player of Experts, Digby Adams was given the leeway not accorded to residents or regulars. So when he got up to speak, his audience was prepared to be patient and hear him out. He consulted his notes.

"I'd like to say a few words first", he said, "about a project close to my heart. As you know," he said, "I am helping out with a film – or rather what we call a visual documentary – for DanAid. The filming will be focussed on the results of the evaluation's key parameters as identified by the Paris Declaration

(Ownership, Alignment, Harmonisation, Managing for Results, Mutual Accountability), and the discussion of these will provide a framework upon which the narrative of the film will be built. The hypothesis of the film is that by following (filming) programme implementation activities during a one-year cycle, typical aid effectiveness dilemmas will automatically unfold such as the ones presented below based on rural water sector experiences in Benin."

Digby turned over a page. His audience was getting restless.

"Then there is some stuff about dilemmas, which I don't need to go into – ownership dilemmas, alignment dilemmas, harmonisation dilemmas and so on."

"What is a dilemma?" asked Mildred, looking up from her knitting.

"It is a polite word for a problem," said Digby. "Otherwise known as a challenge."

"The audio-visual document will be about GOAT – Guaranteeing Ownership of Africa's Transition – a process, not an objective, which was to have been symbolised by Dolly, God bless her. We will be using funds that were set aside to provide a visual record of the old Kireba."

He went on: "The evaluation of the implementation of the Paris Declaration, and the lessons learned from this first phase, present us with a historical and unique opportunity to communicate and disseminate the process and its findings to the multiple constituencies that stakeholders represent – both inside and outside the 'industry'."

The group started to shuffle restlessly but courtesy demanded that Digby be given a chance to outline his project.

"Nearly there," he said.

"Kuwisha, you will be glad to hear, is at the forefront of the aid effectiveness agenda having piloted many of the latest instruments/initiatives such as a home-grown Poverty Eradication Action Plan (PEAP), Joint Assistance Strategy, Partnership

Principles, Delegated Cooperation, General and Sectoral Budget Support, Sector Working Groups (SWG), Division of Labour. What is more, DanAid has recently restructured its embassy to align the pillars of Kuwisha's PEAP with the overall purpose of enhancing alignment – one of the key aid effectiveness parameters."

It was all getting too much for his audience.

Furniver led the barracking.

"Stakeholders, ownership, practical action-oriented roadmap . . ."

"Overcome dilemmas and respond to the challenge . . ." followed up Lucy.

"Of home-grown results-based management . . ." chipped in Pearson.

Digby continued unabashed.

"Fortunately, the scheme will be led by the talented Poppsy Jinkke, who has worked as an institutional expert in Africa in many different capacities. I am pleased to say", said Digby, "I have her card and I now propose a further round of Experts."

He slapped it on the table triumphantly and declared:

Poppsy Jinkke
Senior Executive Director
Institutional Expert
Cross-cutting Specialist Consultant

"I reckon that's a genuine six-pointer, even allowing for the fact that DanAid is involved."

They all had the good grace to join in the laughter.

25

The bus crawled along the route to the church. While Furniver was preoccupied by the game of Experts, Charity Mupanga contemplated her future, or to be more accurate, their future.

She felt a huge responsibility. On her decision rested the happiness of her dear Furniver. She knew she could never leave Kuwisha. She certainly could not imagine living in England. She shuddered. True, her only experience had been a long time ago, when she joined her late husband David for three months in the summer of his ordination at the Leeds College of Theology.

She had never forgotten her astonishment when, in the middle of a grey and rainy day in June, she had been told that this was indeed a British summer. And on their only outing to London, she had watched people disappear down holes in the pavement of busy streets.

"Just like worms," Mildred had commented, and then held her tongue.

As far as Mildred Kigali was concerned, the great puzzle was how Kuwisha had been colonised by such dreary people. To learn that they lived like worms came as no surprise.

Charity confided her worries to Mildred, who had joined her on a seat away from the crowd that had gathered around the game: "I don't know what to do about Furniver. I know he's not happy. He wants a decision from me – and I'm still not sure."

"Tricky," said Mildred, who put aside her own concerns. "Very tricky."

"I know it is tricky," said Charity, a trifle sharply. "What I want to know is what I should do about him."

Mildred nodded.

"It reminds me of when I met Didymus. He was a young man and I . . ." Her eyes closed as she began to recall the single-minded courting that her dear husband had undergone in order to win her hand.

"He was from the district on the other side of the river and the people in my village were very unhappy that a stranger should be taking one of their women."

Charity interrupted.

"Yes, Mildred," she said. "I know the story. You've told it many times. Even street boys know the story. But unlike Didymus, Furniver is not from the other side of the local river. We know that Didymus swam across the river to court you although it was flooded. My friend Furniver is from the other side of the ocean, and the ways of his people are very, very strange. What is more these people look very odd because under our sun their noses and knees become pink."

Mildred again nodded. Though she kept her counsel on the subject of Furniver, her views were strong and forthright.

"If he loves you and you love him that is enough. And that is all I have to say."

"Not so simple," said Charity. It was more than the relationship between two people, which was difficult enough at the best of times. She and Furniver both had cultural baggage, to which both had to adapt; and not only cultural baggage but other practical concerns. Could Furniver tolerate the heat and the mud and the flies and the mosquitoes and all the other *goggas* (insects) that went with life in Kuwisha, alongside the wonders of nature and the beauty of the countryside?

It was Mildred's turn to interrupt.

"The best way of knowing a man," she said, "is to know what he dreams."

"Dreams?" said Charity, slightly shocked. "Dreams are private business and best kept private."

Mildred persisted. "There are dreams and dreams," she said. "Some dreams might be private, but other dreams need to be shared. Why not ask Results Mudenge? He is very good at the dream business."

Charity was about to dismiss the suggestion but paused. Mildred was a wise woman, albeit with conservative views. As far as she was concerned all men were driven by base needs, interested only in steamies, the inevitable outcome of hanky hanky. Even Mr Kigali himself had succumbed to the primeval forces of nature and asserted his marital rights, and they'd been blessed with seven children.

Mildred's view was straightforward: Charity and Furniver should together seek the inspiration and comfort of the Church of the Blessed Lamb.

"Dreams," said Charity thoughtfully. "Dreams. You have made a good suggestion. I will seek the help of Mr Mudenge."

26

The door of the car that had drawn up outside the chapel shut with a deep "thunk". The irreverent, the agnostics and the atheists in the congregation opened their eyes to catch sight of whomever it was that had arrived late.

There were two clues.

The sound of the "thunk", solid, comfortable, satisfied, was usually made by the door of a substantial car. No one was in any doubt that the visitor was a VIP, for only VIPs were allowed to park in the space that was so close to the church, a space demarcated by a sign saying *No Parking*, and another hand-lettered, which urged citizens to *Keep Kuwisha Clean – Place Your Litter in the Bin*.

Below, in slightly bigger letters, a second line declared: *Another private sector sponsored by the Impala Club of Kuwisha.*

Since there was no bin in sight, conscientious citizens tossed their rubbish onto a pile at the foot of the notice. Others ignored the request altogether.

A second "thunk" gave a further clue to the occupant. The first time the noise was heard it was surely the chauffeur, who must have got out to open a passenger door.

Then there was the sound of gravel under a car tyre, as a heavy vehicle manoeuvred its way to the exit, moving without interruption. Those in the congregation blessed with sharp ears could hear the clang as the single bar gate, operated by the policeman on duty, dropped back in position.

By now most of the assembly had abandoned their prayers and were looking in anticipation at a side door used by such eminent local Christians, including the occasional Cabinet minister, who every Sunday ostentatiously paid their respects to Our Lord.

At any moment the side door to the cathedral would open, and the VIP would make his way to the front row pew.

The bishop of Central Kuwisha glanced at his watch. The minute of silent prayer could be extended, providing time enough for the late arrival to get to his seat.

The watcher would have seen a small, frail figure enter on the arm of his companion. Leaning heavily on his ivory-handled walking stick, he adjusted the red rose in his lapel. He paused, letting his eyes, protected by sunglasses, adjust to the darker interior of the church.

The distance from the door to the front bench was no more than ten paces, each of which seemed to be a mile for the old man.

There was an audible intake of breath from the congregation as he stumbled, recovered and tottered towards the vacant seat on the front row, marked "Reserved". The old man wiped his brow with a red silk pocket handkerchief which matched the rose in his lapel, carefully refolded it, and put it back in the breast pocket of his pin-stripe suit.

The Life President Dr Josiah Nduka, Ngwazi Who Mounts All the Hens, founder of the nation and its leader since independence, had arrived.

"Let us pray for the soul of the dear departed . . ."

The bishop of Central Kuwisha, Alphonse Chitende, hands folded in prayer, stood in his purple vestments alongside the plain wooden coffin. At its foot lay a simple arrangement of freesias; at the head was the big Braun radio.

The radio's silver-coloured frame gleamed in the shadow of the curtain that concealed the entrance to the furnace. Boniface Rugiru had been up half the night, polishing, polishing, polishing, in loving memory of the deceased. A bulb lit up the yellow, green and red glass panel which gave the location of scores of stations, names that evoked the history of the empires that once ran Africa.

Although it was 50 years since he first set eyes on the great beast of a radio, Rugiru could still recite, in order of their appearance on the panel, the names of these exotic locations, learnt at the age of 14 when he began work as one of several "small boys" employed at the Thumaiga Club. Unaware that he was producing a litany of colonial dominance, ignorant of any political significance, he had turned the names into a song, which he sang as he dusted and swept the Club quarters of the member to whom the magnificent machine belonged.

He had sung that same song the night before the service, sometimes as a mournful dirge, then changing the beat so it became a defiant chant which halted the tears that had started to roll down his cheeks.

Jo'burg, Cape Town and Salisbur-eee.
The world is watched by the BBC,
Pretoria, Bulawayo, Nairob-eee,
Wherever in Africa you may be
Bloemfontein, Gwelo even Umtali,
You cannot keep a secret from BBC . . .

It seemed only yesterday that he had been a Thumaiga Club *toto*, prancing around the radio, flicking his yellow duster at imaginary enemies. Sometimes the boy bent low, and then exploded into a frenzy of dusting, sometimes he stood still while the yellow cloth seemed to take on a life of its own as it flew over the surfaces, turning into gold ingots the brass catches on the windows that overlooked the flower beds, patches of colour in the green grass.

One day, he had been interrupted by the Club's shoe boy, an ambitious youth who made no secret of his ambition to become the deputy linen manager by his mid-twenties.

"I see you, Rugiru, dancing the tune of the *mzungu* and singing in their praise."

Boniface had defended his position, getting a bloody nose for his trouble, but eventually forcing the boy to sing the song, standing with bowed head in front of the all-powerful radio.

It was not long after this that he had discovered the radio manual.

The right-hand drawer of the desk in the room was usually locked. This day, however, the key had been left in the lock. Rugiru looked through the window, across the flower beds to the gravel car park and checked that the member's old Mercedes had not returned. Then he did what any 14-year-old would have done. He opened the drawer.

Most of the papers were bills, along with a couple of letters, and a manila envelope. Inside the envelope he found the photograph that had shocked, thrilled and amazed Rugiru in equal measure. He looked at it long and hard, then put it back in the drawer. It was not his business. Settler society would neither understand nor forgive the intimacy that it conveyed. But the instruction manual for the radio that topped the pile was another matter.

He had checked again that the car was not in its usual spot and settled down to study the document that would initiate a novice into the mysteries of the machine.

"To operate the instrument", the instructions began, "slide down the on-off switch to the 'on' position. Turn the rotary knob marked 'volume' clockwise to increase the 'volume of reproduction'."

He had read on, entranced.

"Instrument," he murmured. This was no common or garden radio. It was an instrument, which dominated the room, sitting solidly atop a bookcase, like a castle on a headland. Although it was called portable, powered by no fewer than six large batteries, it was the size of a small suitcase.

This was no mere radio. It carried the voice of the world, the BBC, which boomed in from London. It was indeed an instrument, a veritable musical instrument, like an old violin, that had to be coaxed to life with the aid of fine tuning and adjustment of the aerial.

Enthralled, the young Rugiru read on: "The instrument is equipped with a telescopic dipole for the FM band, a telescopic antenna for SW bands, and a ferrite antenna for LW, MW and SW 8 bands."

On some days he would come into the room to find the Braun had been moved from its usual place on top of the book-case, where it stood as a defiant rampart against ignorance; instead it was on the bedside table, a reliable companion during the lonely hours of insomnia.

Decades later, in the era of computers and internet, mobile phones and radios that could fit in the palm of a hand, the appeal of the old instrument was as powerful as ever, evoking the past, and redolent of a conservative authority that had long passed.

In short, to call the majestic Braun a "radio" was like calling a Rolls Royce a car.

The congregation had stopped coughing and sneezing, scratching and fiddling, and in response to the bishop's call, bowed its collective head. In the minute of silence that followed, they no doubt contemplated the vicissitudes of life, its unpredictable or transient nature, relieved only by their certainty that the arms of our Lord would embrace them at the end of their earthly toil.

At a signal from the bishop, Boniface pressed a switch on the panel, and the throaty chant of a guerrilla song rang out, filling the chapel with memories of Kuwisha's fight for independence.

"Odd choice, the last thing that I would have expected," Furniver thought to himself.

Rugiru lifted his eyes to the ceiling, and held back a cheer. The system really worked! He limited himself to another grunt of satisfaction, which prompted a further look of concern from Charity.

How he wished that the radio had been left to him, a gift that he would have treasured for the rest of his days. The thought of it being consumed by the flames along with his friend caused anguish in his heart. This time Rugiru was unable to hold back a sob of distress.

"Poor Rugiru," Charity Mupanga said anxiously. "Poor Rugiru."

"Poor Rugiru," echoed Results Mudenge, who was sitting next to Philimon Ogata.

Only six months ago Ogata had buried his wife; his racking cough suggested that he had not long to go himself, but he turned a deaf ear to appeals that he stop smoking.

Mercy Mupanga, who ran Kireba's only medical clinic, was next to her cousin, Charity Mupanga, alongside Edward Furniver, who had squeezed into his only suit, as befitted the manager of Kireba's Co-operative Savings Bank.

On the same row, sitting ramrod straight, was Didymus Kigali, a senior elder of the Church of the Blessed Lamb, a distinguished figure in his suit, handed down to him many years ago by a former employer, and ironed that morning by Mildred.

Neither showed their advancing years.

"Not a bad turnout," murmured Furniver.

"Shush," admonished Charity, and gave his hand a squeeze.

Furniver shifted his haunches, made numb by the austere wooden bench. How on earth did Mr Kigali manage to remain so still?

Not a seat to spare. Not a bad turnout at all, even after taking into account that two rows were occupied by slack-eyed street children, their number swollen by the promise of free dough balls, as requested in the last will and testament of the deceased.

A few benches in front of Furniver the street urchins scratched their scrawny flanks, picked their noses and explored their nostrils with probing index fingers. Every now and then they searched their curls – many of which had an orange tinge, a sure sign of malnutrition – giving little grunts of satisfaction when they trapped head lice. After crushing the creatures between nails of forefinger and thumb with an audible click, their fingers moved on to explore different locations around their skinny frames, from armpits to toenails, and on to more intimate crevices.

The Mboya Boys, who had to be dissuaded from bringing their football team banner, had gone to great lengths to dress for the event. Most of them wore all the clothes they possessed, partly because they could afford no more than a single outfit, and partly because if they had an extra shirt or pair of trousers, they lacked a safe place in which they could store them.

All the while they watched the proceedings, like drunks checking their change, with bemused and befuddled concentration, pupils dilated and eyes red-rimmed. Every now and then the boys took deep sniffs from the tubes of glue that hung round their necks, and licked their lips in anticipation of the dough balls that had been promised them.

Far too much time, however, had been spent trying to persuade them to leave their glue bottles at the door, and not enough time ensuring that they were upwind of the congregation. Instead they had been seated downwind, at the main entrance, where the breeze carried the powerful odour of tyre smoke and stale perspiration under the nostrils of the dozen or so members of the diplomatic corps in attendance.

One boy in the group seemed marginally more alert than the rest. Rutere's heavy-lidded stare fixed on a guest several rows in front of him. The lad was dressed in an Arsenal shirt which, judging by the way it clung to his bony chest, suggested it was damp, and had been washed that very morning; the shirt was several sizes too big for him, falling almost to his knees and all but concealing a pair of shorts.

"Rutere," hissed a fellow street boy, "where is Ntoto?"

Rutere thought about boxing the boy's ears for asking such a cheeky question, but decided against it.

"Coming later."

Rutere looked around, mentally marking the route to the nearest exit and congratulating himself for selecting the seat at the end of the row nearest the entrance to the chapel.

His finger traced the rim of his nostril as he looked with fear and loathing at the back of Mayor Guchu's head, propelling dark thoughts in the man's direction. One of Guchu's bodyguards turned and spotted Rutere, and glared at the boy, mouthing the words:

"Mupanga's rats!"

Furniver followed the direction of Rutere's stare.

"Who invited that awful bugger?" he asked Charity. "Fact is," he said, "Guchu is a grade A shit. Whether he is Nduka's bagman, I don't know. But the finances of the City Council are a disgrace, and Guchu has been milking the books for ages."

Charity chipped in: "Poor secretaries. All who work in Guchu's office leave because they are with child, and Guchu is their father."

"So who invited him?" Furniver asked again.

"He just came," said Charity. "One does not get an invitation to a funeral. Perhaps he came with the president?"

"Whatever," said Furniver. "He's a very nasty piece of work."

All the while Rutere's finger was furiously working its way round his nostril.

Furniver resumed watching him with a combination of fascination and distaste.

"Bloody Rutere! Wish he'd stop picking his nose."

The Kireba Youth Choir got ready to sing, all loose wrists and extended fingers, looking more like a basketball team than semi-finalists in the All-Kuwisha interdenominational church choir competition for the second successive year.

Their skinny frames came alive under their ill-fitting jackets and shiny polyester black trousers, and their hips began to twitch in time to the music, not so much suggesting a life of their own, but an assertion of life itself.

The few whites in the congregation sat in uncomfortable, self-conscious silence; the rest of the assembly joined in the singing with gusto.

Furniver gave a cough of approval. Who would have thought it? Word of his friend's generosity in funding the township's only clinic, as substantial as it was unexpected, had spread through Kireba like a bush fire during a drought. The people of Kireba showed their appreciation in the only way they could, murmuring as they filed past the coffin: "*Hamba gahle*, old man, go well."

The service was brought to an end with a second round of BBC time pips.

The final *Peeep!* sounded, and Rugiru pressed the button on the panel that controlled the tape recorder linked to the organ speakers. The foot-stomping throb of the old guerrilla marching chant burst out, and for a few minutes the congregation was transported back to Kuwisha's long struggle for independence from Britain – or the *Breetishi*, as the colonial power was commonly referred to.

Charity smoothed her dress, collected from the dry cleaner that very morning by one of her rats, and sat up straight-backed and broad-shouldered.

Alongside her, Furniver sat and looked around.

"Where is Ntoto?" he asked Charity.

"I thought he was with Rutere," she replied.

Next to him, Pearson, head bowed, held Lucy's hand.

Furniver's attention continued to be attracted by the activities of Rutere, prompting him to turn to Pearson and exclaim: "Look! Look. Look at that little bugger. If he's not picking his nose, I don't know what nose-picking is! Watch his finger," he whispered excitedly. "Just watch . . . there it goes, inside . . . Got the little blighter on toast," he said. "You are my witness."

It was one thing they agreed on.

Rutere might be clever; indeed, he was as sharp as a tack. But their analysis of the actions of his forefinger led to one conclusion. The boy was an inveterate nose-picker.

In an elaborate mime, Pearson tried to attract the attention of Charity, who was engaged in silent prayer. His forefinger simulated Rutere's thrust, circle and probe, thrust, circle and probe, though when it came to the circular motion that was the characteristic of the boy's habit, his own aperture was mean and narrow by comparison to Rutere's majestic flared orb.

He nudged Charity, determined that she should open her eyes and see for herself what was happening, while continuing to mimic the street boy's actions.

Whether by accident or design, Rutere's timing was perfect. As the bishop called for the prayers for the soul of Kuwisha's son, Rutere's piping voice carried clearly around the chapel.

"Furniver is nose-picking!"

Didymus Kigali got to his feet, but instead of climbing the few steps that led to the front of the pulpit, stood at the bottom on a raised platform that made up for his height and allowed the congregation to see him.

Kigali's sermon would be the highlight of the service. Rugiru wished that his wife Grace could have been with him instead of tending to one of their fever-ridden children. Two were already "in the arms of Jesus", helped on their journey by Philimon Ogata, and a further two were studying abroad, one in England, one in Texas.

Furniver looked on with admiration as Kigali made his way to the pulpit.

Every day he saw Kigali as his steward, dressed in his starched white shirt, matching shorts that came to his knees, and white plimsolls. This time Didymus Kigali was in a suit, as befitted a senior elder in the Church of the Blessed Lamb, the fast-growing fundamentalist Christian sect affiliated to the Kimbanguists of Congo.

It was a most unusual step for an elder to participate in a conventional church service, for it went against all the sect's principles.

One of the tenets of the Lambs' faith was that worship of the Lord should not take place in a man-made structure. The hills are our altar, the trees our shelter, the skies our roof, as their creed put it.

But not only was Kigali prepared to attend the service, he was ready to deliver an admonition.

The congregation sat in happy expectation of what was to come: the bishop would lead the way, his conversational style in contrast to the delivery of Kigali. The difference in stature had been noted, the bishop of substantial girth and a light voice, whereas Kigali was modestly built but possessed a powerful bass.

Brows were mopped, scratching was frequent, as were the coughs, but any physical discomfort was forgotten in the atmosphere of keen anticipation.

As he approached the pulpit, Kigali passed Charity Mupanga and the two exchanged a murmured greeting. Kigali had shared her sorrow over David's death and had also attended the funeral of her dear father, Harrods.

No one knew for sure what year Kigali had been born, though he claimed to remember the great migration of the animals, at the time of the drought. This would have made him at least 70 years old.

My, my! Charity clicked her tongue in admiration. Seventy years! Born not long after the arrival of "Europeans", the white folk who came to Kuwisha and made farms on what they called "virgin land", where they grew tea and coffee.

Strange to think that her father and the *mzungu* whose death they were about to mourn and whose life they were to celebrate, were almost contemporaries. They could have known each other! Well, she looked forward to the bishop's eulogy and to Didymus Kigali's admonition. Perhaps they would try to explain how these two men could have such different lives, both rising to the top of their professions yet remaining so far apart on society's scale of values.

Her father, a young man from the bush, who had sought work in the city, had served the British High Commission for 35 years, entering service as a "brush man", whose sole responsibility was to clear the driveway of leaves. By the time he retired, he was head gardener.

And the British High Commissioner, even, called him *mzee*, the term of respect accorded to wise old men.

Charity bowed her head, closed her eyes and tried to shut out the outside world, and to block her ears to the growl of traffic and the cries of the *matatu* boys. She felt at home here in the cathedral where her dear late husband David had delivered his last sermon. Was it really five years ago? It could have been yesterday, for the words came back to her . . .

"They say there are no atheists in the foxholes of the front line of war. So is it in Africa, where those of us who live on the continent daily thank God, or Allah, or the ancestors, for delivering us from the perils that surround us."

It was a sermon that had touched the lives of everyone, rich or poor. With wit, charm, and compassion he attacked government incompetence and the endemic corruption that was destroying Kuwisha.

And as the sermon's fame spread, so did the sobriquet "bishop of the battered, shepherd of the shattered".

A few days later, Bishop David Mupanga was dead, killed in an accident of the sort he warned about in his sermon – or, as many believed, assassinated by the Public Relations Unit; members of which had been present throughout David's sermon, ostentatiously talking into lapel microphones, murmuring behind a cupped hand.

The abiding memory of that day, however, for Charity at least, had been the looks of confusion, shame and ultimately joy on the faces of the half dozen members of the Special Branch Unit whose full-time job was to monitor David's movements.

At the end of his sermon he had stepped down from the pulpit and embraced the men who had surrounded the pulpit in a heavy-handed attempt to intimidate him.

"Let us pray," said Didymus Kigali.

And then, without notes, he began to speak, and his rich, resonant tones filled the chapel.

27

"We are here to say farewell to a man of opposites," Kigali began.

"To some, who saw him only as the retired district commissioner, he was a racist. But to Boniface Rugiru he was a good friend, and he trusted Rugiru to make the arrangements for his final journey. And when I last looked at him, Rugiru was a black man. To some, the Oldest Member was a racist. But if he were a racist, why did he leave his money to Kireba? Why did he insist on dough balls for the street boys?"

There was an outbreak of clapping from the boys. They were now prepared to accept that they would, definitely, be given dough balls. If Didymus Kigali had said so it must be true.

"There is one thing that cannot be doubted. The Oldest Member was never corrupt. This I know for sure. When my father had two cows stolen, he went to seek justice from the local district commissioner, the man we knew as the Oldest Member."

There were whistles of astonishment from the audience. This was the first time Kigali had disclosed a personal link with the deceased.

"Never did my father have to pay for justice, like the people have to pay the magistrates today. Never. True, the deceased did not say sorry for serving the British, but he did learn our language. Never did he express regret for serving as an officer in the colonial army that tried to crush our nationalism – although he fought bravely for freedom in the war against the Nazis."

"Never," echoed the congregation.

"Never," said Rugiru. "Never. Never did he stand up and say that colonial rule was wrong."

"Never," the congregation roared back.

"But together we defeated the British. Together we gave them a good hiding. Together we hit them for a six."

The mood changed in an instant, and the congregation let out a collective roar of laughter, apart from the street boys, who looked baffled by the proceedings.

"Today we suffer from a different disease," Kigali continued. "The British have gone. Gone forever, though every now and then they send their dogs to mark the territory they think they own."

Mr Kigali then imitated the action of a dog lifting its leg, his expression solemn.

The congregation burst into applause, and roared its approval.

"Colonialism has been defeated! But corruption has taken its place, and it destroys our lives. Our brother was indeed a racist – but he was not corrupt. Like you and like me, he was a flawed man, but he was an honest man."

Kigali then reached into the pocket of his suit and took out a piece of paper, which he waved at the congregation.

"I expect", he said, "you know what this is. It is the last sermon of my dear brother in Christ, the late Bishop David Mupanga, whose words are as important today as when he first uttered them.

"Let me remind you of what he said. He said there are no atheists in the trenches of war and suggested that that is why we so often thank God if we live in Africa. But whether we live here, or whether we are regular visitors, we thank God, or Allah, or the ancestors, for our many deliverances, with fervour and humility."

The congregation murmured its support and understanding and Charity shut her eyes and imagined herself back amongst the congregation on that day, listening to the rest of the sermon delivered in David's confident, deep voice.

"We thank God when we arrive safely at our destination, whether by car or train or ferry or aircraft. We thank God that the car's brakes did not fail during the long journeys on Africa's potholed roads; we are grateful that our driver spotted the lorry that was parked ahead without tail lights; and we give thanks that the over-loaded ferry did not sink."

"Thank God," said the congregation.

"We give especially heartfelt thanks when we arrive safely at our destination after travelling at night, unmolested by the armed robbers who make their living along the highways, who so often seem to be dressed in uniforms stolen from the army or the police force."

"Thank God!" cried the congregation.

"We live with risk, some more than others, but we all live with it, whether it is the risk of Aids, or the risk of a car accident because we lack spare parts, or the risk of malaria, or even worse, catching malaria that has learnt to defy pills. We thank God.

"We thank God when we have the energy to face the day, that we do not have bilharzia, or other intestinal worms or parasites that suck the vitality of their victims.

"We thank God when a child enjoys a birthday, and we thank God if he or she survives the hazards of being young in Africa. We thank God if our children are lucky in Africa's lottery. We thank God if they are not one of the 3 million children who die each year from preventable diseases before they reach the age of five.

"We thank God if they emerge numerate or literate. We are particularly thankful if it is a girl who survives, because for her the hazards of life are much greater.

"We do not despair because that is a cardinal sin. We try not to succumb to fatalism but instead, if one is a Christian, one soon learns from the wisdom of another faith, and utters a precautionary word that reminds one of human frailty: *Inshallah* – God willing.

"We thank God for a decent meal because most of the 700 million souls who live on our continent go without adequate nourishment.

"We thank God if we live in peace because millions of us have lives made hell by war. We thank God if we have clean water to drink, because most of us do not and we consider ourselves fortunate if we do not have to walk miles to fetch it.

"We thank God if we are not a refugee, on a continent where millions have been forced to flee their homes, seeking sanctuary within or without the country that is our home.

"So in Africa we thank God, or Allah, with unusual frequency and we are especially thankful if we end the day alive and well, with a meal in our stomachs, with a bed to sleep on and our loved ones safe. Above all, we thank God for our friends."

And with these words, Didymus Kigali, elder in the Church of the Blessed Lamb, stepped away from the pulpit and took his place in the front row.

President Josiah Nduka turned to him and, hand outstretched, leant across and muttered in Kigali's ear:

"Well done, Kigali. Good stuff. As you say, corruption is a great evil."

28

Mayor Guchu, rolls of flesh bulging above his collar, made his way to the exit of the chapel, where he and other VIPs waited for their cars to turn up. He was surrounded by his security guards who looked longingly at the street boys, like obedient guard-dogs spotting stray cats.

"Mupanga!"

Guchu's call reached the ears of Furniver and Charity who were shaking hands with departing mourners. At first she ignored the cry from the man she loathed.

"Mupanga!"

It was not so much called, as hissed – a remarkable achievement, given there was not a sibilant syllable in her name.

"Mupanga!"

Then one of Guchu's aides, a man in his mid-forties, slim, medium height, eyes concealed behind dark glasses, mobile phone in a pouch attached to his belt, took up the cry: "Mupanga!"

This time the syllables were enunciated carefully and separately as his tongue rapidly licked each corner of his lips, flicking to one side and then the other, like a lizard in anticipation of its prey.

"Mu-pang-a!"

The syllables emerged into the open air, where they hung, redolent with contempt.

As Guchu looked on, with a smirk on his face, the aide handed her a brown envelope, with her name typed below the words that had been printed in large bold letters: **Official – City Council.**

Charity had been half expecting some form of retaliation or punishment for the fact that she had long been a thorn in the side of government. There were two weapons frequently used against "dissidents" by the ruling party of President Nduka: tax returns were inspected with especial thoroughness, and foreign currency transactions were scrutinised. If the letter of the law was followed, it was an offence to possess any currency other than *ngwee* unless it had been purchased at a bank.

Charity had taken great care to keep her tax obligations up to date, and the accountant who checked the books of Kuwisha's co-op bank, ran a sharp eye over her returns for nominal fee.

As for foreign currency transactions, she was equally careful. Every now and then a foreigner who visited her bar would pay for food and drink in dollars, or leave a donation. These dollars Charity then exchanged for *ngwee* with Furniver, at the official rate. The receipts were kept in the cash box, under the bar, ready for inspection, should it prove necessary.

She looked more closely at her tormentor. There was something familiar about his face. Where had she seen it before? Then she remembered. The man at the shoulder of the mayor at every public function, standing so close that they appeared to share the same neck.

Of course! It was Cedric "Two Head" Moyo, special assistant to Mayor Guchu.

"So what nonsense is this?" she asked.

"Read. It is the law. Just read . . . Mupanga."

Guchu's sidekick had chosen his moment well. As he handed the envelope to Charity, he moved alongside Mayor Guchu, who was waiting for his Rolls Royce to arrive.

It could be seen in the middle distance, about to pull out of the garage where it had been fed by Titus Ntoto.

*

The encounter in the cathedral porch, as they trooped out from the service, had taken Furniver by surprise. A tall man, in his seventies, with a mop of silver hair, approached him.

"Knew your uncle." He held out his hand.

"I say!" exclaimed Furniver, with the enthusiasm with which one greets a stranger who seems to know you.

He bought himself more time.

"I say!" he said again.

Things were getting desperate. Thank God he had been in Africa long enough to set aside some of the characteristic English reserve.

He embraced the man. It was essential to retain the initiative.

"Wonderful to see you here," he said. "Wonderful."

He waited for a clue.

"Oliver was absolutely right."

For a moment Furniver wondered if he was in the right place. Then he realised that the man who was almost universally known as the Oldest Member had been called Oliver by his contemporaries.

"Spitting image of your dad. Hell of a man. Could kill a fly at ten paces with his *sjambok*. Did he ever tell you about the evening when we were posted to Somabula? Gather you're a chip off the old block, eh? Oliver told me about how you wanted to deal with your boy and the *jipu*."

Furniver winced.

"First, take your boy behind the *kia*," said the stranger, hooting with laughter. "Know what you mean, nudge nudge and all that. Oliver seemed to think you wanted to go a bit too far. He was always a bit on the liberal side. Got soft in his old age. Suffocate the blighters. Improve their ironing no end." He hooted again.

Suddenly it all fell into place.

It could only be "Flogger" Moreland. And he knew for certain that he had never met him before in his life.

It would have been discourteous to cut the conversation short, and Furniver had no wish to offend an old settler. He was running out of small talk.

"How did you get here?" he asked.

"Came up from the coast," said Flogger. "First time I've made the journey for ages, and it'll be the last time. Absolute hell."

Furniver gave him an encouraging lift of expectant eyebrows.

"The experience proved something or other. It's the closest thing I know to running a piss-up in a brewery. If you can't make a decent fist of managing a railway, which should be faster than the road route, cheaper than lorries and a great tourist lark, something is seriously wrong." Flogger paused. "And I blame the UN."

Furniver's curiosity got the better of him.

"Sorry, don't quite follow. How can you blame the UN for a local cock-up?"

"If the silly buggers allow their railway line to be run by foreigners there are no opportunities for the locals."

Furniver prodded him for more.

"I took the 1900 from Mombasa to Nairobi, which was running, or to be precise standing, 30 minutes late. On board was the usual gang of rat-catchers: a couple of Brits complaining about the warm beer and a Swedish student – not to mention a Frenchman old enough to know better, travelling with a lithe young companion. Then something in me snapped," said Flogger. "It was not that the beer when it finally arrived was warm; that the toilet had no seat, soap or paper; or that the whole train was filthy from the first-class section to the third-class carriages. It was my fellow foreigners that made me so furious. They found it 'quaint'. And the others said it was 'all rather unusual'. One told the rest of the carriage that she'd travelled on 'more challenging trains' in India. It made me feel bloody ashamed," said Flogger. "I resented Kuwisha being patronised by tourists, however well meaning. I don't want to read guide books which talk about 'hearty cooked meals, served by white-coated attendants', who 'make eating in the dining car an experience in itself'."

By now, Flogger was well into his stride.

"It was bloody sad, not quaint; it was typical, not unusual; and it was bloody dispiriting, not challenging.

"Forty-odd years after independence," he continued, "Kuwisha's railway has been run down by an elite with their bums in the butter and their money in road haulage."

Furniver thought the man would never stop, banging on about the squalid state of the national train service and the run-down state of facilities in general.

"I'm staying at the Thumaiga Club," said Flogger. "See you there. We can have a long chat over a G and T."

There was only one response. Furniver hugged him again.

"Absolutely right! See you there. Absolutely," said Furniver and vowed he would go nowhere near the place until Rugiru had told him that the coast was clear.

29

The service, widely regarded as a triumph for Boniface Rugiru, had ended on a sour note for the man himself. Indeed, it was only through the exercise of considerable self-discipline that he was able to conclude his final duties.

While Charity was being served with official papers that threatened the very existence of Harrods, Boniface Rugiru stood at the top of the steps and shook hands with the mourners as they filed out. The event had been a tremendous success, if that was the right term to use. It had gone without a hitch and Rugiru graciously accepted the congratulations offered by all and sundry.

But far from feeling the benefits of catharsis that a good funeral send-off should provide, he looked deeply distressed and several of the departing congregation commented on this. They put it down to the stress of the occasion and the pain of his loss. Boniface chose to keep silent about the theft of the radio.

Silence was the only way to cope.

Had he not stayed quiet, he feared he would have been unable to maintain his relative equanimity and would have broken down in tears of rage and frustration.

"It was so quick," Boniface later told his wife, who was still tending their fever-struck youngest son.

"In one shake of a duck's tail, the radio, it just disappeared."

As to the culprit, he had his suspicions. The crematorium's gardener and odd-job man, an Okot, was at the top of his list. After all, he was from the north of Kuwisha, and from the clan of the same name. Rugiru shared his suspicions with his wife that evening.

Part of his case against the man, he acknowledged, was based on nothing other than prejudice.

"But the main reason", continued Rugiru, dipping a ball of *nshima* into the tasty goat gravy made by his wife, "is that you can never trust an Okot man."

He was already due to return to the crematorium the next day to collect the Oldest Member's ashes. Now that sad journey had an additional purpose. He would chase the Okot man, and with the help of our Lord, recover the radio.

"You will be lucky," said his wife. "This is Kuwisha. Okot has probably sold the radio already."

"I tell you," said Rugiru, "I will find that thief tomorrow and I will complain directly to the manager of the crematorium about the staff that he employs. Disgraceful!"

The next morning Boniface Rugiru, dressed once more in his senior bar steward uniform, mounted his bicycle and set off for the crematorium, determined to confront the general manager. His fury and his shame had not diminished overnight, although his wife had counselled restraint. He knew that the chances of recovering the Braun radio were negligible. Whoever had stolen it would almost certainly have sold it by now but he was determined that the culprit would not get off scot free.

As he approached the grounds of the chapel of the crematorium, he was greeted politely by the gardener, who waved from a far-off section of the Garden of Rest, where he was tending a flower bed.

Rugiru returned the greeting with a curt nod, so curt as to be almost rude. Any doubt that he'd had as to who was responsible was removed by this outrageous behaviour. Only an Okot could be so hypocritical!

His wife Patience had not improved his mood that morning when she had defended the Okot clan, doubtless because her clan were closer to the Okot people than his own, which hoarded memories of raids on cattle as fresh in their mind as if they'd taken place yesterday.

Rugiru propped up his bike against the railings outside the manager's office, locked it and took his seat in the office from where he could keep an eye on the bicycle.

"Mr Chipanda will see you now," said his secretary.

Rugiru scowled. The name was a giveaway. He must be a Lua. If the Okots were thieves, the Luas were certainly as bad. The combination of the one lot's thievery and the other lot's cunning was formidable and Rugiru regretted he'd left his stout stick behind.

"He will see you now," said the secretary again.

Rugiru wanted to get it over as soon as possible and entered the office.

"Gideon Chipanda," the man held out his hand, which Rugiru shook reluctantly.

"Mr Chipanda, I've come to see the Okot man. I am very . . ."

Chipanda intervened.

"Let me call him now," he said. "And you can thank him for yourself. Perhaps, even, you will want to give him a small present?"

Rugiru was nonplussed. If there was anything he would give this audacious thief it was a good kick up the arse.

"Let me go and call him," said Chipanda. "I'll be back in a minute."

More than ever, Rugiru wished he'd brought his stick. He cast his eyes around the modest office and saw on the desk of Mr Chipanda a well-thumbed copy of a book, whose title, on closer inspection, Rugiru was able to read: *Running a Crematorium: A Basic Guide.*

Before Rugiru could make a closer examination, Chipanda had returned but noticed his interest in the book.

"My bible," joked Chipanda, adding: "The Okot man, who is a very good gardener by the way, will be along any minute.

That book," he said, shaking his head in admiration. "That book is excellent. Many times I have consulted it and every time it has come up with the answer to my problem. Or", he said, "given me a warning of what could become a problem. You will not believe, Mr Rugiru, some of the requests that we get from our customers. Or, I suppose I should say, relatives of some of our customers.

"Sometimes people want company on their last journey. Many settlers want to take their dogs with them. I myself do not want my dog to come with me, wherever I am going. But the settlers want their dogs. I myself would choose my favourite cow."

At this point the secretary put her head around the door.

"The ashes for the late Mr Smeldon are ready for collection," she said. "Are you sure, Mr Rugiru, you don't want tea? I am told it was a very good service."

Rugiru shook his head. Things were not proving quite as he had anticipated.

"Tea, Mr Chipanda?"

"Yes, please."

Chipanda picked up the booklet.

"Let me read to you", he said to Rugiru, "the section which was so helpful in preparing for yesterday's sad event. It is called *The Case of The Exploding Bullet*. 'It must be stressed', wrote the author of this book, 'that the habit of mourners in Karimoja, where cattle rustling is very bad of placing of a live bullet in the coffin out of respect for the occupant is to be discouraged. There have been reports of injuries caused – though thank God no fatalities – by bullets exploding after the coffin has been consumed by the fire. On one occasion, sad to relate, there was a serious misunderstanding between rival groups and there was an exchange of fire between bodyguards in the congregation.' "

He chuckled. "As for batteries, they also explode. And when I saw that the radio was going into the fire, I had to signal to the Okot man to catch it in time. The batteries would certainly have exploded and many people might have thought they were bullets, and with the president himself attending who knows how his bodyguards might have reacted."

Mr Chipanda chuckled again.

"I was a bit surprised that your friend did not leave instructions for the radio to be removed. He had thought of everything else. So, Mr Rugiru, you can understand that we were saved from great embarrassment by our friend the gardener."

The secretary brought in the tea and returned a moment later with an urn containing the ashes of the Oldest Member.

"Here we are, Mr Rugiru," she said, handing over the urn.

Behind her stood a beaming Okot man. He handed over, respectfully bowing as he did so, the Braun radio. At the same time, Chipanda gave Rugiru a handwritten note.

"He asked me to give it to you when I handed over the ashes. He was most insistent. No radio, no note. Any idea why, Mr Rugiru?"

Rugiru shook his head. He read the note:

Dear Rugiru,
We hit 'em for a six! Look after the radio.

"It was very embarrassing," said Rugiru to his wife that evening.

"Surely you were very pleased, my husband, because you now have the radio back. The Okot man was not stealing, he was helping. And even Mr Kigali says you can keep it."

She might have stayed silent, for all the notice Rugiru took of his wife's words.

"Very, very embarrassing," said Rugiru, "I had to thank an Okot man."

His wife sighed. "There is a message from Mrs Mupanga," she said. "They will pick us up tomorrow at the Thumaiga Club."

"An Okot man," Rugiru repeated, shaking his head.

What was the world coming to?

There was one thing that always puzzled Nduka. If the reforms, insisted upon by the West, were so obviously in Kuwisha's interest, why did they bribe his government to implement them?

An IMF deal could easily bring in $250 million – but when you included the World Bank loan that followed, funds from the European Development Bank and bilateral offerings from the donors, a deal that was done in their own interest could easily generate a billion dollars. The ways of the West were indeed strange.

Still, who was he to complain? All it would cost was a memo and a few promises.

Berksson had asked for a letter to all the participants and he had promised to deliver it by the next morning.

"Progress on the project to rebuild Kireba," he wrote.

"I wish to congratulate all involved in this great scheme to transform Kireba. Such is the progress, that we feel that posterity would not forgive us if this historic opportunity was not grasped to the full.

"Not only does it envisage the building of 500 flats, we plan to have a market and a crèche as well as a community centre."

"But more than this, we need to seize a once-in-a-lifetime opportunity to turn Kireba into the hub of a regional transport system which will include rail and road links to the coast.

"We know we can count on your governments' support when we put this to the World Bank and other funding agencies.

30

She had to decide, and soon. To delay was not fair to Furniver. Would he join her on the *shamba*, helping to cultivate the coffee for which Kuwisha was famous, and care for the cattle? Or would they go their separate ways, retreat into their separate cultures and traditions?

Charity looked into her heart. The answer to him, she feared, had to be no.

Much as she loved Furniver, she could not live in England and be the same person. And if this were true of her, why should it not be true of Furniver? Did he not find the heat oppressive? And did he not hate the mud?

As to other differences, she could live with them: the extraordinary fact that Furniver's children were growing up without knowing their father; that they had to endure the apparent absence of an extended family, poor things.

But before she finally acted, she should give Mudenge a chance.

Mildred was right. It was time to consult, for the second time in a matter of days, Clarence "Results" Mudenge.

"I can promise you," he said at the end of the consultation, "that either I get the results or you get your money back."

At the first session Mudenge had listened carefully, interrupting only to ask pertinent and penetrating questions that opened her mind.

"Yes, Mrs Mupanga" – he always addressed his customers as Mr or Mrs, a courtesy that Charity appreciated – "I must speak frankly. It is clear to me that there is a problem here. But like all problems, there is usually an answer – although

I must tell you that it might not be the answer that makes you happy."

Charity nodded her agreement.

"First, as Mildred told you, I need to know about his dreams."

"That is easy – he is always dreaming. He talks about coffee grown without insect killers on the *shamba*. I tell him that's fine but it will be his job to catch the *goggas* that eat the leaves and the coffee berries."

She spoke with passion, leaving Results in no doubt that the subject was a delicate one.

"He dreams about power from the sun, about storing rain water. Oh yes, he is a man who dreams all right . . ."

"That is a good start", said Mudenge, "but I am looking for other dreams. For proper dreams. The lion and the tortoise both dream . . ."

Charity looked at him sharply. Was he making fun of Furniver, who had filled two notebooks with Kuwisha proverbs before realising that most of them had been made up by Pearson, in a ridiculous competition with Shadrack, his steward?

"The dreams you mention are very interesting, but they are hopes and not so much dreams," Mudenge continued. "I want to know his sleeping dreams."

Charity was shocked.

"That is private business for any man."

"Or woman," replied Mudenge. "The fact is, Mrs Mupanga, our dreams tell us a lot. Please, think very carefully about Furniver's dreams and I think we will find they have the answer to your problem."

Results Mudenge studied Charity Mupanga. Not for the first time, he acknowledged that she was a fine woman indeed, with a strong handsome face, a throaty laugh and all the assets of a woman of Kuwisha.

"But I promise you the dreams will stay private. That is my business."

31

The pump boy had behaved just as Ntoto had anticipated.

The two had arranged to meet beyond the forecourt. In one hand the boy had a tattered oily rag, and in the other a fluorescent jacket, the badge of office that made the wearer all but invisible, for he was seen as a mere petrol dispenser and windscreen cleaner.

The agreed fee for the job was 100 *ngwee*, which Ntoto had persuaded Furniver to lend him from the bank's entrepreneur fund, promising that the money was needed as a down-payment on a pair of pliers that he would use to set up his business as a wire toy-maker.

The boy shuffled nervously. It was all very well to devise the scheme for extra cash when polishing a succession of car windows and dreaming of what you could do with the money; but with Ntoto standing in front of him it was a very different matter.

The captain of the Mboya Boys' football team had a formidable reputation as a thug on the field and a bully off it.

"We agreed," said Ntoto, "100 *ngwee*."

"The petrol captain wants his share," said the boy nervously. "That is 25 per cent."

Ntoto said nothing, though his eyes and his chilling stare spoke volumes.

The petrol boy dropped his gaze and coughed nervously.

"Very well," he said. "This time I will do it for 100 only, as a favour."

Ntoto's eyes looked through the boy, with underlying menace. He counted out the notes and handed them over.

"Show me the polishing rags and give me your jacket and cap."

"And we share tips," said the boy, a tall skinny youth who was suspected by the Mboya Boys of being a sympathiser of *mungiki*, if not a member of the fast-growing sect.

"Rubbish," said Ntoto. "Just rubbish. All tips are mine and that is what we agreed."

He then made a calculated gamble.

"If you think I will give you tips our agreement is broken," and he threw the peaked cap at the boy's feet.

"Pick and give it," he demanded. "Pick and give it or we finish."

For a terrible few seconds the boy seemed ready to call Ntoto's bluff but then reluctantly and sullenly bent down, picked up the cap and handed it to Ntoto.

"Your pump is number three, over there."

Ntoto looked at the clock on the forecourt. It was 10.30 a.m. and the service was due to start any minute now.

"Why are you wearing that cloth around your head?" said the pump boy nervously.

"Toothache," said Ntoto. "Very bad toothache. Where can I leave my lunch?"

The petrol boy gestured towards a waste bin next to one of the pumps.

"It'll be safe in there."

Ntoto removed the small sack from his baggy shorts, dumped it in the bin and covered it with the sheets of a discarded newspaper.

The oily forecourt of the garage had four petrol pumps and two pumps for diesel.

Ntoto took the rag, the bucket of soapy water, and the peaked cap with the sign "Lucky Lucky Motors" on the brim. So far so good. Although there was only a slight chance that he would be recognised by the other petrol boys, the less time he spent on the forecourt the better.

As the official pump boy left Ntoto to it, and made his way across the road, Ntoto could see in the distance the four-wheel drive that invariably escorted the mayoral Rolls approaching. Jamming the cap on his head, pulling the peak as far down as it could go, obscuring his face, clutching the can of soapy water in one hand and the oily rag in the other, he trotted to the entrance to the petrol station and waited for his quarry. The Rolls Royce rolled to a halt like a beast approaching a watering role, but without fear, replete and well groomed.

Mounted on the short flag holder on the right of the bonnet was the mayoral insignia.

Ntoto looked out from under the peak of the cap and to his horror saw that the man sitting alongside the driver was none other than his old adversary, Sokoto, who had been responsible for beating him in the presence of the mayor. Too late now to have second thoughts. The huge vehicle drew to a halt. Sokoto, to Ntoto's enormous relief, immediately set off for the Gents.

Ntoto went to the petrol pump.

"Where is the regular pump boy?" asked the driver.

"He is sick, suh. I am his deputy, suh."

Ntoto then gambled on his knowledge of life in Kuwisha and added, "He told me about your discount, suh."

Whatever doubts the driver may have had were dispelled.

"Don't loaf! Fill her up, boy."

He wound up his window again and got out of the car, slammed the door shut and went off to join Sokoto in the Gents. This was a stroke of luck for Ntoto, for the riskiest part of the operation was about to begin. He thrust the nozzle of the pump into the tank, turned the machine on to automatic and retrieved the sack from the bin, a couple of paces from where he stood.

A tug of the string at the top opened the bag. Quickly, he turned the pump back from automatic to manual, pulled out the nozzle and poured the contents of the sack into the tank of the Rolls. He was just in time. The driver returned and signed the chitty, which Ntoto had prepared.

"This includes discount?" he asked.

Ntoto nodded.

As Sokoto left the Gents, he motioned to the driver, indicating that he would wait for the car at the point where the garage met the main road.

The driver took a hard look at Ntoto.

"Have I seen you before, boy?"

Ntoto hesitated.

The cuff that followed caught him by surprise and sent him reeling. He contained his rage.

"Sorry, suh. Sorry, suh."

The driver gave Ntoto a final clip over the ear for good measure, stepped back into the car and drove off, collecting Sokoto on the way.

Ntoto did not wait. He abandoned his peaked cap, dumped pail and cloth, disappeared in the direction of the toilets, made his way across the busy main road and concealed himself in the branches of one of the trees that lined the avenue. From there he watched and listened.

He tensed in anticipation. If it was going to work, it would work in the next 100 metres of its journey. For a terrible moment he thought he'd failed.

Then he heard the sound that signalled success. Above the noise of the traffic, the Rolls backfired once, twice, three times, like the cough of a wounded buffalo.

It continued on its journey, coughing, jerking, rallying, seeking shelter, before coming to a shuddering halt, dying at the very feet of a distraught Mayor Guchu.

The sugar had worked! The maintenance manual was right! Dirt in the carburettor could be a problem – and sugar did the most damage.

A few minutes later Ntoto was joined by Rutere, who had left the chapel and was waiting for him, panting, concealed by a bush on the far side of the road.

Rutere, his heart bursting with pride at his friend's cunning, described the scene at the chapel.

"We could hear the car coughing, like this . . ."

Rutere made a rasping noise in his throat.

"Guchu heard the cough, and was looking, looking."

Again Rutere acted out the part, raising his hand to his forehead, and peering out, like a man scanning the horizon.

"Next, more coughing, like that Aloysius Hatende. Three times, maybe four times, all the time the car is struggling to reach Guchu, struggling, struggling."

By now Rutere was beside himself with pleasure.

"And then, my brother, when it reached its master . . ."

Rutere hopped from one leg to another, hugging himself with delight.

"When it reached the feet of Guchu, it died, at his feet. And then, and then, that boy called Cephas, who we said stole the sugar, the boy who loves Arsenal so much, Cephas began singing, like they sing in England, all pointing their fingers, and singing."

"The song he sang was so good, soooo good, all the boys started singing at Guchu."

Rutere completed his performance singing the song himself, his thin, reedy voice surprisingly loud:

Guchu, your car's dying!
Guchu, why you crying?
Guchu, you're rubbish
Guchu, your car's dead!

Ntoto joined in.

Arms slung around each other's bony shoulders, the boys set off back to Harrods, singing their defiance as loud as their lungs could manage.

Guchu, your car's dying!
Guchu, why you crying?
Guchu, you're rubbish
Guchu, your car's dead!

And every five minutes or so, the two boys danced, their stick legs stomping, pot bellies shaking, and elbows pumping, they celebrated the humiliation of the street boys' enemy.

As the boys took the backstreet route to Kireba, Rutere asked the question that had been on his mind.

"Will the pump boy tell? Guchu can find us, for sure."

Ntoto had thought about this.

"What can he tell? He is better to keep quiet. If he says he sold his job to me, Titus Ntoto, captain of the Mboya Boys, he will be punished for being stupid."

"The garage manager will not sack him, because he is Guchu's nephew. And Guchu will beat the boy," added Ntoto, matter of factly. "Guchu will maybe even disappear him. So the boy will have to stay quiet. And if he is a problem to me, I will say that he helped me do it."

Rutere beamed.

"Clever. Very clever."

Ntoto had left some good news for last.

"And Rutere, there is sugar left over – enough to make a bucket of *changa*!"

32

It was time to tackle a difficult matter. Didymus Kigali had never broached the subject of his retirement. And why should he? Indeed, it sometimes seemed to Furniver that his steward was, if not getting any younger, not getting older. Nevertheless, Furniver was determined to raise the issue, delicate though it may be for all concerned.

"Had a session with Mr Kigali," he told Charity. "Message didn't get through, I'm afraid."

"What do you mean?"

"Well, I wanted to break it to him gently, and I thought I had hit on a wheeze . . ."

He recalled the exchange.

Furniver had got up from the breakfast table slowly, and held his hand to the small of his back, as if the burden of advancing years was getting too much for him.

"I'm getting old, Mr Kigali, getting old. Jolly good admonition, by the way. Really first class . . ."

Mr Kigali nodded sympathetically.

"Suh. Yes, suh. You are getting old." He clucked concern. "You will need me to look after you."

This was not what Furniver had in mind. He thought that if he showed the strain of years in his late forties, it might encourage Kigali to do the same. He was wrong.

He decided to approach the matter more directly.

"As you know, you have earned a decent pension and a gratuity, and I'll throw in a goat, perhaps from Digby."

Didymus gave him what could only be called an old-fashioned look.

"I think we need to seek the help of the Good Lord," he said. "Let us pray."

Furniver had no option but to join the old man, who had dropped to his knees, and cradled his head in his hands.

"What else could I do, I ask you, it wasn't easy getting up again off my knees, but old Didymus popped up and down as easily as a cork in water."

Charity looked at her friend sceptically.

"I hope you gave him the right end of the stick," she said, brushing her teeth with the splayed bristle of a chewed-up wooden twig.

"Well, I broke the news to him. He didn't seem to take it all in and was remarkably cheerful. I had thought the old chap intended to work till he dropped and that the prospect of sitting on his bottom watching the world go by filled him with horror."

Furniver frowned. "Really odd. Perhaps it was too easy," he said. "Don't understand it. Far too cheerful."

Charity looked at Furniver pityingly.

"Don't you know that he and Mildred got compensation for their plot?"

"Blow me," said Furniver. "How did he manage that?"

Didymus, himself, appeared just as he spoke.

"How on earth, Didymus, did you get compensation for land which, as far as I know, you don't own?"

Didymus looked at him sternly.

"No one owns land," he said. "It is leased for the duration of the Lord's wish and Mildred and I have lived in that same place for many years now."

"So where do you plan to spend your retirement?" asked Furniver.

"Where do you think?" said Charity. "On the *shamba*, of course. Kigali has ordered the corrugated iron roof for their new house and said it will be much easier to work for you since he'll be living so close."

Didymus nodded his assent vigorously.

Charity gave Furniver one of her looks. "When we talked about arrangements for Kigali's retirement, I hope you didn't think . . ."

Every now and then, Furniver realised, one had to accept the hand that fate had dealt one. There were worse things in life than to be looked after by a man who dressed like a cricketer and who was determined to defy the years. Assuming, of course, he and Charity ended up together, a prospect which seemed far from certain.

33

The envelope presented to Charity by Two Head lay on the table at Harrods.

Looking back, Charity blamed herself for overlooking the obvious: if you don't pay a bribe in Kuwisha, running a business – any business – is impossible, and she should have known this better than anyone.

If Harrods came to an end, as now seemed inevitable, she had only herself to blame.

Furniver disagreed.

"Had you paid a bribe", he said, "you might have bought a bit more time, but you would have lost your principles, dirtied your hands, and they would still have got you in the end."

"I still feel stupid, Furniver, I should have guessed. And as you English say, forewarned is forearmed. I should have tried harder to get the Zimbabwe toilets in place. Good toilets would have made a difference."

They were sitting at dusk on the brick patio which Furniver had helped build – or, rather, he had supervised the team of street boys assembled by Ntoto and Rutere. Although he had been wearing, at Charity's insistence, a floppy canvas hat, it had not stopped his nose from blazing like a beacon by the end of the day.

"Read out again what that notice says," requested Furniver.

Charity read extracts from the two-page document.

Health and Safety Regulations, 1961.
Name of establishment: Harrods International Bar (and Nightspot).

Owner: Mrs Charity Mupanga.

Manager: Mrs Charity Mupanga.

Location: Kireba East.

The above premises were inspected by the staff of the Council and the following defects were registered:

Bar – no licence.

Television – no licence for public entertainment.

Water – no running water.

Electricity – illegal connection.

Toilets – no toilets.

By the authority of the statutory powers invested in me, I Willifred Godwin Guchu, hereby order the closure of the Establishment known as Harrods International Bar (and Nightspot).

Grounds for closure: inadequate sanitation.

The owner and other interested parties have the right of appeal. This right must be exercised within seven days.

Charity threw the document down in disgust.

"I am tired of this nonsense, Furniver. Tired and sick."

Furniver retrieved the document and studied it. There seemed no room for any manoeuvre. He looked through it one last time.

Suddenly it struck him.

"Hang on a mo," he said. "I'm not a lawyer but I think you could buy a bit of time. Time in which we could erect the Zimbabwe toilets. It's worth a go. Have a close look. What do you notice?"

Charity looked baffled.

"Just read it again, and think about your late father."

Suddenly the penny dropped. Furniver had a point.

"But I have no money for lawyers," said Charity.

"You must speak in your own defence," said Furniver. "We cannot let Guchu win so easily. Let us call Mudenge and between us we can prepare for your case. When does it start?" He checked the document. "Time we got to work."

It was proving difficult for Pearson to get a word in, but he was determined to keep trying. He had barely begun when the first interruption came.

"So this *Financial News* chap, Mark Webster, who eventually left to work in television, he went off to see the US ambassador in Kinshasa. Wanted to know what he thought about Mobutu's latest reshuffle.

" 'What do you get when you shake up a can of worms?' the ambassador asked him . . ."

But before Pearson could deliver the punch line, the table came alive, their comments triggered by the subject of worms.

"Worms! I do not like worms, snakes and worms, flies and mosquitoes," said Charity. "Snakes and worms."

Mildred Kigali, who had joined them for her tea break, intervened.

"Scorpions are worse than worms."

"For God's sake, let me finish what I was going to say," said Pearson.

Furniver interrupted. "Worse than snakes?" he asked.

"Nothing is worse than snakes," muttered Ntoto. "Nothing."

"Crocodiles," said Mildred. "When I was a girl, at the time of the Great Floods and Mr Kigali was still a . . ."

Pearson refused to give up.

"So the ambassador asked: 'What do you get when you shake up a can of worms?' And he answered his own question: 'Dizzy worms!' "

Ntoto displayed a trace of interest.

"Perhaps he was talking about *mopani* worms. Fried *mopani* worms. With salt."

He smacked his lips.

"Silly buggers," muttered Pearson.

He stood up, stretched his legs, and went over to the bar to check on the progress of his order for roasted chicken necks, and to collect another ice-cold Tusker.

Charity looked at Furniver and giggled. "Shame on you, teasing him like that."

Mildred was unforgiving.

"This worm business. I have heard from Pearson about this worm business before," said Mildred. "He thinks he is being very clever! He thinks we don't know that he is talking politics when he speaks about these worms. Yes, all politicians are worms, all lawyers are worms, all are very confused. Journalists, even, are worms. Sometimes it seems that Kuwisha is all worms. So where is the answer? He does not tell us how to get rid of these worms. All his words . . . just useless."

There was no reply from her audience, only a general muttering and shuffling of feet.

Just then Cecil returned to the table, carrying a Tusker and a saucer of freshly roasted and salted groundnuts in time to hear Ntoto declare: "Worse than worms. Worse than worms are tape worms."

Voices were raised as Rutere and Ntoto clashed over whether the tape worm qualified as a worm, or whether it should be treated as a sleeping snake.

The boys finally agreed. As Ntoto observed: "You cannot eat tape worms," said Ntoto. "They eat you."

Rutere was suddenly struck by another candidate for condemnation.

"Jiggers," he said, and showed off the hole in his big toe.

"Get your feet off the table," said Charity. Cyrus Rutere belched, a long and rumbling eructation that came from the bottom of his round belly.

"Beg pardon," he said, just as Charity had taught him, and added, as if by way of explanation: "Goat meat. Very sweet."

Digby winced as the aroma of Rutere's last meal wafted across the table.

"Poor Dolly! Poor, poor Dolly," he sighed.

34

The hearing took place in the Kireba magistrate's court, a nondescript building on the edge of the slum. It had once been whitewashed, years ago, and since then the colour had changed to a grimy off-white atop a band that had been stained red by the ochre soil that surrounded it.

The duty magistrate was Josiah Buruna, a grey-haired man in his early forties, who had been passed over for promotion – the consequence, it was claimed, of his refusal to be "helpful" or "sympathetic" to government supporters who had lost at the ballot box.

"Silence in court," he ordered.

"Where are the enemy?" whispered Furniver, who had made a point of turning up early.

Results Mudenge, present to lend moral support, looked grim.

"Outside, waiting. They are showing they are boss by coming in late."

The packed courtroom let out a collective gasp of dismay as the state team entered, led by none other than Newman Kibwana, a state counsel no less, accompanied by his junior, Miss Patience Kola, the instructing solicitor, and a clerk weighed down with files and legal tomes.

Mudenge nudged Furniver.

"That Kola, she has been allocated a place on the new Kireba housing list."

"You are late, Mr Kibwana," said the magistrate.

"I apologise, your honour, there was a call from State House – they are very interested in this case and very concerned about the outcome."

"I care not a fig the reason. You are late. But I note your apology."

"Thank you, your honour."

Buruna nodded.

"Now then, I must ask you this question. While I do not know the applicant personally, I have on more than one occasion taken tea and enjoyed a dough ball at the establishment you seek to close. So I feel obliged to ask: do you wish me to recuse myself?"

"He's offering to stand down. If the verdict went against him, Kibwana could claim the judge was influenced by personal contact," whispered Furniver.

Kibwana did not hesitate. Confidence personified, he declared: "Not at all, suh."

"I assume that the State has no objection to Mrs Charity Mupanga representing herself, accompanied by Mr Edward Furniver and Mr Results Mudenge?"

"No objection."

"Mr Kibwana, will you set out your case?"

Kibwana was good. Very good.

"I, too," he began, "have taken tea served by Mrs Charity Mupanga, and I too share the general esteem of her dough balls."

"But I count myself lucky," he continued, "that given the state of the toilets I did not have any trouble with my stomach afterwards."

The magistrate was not amused.

"I must warn you, Mr Kibwana, that this is a serious matter and there is no room for jokes."

Kibwana seemed about to reply but checked himself.

"I will set out the State's case as briefly as possible. A bar is a public place. There should be toilets. There should be water for washing hands. There should be a licence for a television which is watched by the public. But above all, there should be toilets.

"But there are no toilets. Or, for I must be fair, there are holes in the ground which are treated as toilets. They attract flies, and spread disease. No one can disagree with that. Our client, Mayor Guchu, seeks only to apply the law in the interests of the public.

"I wish now to call the inspector of public health who visited the site and has reported on the conditions he encountered . . ."

Charity gave Furniver's hand a squeeze and stood up.

"Your honour, I do not want to waste the time of this court. I have read the inspector's report. I do not challenge the finding. But I move to dismiss the case, and seek costs."

"Mrs Mupanga, you must give reasons."

She pretended to confer with her team. Mudenge had assured her that Kibwana would be unable to resist taking the stand.

"Try it," he urged, "just try it. I know Kibwana – he is a show-off."

"Can I ask for Mr Kibwana to be a witness?"

Whatever his personal sympathies, this was too much for the magistrate.

"Mrs Mupanga, Mr Kibwana is here in his professional capacity . . ."

Kibwana intervened. As Mudenge had suspected, while he was a clever man, he was unable to resist showing off his cleverness.

Making a great play of removing his wig and gown, he said to the magistrate: "If it is of any help to Mrs Mupanga, I will take the oath and enter the witness box. Anything that serves justice has my support."

"Very well. It is most unusual but the court neverthe-less thanks you for your public spirited gesture. Please take the oath." Kibwana was sworn in.

"Mr Kibwana, you want Harrods closed. Is that correct?" asked Charity.

"No, that is not correct. I have no view on the matter. I am simply here to make the case for the State."

Charity persisted. "Do you have any interest in the outcome?"

"Madam. The Kireba Residents' Association has done me the honour of electing me their chairman. Since office holders must have residential status, I have accepted a plot allocation."

"The KRA are a front for Nduka," whispered Mudenge.

"You and Miss Patience Kola . . ." said Charity.

"That is enough, Mrs Mupanga," said the magistrate. "I cannot allow this questioning to continue. It is not relevant to the case."

"I am sorry, your honour, I have just one or two more questions.

"This order of closing is for Harrods International Bar (and Nightspot)?"

"Yes," said Kibwana.

"Not for any other place in Kireba?"

"No."

"Not for the closing of the Drink Cheap Shebeen? Where they serve *changa* that poisoned many people? And which has no toilets?"

"No."

"Not the Lazy Licka Saloon Entertainment Bar, where they fry their dough balls in bad cooking oil?"

"Enough, Mrs Mupanga. Come to your point or this hearing is over."

"I want to be certain, your honour. The paper says you want to close Harrods International Bar (and Nightspot). That is what this paper says?"

Kibwana gave a theatrical sigh.

"Yes."

"And no other place?"

By now Newman Kibwana was getting irritated.

"Can you read, Mrs Mupanga? Or should I read for you?"

Charity could have cheered. Kibwana was about to fall into the trap so carefully prepared by her team the night before.

"Please read," she said.

With a sigh of irritation, Kibwana read out the closure order for Harrods.

Charity drew herself up. "Phauw! Why are you beating a dead horse, Mr Kibwana? Harrods is already finished. It is closed. There is no more Harrods. It is air force. It is over. And that is why the case should be dismissed, your honour."

The magistrate intervened, with an edge to his voice that suggested he had lost all sympathy for Charity.

"This is foolish talk. Mrs Mupanga, I myself took tea at Harrods last month."

"No, suh, not at Harrods."

It was time to play the only ace in her pack.

"Harrods was closed, many months ago, suh, by lawyers from London. I can show you all their letters telling me I must close my bar. Those cheeky men from London said they owned the name Harrods, even though it's the name of my late father, and I had to close Harrods."

She flourished a file, which had the correspondence between the London lawyers and Edward Furniver, who had acted as her representative in the case.

"Harrods is closed already," she said.

Charity handed the file to the magistrate, who studied the contents.

"Mr Kibwana, Mrs Mupanga appears to be correct. These papers confirm that Harrods ceased trading."

"With respect, your honour, Mrs Mupanga is wasting the court's time."

Charity drove home her initiative.

"Suh. I submit, your honour, that the State has been lazy. The place you call Harrods no longer exists. It is now called Tangwenya's International Bar (and Nightspot). And when we launched, we had a special offer of 10 per cent off Tuskers. If

Mr Kibwana knew his business he would know that Harrods is gone. No more. Finished."

She then began the paragraph that she had prepared the night before.

"I submit, your honour, that this is a sad case of mistaken identity. If the order is against Harrods, there must be another place in Kireba of this name. The place I run, where the food is so good it waters your mouth, is called Tangwenya's International Bar (and Nightspot)."

"On these grounds, Mr Magistrate, I call for the charge to be dismissed. At the very least I appeal for an adjournment until Monday. Then the government must do its work properly. In the meantime let them stop harassing me."

"I am sorry, Mrs Mupanga . . ."

Charity's heart fell – and then lifted.

"As much as I would like this case to come to a speedy conclusion, the court cannot reconvene on Monday. We are on duty elsewhere. May I suggest the following Wednesday instead. Mr Kibwana?"

Newman Kibwana made a final effort.

"I will take instructions, your honour, but it would not surprise me if my client sought satisfaction in a higher court."

Josiah Buruna looked at him coldly.

"First, Mr Kibwana, you have to finish with my court, and you will only be finished on Wednesday next week."

As Charity left the court she was surrounded by men and women who were determined to celebrate a rare and wonderful victory. Provided the rains held off, by next Wednesday the concrete base of the Zimbabwe toilets would have set, and the structures put in place. The mayor would then surely have to think again.

A group of young men from the Mboya Boys' football team hoisted her up onto their shoulders and paraded around the red-earthed yard, singing as they did so: "Mupanga *tosha*! Mupanga *tosha*!"

"Let us celebrate!" cried Charity. "You are invited to come and enjoy a discount at Harrods." She paused. And amidst much laughter corrected herself. "Tangwenya's – at Tangwenya's International Bar (and Nightspot). With a free dough ball with first orders."

That night Charity and Furniver looked back over the day's events.

"Well done, my dear," said Furniver, giving her hand a squeeze.

"What have I done well, Furniver? What?"

"You have bought time. And in that time, much can change. You know," Furniver continued, "the English say you can win a battle but lose the war."

Charity nodded.

"But sometimes you can lose a battle and win the war. You have won a battle – now you must fight and win a war."

Charity squeezed Furniver's hand in response to show her love, but she was not going to let him get away with these masculine sentiments.

"That is the language of men. Fighting, always fighting, talking of war and such stupidity.

"We have too many dizzy worms in Kuwisha. Too many dizzy worms."

The sun rested on the horizon, like a luscious, juicy mango ready for plucking. An evening breeze provided respite from the usual stench, and carried the distant sound of the BBC time pips and the jaunty strains of "Lillibullero".

Charity Mupanga looked across the valley, crammed with shacks and shanties, and beyond, over the dam and above State House, and further to the distant hills soon to disappear from sight as dusk changed rapidly to darkness.

She turned over a maize cob roasting on the brazier between them and Furniver took a sip of his beer.

Mudenge had counselled patience, dreams take time to surface – but life did not wait for dreams.

It was time for some frank talking.

Charity looked into her heart and once again it seemed the answer was "No". Much as she loved Furniver – indeed, precisely because she did love him – she could not live in England and be the same person.

And if this were true of her, why should it not be true of Furniver? Did he not find the heat oppressive, as oppressive as she found the summer greyness of England? And did he not hate the mud?

As to other differences between their cultures, she could live with them: the extraordinary fact that Furniver's children were growing up without knowing their father; the apparent absence of an extended family, poor thing; and the general arrogance of their pink race, who believed that the world began in London.

For the second time Charity lacked the resolve to give Furniver the bad news.

35

A dozen or so of the foreign correspondents based in Kuwisha gathered at Lucy's Borrowdale home for the long-anticipated briefing on the role of the new ambassador. They sipped cups of coffee, kept a wary eye on her notoriously bad-tempered dog Shango, and, whenever possible, looked down the front of her T-shirt.

Digby had turned up as arranged, and when he saw the assembled journalists was ready to turn tail.

"Any news on the goat?" asked Lucy.

"You mean Dolly?" said Digby.

"Yes. The goat," said Lucy, in a tone that brooked no challenge.

"Couple of sightings, still alive according to some of the boys. But Rutere and Ntoto don't seem to be very hopeful."

Digby sniffed the air.

"Don't want to be rude, but what is that awful smell?"

"Shango's meat, just delivered."

"No wonder that dog's breath clears a room," said Digby, mournfully.

"So what do I tell them?" He looked over his shoulder at the assembled press corps. "I can't tell them I've lost the goat. Half of them would never believe me, and the rest would never forgive me – and they'd all take the piss out of me . . ."

He appealed to Lucy.

"What can I tell them? As it is they're expecting George Clooney."

Lucy looked at him without a shadow of sympathy. "I don't care what you tell them," she said. "But somebody's got to tell them something – and you've got to do it."

Digby thought long and hard, and was thinking about making a run for it, when a car drew up carrying David Podmore.

"Oh Christ," said Digby.

Podmore came into the room, his bottom wagging, like a Labrador with a bone.

"Sorry I'm late. Held up by this Kireba rebuilding project." He rubbed his hands together. "Where's Dolly? Been looking forward to meeting her."

His nose wrinkled. "What's that frightful pong?" he asked. "Not Dolly, I hope?"

Digby took him to one side and, blushing with embarrassment, confessed to his loss.

"What should I do?" asked Digby.

Podmore looked thoughtful.

"Two principles, old boy, when dealing with the reptiles. Never tell them the truth. They won't believe you. Or they spill the beans, breaking deadlines, ignoring embargos. Second rule. Never admit a mistake."

He thought for a few moments.

"I've got an idea."

He went through to the kitchen and re-emerged with a bulging plastic bag, and thrust it into Digby's hands.

Shango growled.

"Look out for that dog," said Podmore. "He's an evil, cunning brute. Right. This is what you say . . . and this is what you do."

A few minutes later Digby composed himself for what would be the toughest test he'd encountered in his distinguished but short career. He stood up in front of the journalists, his expression sombre, his eyes mournful.

"Thank you for coming. The good news is that George Clooney and Mia Farrow have sent a personal message of support for our work in 'Kuwishaland', and hope to 'visit with us' in the near future."

The announcement was greeted by a rumble of complaints, and the sound of notebooks being closed.

"The sad news is that I had hoped to introduce you to the WorldFeed roaming ambassador, Dolly. I am sorry to say that while she is present in the flesh, her brave spirit is elsewhere," said Digby, his voice cracking under the evident strain.

He paused: "Meet Dolly!"

He tossed the plastic bag onto the floor in front of him.

"At least, meet what's left of her . . ."

Shango pounced on the bag, growling furiously, and even hardened hacks recoiled as he buried his snout in the bloody intestines that spilled out.

It was a slow news day and foreign news desks across London were looking for a decent colour story. The *Daily Telegraph* and *The Guardian* both got to work.

"Aid worker's ordeal," ran the *Daily Telegraph* headline in the story that appeared the next day.

"Starving children in Africa's most notorious slum yesterday ambushed aid worker Digby Adams on his way from the airport to the city centre, driven by hunger and desperation. Their target was a rare breed of goat that ironically Adams had brought to help the people of Kuwisha . . ."

" 'They tore Dolly apart, the poor, starving little blighters,' said Adams, visibly moved at a press conference yesterday. Adams, a veteran of Africa's aid business, told the *Telegraph*: 'Never have I known such ferocious hunger. It was worse than Darfur, worse by far than the Eastern Congo.' "

"He made it clear, however, that what he called a 'grim episode' would only reinforce his determination to free the people of Kuwisha from what he called 'the yoke of poverty'."

" 'I see myself,' he said, 'as a foot soldier in the front line of the battle against disease and deprivation.' "

The Guardian report took much the same line, except it blamed external debt for the economic conditions that led to the children's attack.

When Digby met Podmore the next day, he was effusive in his thanks.

The First Secretary shrugged. "It was nothing," he said. "By the way, have you ever thought about working in the Foreign Office? There'd be a role for you in news department. Let's talk about that over a spot of lunch?"

David Podmore settled back in the wicker chair on the veranda of the Fairview Hotel, took a long draft of his Tusker, smacked his lips and surveyed the scene.

"Look," he said. "Just look around you."

Digby followed his instructions. From their table on the veranda they had a clear view beyond the road and the university onto the purple hills that marked the start of the Rift Valley. In the foreground, vendors sold batteries, plastic knick-knacks, screwdriver sets and apples; at the taxi rank, drivers of run-down, rusting and battered taxis solicited for custom; ice-cream sellers had insulated cartons strung from the handle bars; newspapers were being sold on the corner; and everybody seemed to be talking into a mobile phone.

Podmore called for a menu. "Look around," he gestured. "See what I mean? You are looking at the indigenous, *wananchi*, masses, *povo*, men and women in the street, call them what you will. What do they have in common?"

He leant forward, and lowered his voice.

"They all work bloody hard. Problem is, they are all affected by the politics of the foreskin. Divides the whole country. When will they find more to their politics?"

"You'll have to explain the foreskin bit," said Digby.

"Luolanga are circumcised; Kuolanga are not. Or is it the other way round? Doesn't matter. One lot won't vote for the other. And it goes further and deeper than that. It will be the basis on which the office messenger got his job."

"Good Lord," said Digby. "Sounds like Northern Ireland."

They studied the menu.

"S'pose you've seen the papers?" asked Podmore. "Lot of fools playing silly buggers at your office in Oxford, at WorldFeed."

He pointed to the headline in the *Nation*.

Goat link to N-East drought
Animals blamed for warming emissions

"Seems that a radical breakaway faction from WorldFeed calling themselves Vegetarians for Ensuring Africa's Liberation are demanding a halt to your goat scheme."

"Apparently they got hold of a research paper prepared for a global warming summit that claims that the drought in the north-east is caused by tens of thousands of the blighters, all farting away. Between ourselves our chaps are getting reports of mobs rounding up goats in several villages."

"Any word on Dolly?"

Digby shook his head.

"Let's face it," said Podmore. "She's probably being prepared for the pot as we speak. Fancy the asparagus? No? Don't be put off your tucker, old boy. This is a tough part of the world . . . sure you won't change your mind?"

Podmore continued to study the menu, while attempting to light a cigarette. The match flared briefly and died. Podmore flicked it away, and tried again, with the same result. The third time, the match head broke off, fizzed across the table, and landed on Digby's napkin. By the sixth match, the cigarette was lit.

Podmore took a notebook from his jacket and jotted something down.

"That's it. I'm downgrading the buggers."

Digby looked puzzled.

"One of my rules on Africa. Podmore's Principles. The matchstick business came to me when I realised there was a connection between the state of the country I happened to be in and the quality of locally made matches. In South Africa, they're pretty reliable. Seldom need more than one match to light your fag. Though I'm keeping my eye on them," he added darkly.

"As for Kuwisha, I had them down as four to five sticks to light a cigarette, not good, but better than the African average. Not any more."

He took a mouthful of Tusker.

"I'll announce it at the European Union meeting this afternoon. As from 4 p.m. today, Kuwisha is a six-stick state. And that means trouble ahead . . . are you sure you won't share some asparagus? They do a marvellous vinaigrette here."

"Certain," said Digby. "Really must go. Look for Dolly."

"I'll get you a taxi."

As they walked through the hotel grounds to the rank, Podmore kept talking.

"Let me tell you a story, but you didn't hear it from me. Crocodile and a hare were both on the banks of a raging river. The hare was trapped because he could not swim. The crocodile, could, of course, swim, but needed somebody to guide him across, so fierce was the flood.

" 'So, how about we help each other out?' said the crocodile. 'You can't swim and I need help in navigating.' The hare thought long and hard. Self-interest would surely rule the day.

"So they set off – with the hare riding on the crocodile's back, giving directions. Half way over, the crocodile flipped the hare off his back and crushed him between his jaws.

" 'Oh my God, why did you do that?' said the hare, as he breathed his last. 'Can't help it,' said the crocodile. 'This is Africa.' "

Digby got into the cab.

"Sorry to miss the asparagus, but I owe it to Dolly. My place is by my goat."

36

Titus Ntoto and Cyrus Rutere sat atop one of the containers that made up Tangwenya's International Bar (and Nightspot) and looked out over Kireba as the sun began to set. Although they were safe, their celebrations were muted. All they could do was watch as the huge trench diggers rumbled away, night and day, excavating the deep ditch that would effectively slice Kireba in two.

Though they could only guess at the consequences of Guchu's humiliation, their instinct for survival alerted them to impending peril. Like animals cut off from the main body of the herd by an advancing bush fire, they felt a growing unease.

In the meantime, however, they had full bellies, a brew of *changa* that had just matured, glue in their bottles and a dough ball to share whenever they wished. All things considered, life was good.

The boys scrambled down from the container. Usually they were not allowed to sit at the tables.

"For customers only," Charity explained to those who wondered. "When they buy a cup of tea, they can sit. Until then, they are kitchen workers. And anyway", she said matter-of-factly, "they smell."

The rule had been relaxed, however. Although no one said as much, this was probably the last time they would all be together at the bar.

Rutere belched, a long and rumbling outbreak that made the others around the table instinctively withdraw. He patted his stomach.

"We have eaten well," he said.

He belched again. "Beg pardon," he added, just before Charity would have ordered him to say so.

And then, as if by way of explanation, he said: "Goat meat . . . Very sweet!"

Digby, who had arrived just a couple of minutes earlier, winced as the smell of Rutere's meaty eructation drifted under his nose. He had to face it. A goat from England could not be expected to survive the hazards of life in Africa, which ranged from intestinal worms to hungry street children.

Add to that the reports of mobs of goat-fearing youths, determined to round up any strays, and Dolly's fate seemed sealed. He had let down WorldFeed, let down Dolly, and above all had let down the good people at WorldFeed who had placed their faith in him.

He was about to rebuke Rutere when he felt something tugging at the hem of his trousers. Digby could hardly believe what he saw. The amber eyes of Dolly looked up at him soulfully, and gnawed on the cord that led from her neck, under the table, to Rutere and Ntoto. The boys burst out laughing.

"Our friends found your Dolly," said Rutere.

"Foolish!" added Ntoto. "You know nothing about goats. It is not Dolly goat – it is Billy goat!"

Overwhelmed with relief, Digby could not resist giving her a hug and planting a kiss on the end of her golden nose.

Pearson looked on disapprovingly.

"Always thought he had a thing about goats," he muttered. "Mark my words, it'll be donkeys next," he said to no one in particular.

The group sipped Tuskers, and fruit juice and milky tea, sitting in companionable silence, which was broken by Furniver.

"A round of Experts?" he asked, but there were no takers. Instead, they were all preoccupied with the knowledge that Life was soon to carry them to different destinations.

The future of Harrods – or Tangwenya's – was tied up with that of Kireba. The new Zimbabwe toilets might win a respite from the mayor's attention, but sooner or later the bar would have to bow to the inevitable.

Few believed that the people of Kireba could resist the change that was gathering momentum, the remorseless flow of good-will that was about to engulf the slum as it was engulfed by the world of aid and development. Instead they remained silent, each lost in their own thoughts. Radios came to life, lanterns flared, voices drifted across the valley of shanties, and the sound of children playing for a few moments seemed to prevail.

Lucy seldom expressed her affection in public, but now she trailed her fingers through Pearson's hair, and she gave a small murmur of sympathy when they encountered the bump left behind by the rioter's stone the year before.

She had now been in Kuwisha for four years. Long enough to know the questions to ask about aid, long enough to realise that she did not have the answers.

For both Lucy and Cecil, it was time to go home. Time to leave Kuwisha to battle against, or alongside, the army of foreign experts and consultants that occupied the country. There was a new generation, a generation of Digbys, that would take their place.

"We meant no harm," said Pearson, as much to himself as to the group.

"Did we do any harm?" asked Lucy. "We were the workers who followed the circus through town, shovelling up after the elephants. Did we do any harm?" she asked again.

"We didn't do much good, that's for sure," said Pearson.

"All your editorials, news stories and features, Pearson, did they amount to a row of beans?" asked Lucy.

"About as effective, I suspect, as your projects, and the briefings and press releases that you issued in the name of WorldFeed."

But the comments were said in a tone of detachment and neither of them took umbrage at what the other said. They had reached a rare agreement. Neither had much to boast about.

Whether this truce would last, whether it would sustain a life together, who could say?

But as dusk fell at Harrods, and the strains of "Lillibullero" drifted across from Rugiru's shack, and the smell of woodfire and roasting maize filled the air, it seemed to Pearson that a long-term partnership with Lucy was well worth a try.

"What I missed when we were apart", said Pearson, "was the wonderful intimacy of our rows."

Lucy narrowed her eyes. She said nothing, but her eyebrows curved in characteristic fashion, antagonistic and belligerent.

"What?" said Pearson. "What's the matter? It's true, I really missed them."

"Hmmm. Look at me, and say that again."

Pearson looked into Lucy's blue eyes and then had to break away, unable to hold her gaze.

"All right," he said. "I miss the wonderful intimacy of our rows . . . as Joe Slovo said in his letter to Ruth."

"I knew it," said Lucy.

"Knew what?" asked Pearson.

"I knew that you filched that phrase from somewhere. You may be good with words, but you're not that good."

Pearson later told Charity about the exchange.

"When somebody knows you so well . . ." he tailed off.

"Did the words come from your heart?" Charity asked.

"Sort of . . ."

"So what did you do next?"

"I asked if she would stay with me in London."

Furniver seemed to choke on his mango juice.

"Hanky hanky before marriage? You'd better not tell Didymus, he'd have a fit! Why don't you come out with it and ask the girl to marry you?"

Pearson was uncharacteristically lost for words and blushed.

"Actually I did, just now."

"And you, Lucy, tell us," ordered Charity. "What did he say?" It was Lucy's turn to blush.

"He asked me to marry him."

"And?" Furniver and Charity asked in unison.

"Well, I said, sort of, yes. In a way."

"So what are we waiting for?" asked Charity. "Mr Kigali!" she beckoned. "You are needed."

"There is only one condition", said Mr Kigali, "and that is that you are married in the open air because we Lambs believe that the hills around us are God's own church and the mountains are his altar."

Charity clapped her hands with enthusiasm.

"We must strike with the hot iron. Let Mr Kigali give us a blessing from the Church of the Blessed Lamb and we will sing a good hymn. Mr Kigali can then marry you on this spot, now."

Mildred looked on, delighted.

"Mr Digby, sing!" ordered Charity.

Both Cecil and Lucy looked uncomfortable, as if feeling trapped into a ceremony that would in fact be binding by the law of Kuwisha.

Furniver took pity on them and tried to intervene.

"Give them a chance, Charity . . ."

He got no further.

Charity looked at him, eyes narrowed.

"Hanky hanky comes only with marriage," she said firmly. "Only with marriage! I am giving them a chance, a chance to have their union blessed in the eyes of our Lord."

Furniver and Charity volunteered their own wedding rings for the ceremony and Didymus Kigali presided over the exchange of vows.

The simple ceremony took just a few minutes.

"Amen," said Kigali.

"Digby," Charity barked. "Get ready! It is time to sing."

Cecil took Lucy's hand in his. To his surprise she was smiling and the look of worldly scepticism that was usually there on her face had disappeared.

"Sing, Digby, sing!" urged Charity. "You know you sing well for an Englishman."

Digby gave an embarrassed cough. It was a long way from the front line of the battle against poverty in which he had enlisted. But who was he to deny Charity's order?

He made a faltering start.

"What a friend we have in Jesus . . ."

From the newly installed Zimbabwe toilet came help as Aloysius Hatende, who, before driving Lucy and Pearson to the airport, had answered the call of nature, added his baritone to the singing with all the confidence of a seasoned churchgoer.

". . . all our sins and griefs to bear!
    What a privilege to carry everything to God in prayer!
    O what peace we often forfeit, O what needless pain we bear,
    All because we do not carry everything to God in prayer."

"Have a good flight," said Digby. "Travel light, hand baggage only, and wear a suit. That's my tip if you want to be upgraded."

Pearson wondered if Digby was taking the piss.

Lucy got into the taxi.

"Come on, Cecil, we'll be late."

Pearson was about to step into the taxi with Lucy when he remembered that he had a question.

"Just one thing, Digby. When you said that there was an agreement between the BBC and KTV, you hinted that there was more to come."

"Absolutely," said Digby. "Thought I had told you. I had a meeting with Berksson to tie up the deal today."

"So just what is this deal?" asked Pearson.

"That song, the one used by NoseAid on their appeal night . . . We sang a few lines – *Together, together we stand, United, united our land*."

"Don't – it was bad enough the first time I heard it sung by weather forecasters and newsreaders."

Digby beamed: "Berksson and I have arranged for the Kibera Orphans' Choir to sing a new version."

"Hang on," said Pearson. "What choir? The Kibera Orphans' Choir? Never heard of them."

"You will," said Digby, "you will. We're collecting names of members now. Limited to Aids orphans, obviously. Here is the press release I've drafted. And I have asked Sing Africa Proudly to help out, get it started . . ."

Pearson read the release.

Rehearsals would begin in the next couple of days, and WorldFeed was ready to underwrite a European tour.

"Did you know about WorldFeed's backing?"

Pearson looked accusingly at Lucy.

"I told you. Marvellous news. WorldFeed originally offered our support in principle and HQ have now said OK."

"You haven't heard the best bit," said Digby. "The proceeds from record sales and choir appearances will go to an orphans' crèche in the new Kireba centre. Let me sing the first lines of the new version. What's the Swahili word for 'together'?" Digby asked.

"*Torusha*," said Pearson, making it up on the spur of the moment.

Digby began to sing:

Torusha, together we stand
Torusha, Kuwisha, our land

Pearson looked at his watch.

"Gotta dash. Plane to catch."

Their taxi was about to drive off when Digby called after it.

"The president agreed, by the way."

"Agreed to what?" asked Pearson.

"Didn't you know? He agreed to let us call the crèche after him ... the Nduka Crèche for Orphans – Aids orphans, of course."

"Obviously," said Pearson, "obviously."

37

It had been a tiring week and an exhausting day for President Nduka.

His schedule, which would have knocked the stuffing out of a man half the president's age, had left him tempted to take a nap. Meetings with the British High Commissioner and the Chinese trade delegation that morning had been the last straw.

His study was in near darkness, with the only light provided by the fire in the hearth, lit some 30 minutes ago by the kitchen *toto*.

The president breathed in deeply, relishing the aroma of veranda polish, wood smoke and Jeyes fluid.

There was something he had to do before he could rest.

He took out a fountain pen.

There were some lists he enjoyed compiling.

A Cabinet minister led the way, followed by three provincial officials, trouble-makers the lot of them.

He rang his head of security, who impassively studied the names.

"They are to join the shadow cabinet," Nduka chuckled. "Phone when you have made the arrangements."

The man nodded and left the room.

Nduka was tired, tired as an old dog. He rested his head on his forearms.

"Boy! Boy! Bring me my honey water."

But his voice had been reduced to a whisper.

"Where is my honey water?"

The phone rang, several rings, and then stopped.

The small, slight man at the desk stayed motionless. Ngwazi, who Mounts All the Hens, Life President Dr Josiah Nduka, had made his last list.

38

Minutes after Lucy and Pearson had reached the airport, Pearson's mobile rang. After a brief exchange, he turned to Lucy.

"There's a rumour that Nduka has died. The paper wants a leader."

"I'll see you in the duty free," said Lucy.

Pearson sat down at his laptop and bashed away.

"If Kuwisha is to overcome the formidable challenges that lie ahead, all sides must play their part. With the right policies, consistently applied, and rigorously monitored, Kuwisha could yet become Africa's model state."

"Come on, we'll miss the flight."

Lucy ran her eyes over the leader.

"Isn't that pretty well what you said last time?"

Charity and Furniver sat alone at a table at Harrods, like hosts at a dinner party after the guests had departed. Charity returned to a vexed concern, prompted by Mudenge, who had pressed Charity for more information.

"Like most men," Charity had told Mudenge, "he does not say much, especially when we spend more time together. Before he would talk about missing London. Then he talked about missing Kuwisha when he was in London for his divorce. He is very confused."

Furniver responded to her questions with an easygoing tolerant way that was one of the reasons she wanted to share the rest of her life with him.

"Dreams, old thing? You still on about my dreams? My latest dreams?"

Furniver was mildly surprised.

"You still want to know? I've told you that dream about your, er, um, teeth, every now and then. Freudian. Castration complex. Or could be an oral fixation . . ."

Charity interrupted.

"Furniver!" she warned. "No nonsense, no stupid talk."

"Truth is," he said, "head touches pillow, out like a light. Sure I dream, but dashed if I can remember."

These were thin pickings indeed.

"I sleep like a dog, once I drop off. Been a bit worried though. Sometimes I miss London, sometimes I miss Kuwisha. The worst thing is when I am in Kuwisha I miss London, and when I am in London I'm missing Kuwisha. If you get my drift."

This was surely not what Mudenge had in mind.

"Furniver says he sleeps like a dog," she had told Mudenge, who shook his head.

"Every person dreams," he said firmly. "Everybody."

"When was all this missing London? When was he missing Kuwisha?" asked Mudenge.

"As I said, when Furniver was in London, he was dreaming about Kuwisha. When he is in Kuwisha, he is dreaming about London. Very confused."

As soon as the words were out of her mouth, Charity realised their significance. This was the stuff of dreams that Mudenge had been seeking.

It was now clear that Edward Furniver was in that no-man's land, caught between the memories of his English past and the appeal of Kuwisha.

Mudenge chose his words carefully.

Charity should be aware, he cautioned, that Furniver was never going to rid himself of his elemental feeling of belonging to England; but Africa had surely surprised him with the generosity and the warmth of its embrace. He could not desert the continent. Africa was now dear to him.

Of course, he went on, Furniver could never become a "white African" no matter how long he stayed. As a Kuwisha proverb put it, no matter how long a log lies next to the stream, it will never become a crocodile.

And most men and women who claimed to be "white Africans" invariably travelled on a passport issued by Britain or Ireland or France, never sharing the trials and tribulations of someone who was obliged to travel on a passport issued by an African government.

No, Edward Furniver would always be a white man who lived in Africa. Nevertheless, the relationship would be a close and intimate one, continued Mudenge.

And when Furniver travelled, he would return to the continent with a sense of coming home, taken into an embrace of sounds and senses and shapes. Africa's face and body would become more dear and familiar to him, ravaged though it may seem to others, and battered by misfortune, whether of its own or outsiders' making.

But he would hear, and smell and feel Africa's welcome, said Mudenge the high-pitched hum of the Christmas beetle, the chirrup of crickets, the acrid aroma of the *veld* fire and the tang of the air after rain; the spread of the acacias and the *msasas*, the purple jacarandas, the gold of the winter grass and the steel-blue sky; the laughter, the handshakes and the embraces; the liquid vowel sounds of languages, all would be dear and familiar to Furniver.

But at other times, Africa was a giant wounded beast, which Furniver would encounter at his peril. Although he was well-meaning in his concern, he ineptly administered to its needs. He tried to comfort it in its distress, all the time aware that he could be knocked flying with a wave of its paw. And he would not know whether the action had been prompted by an involuntary spasm of pain, or whether the beast was affectionately trying to take him into his arms, unaware of its own strength.

There was no need for Mudenge to say more.

The consultation with Charity was interrupted by the appearance of Furniver himself.

"D'you remember me telling you that old Ezekiel Mapondera negotiated a guaranteed price for his cement order?"

Charity nodded: "That Ezekiel is very smart."

"What I didn't tell you is that he promised to let you have any cement left over from his hen house. Well, the old boy has come up trumps. There is enough cement for six more toilets! Bloody marvellous! We can get to work right away!"

Charity's eyes filled with tears.

"I say, steady on, my dear, no need to blub. I told you it would be okay. I'm as pleased as you are. Know what? I've been dreaming about the bloody toilets."

Mudenge looked at Charity.

"One hundred *ngwee*, please."

He watched, slightly embarrassed, as Charity embraced Furniver with passion and enthusiasm, and then made a discreet exit.

"Steady on," said Furniver, offering Charity his handkerchief. "They are only toilets, after all . . . Anyway, it'll take no more than a few hours to mix and pour the concrete. Then we'll have the new VIP toilets."

"For you, Furniver, they may be toilets only. But for me, they are dreams, fine, fine dreams! Now let us find the rats. The *matatu* will be waiting . . ."

The sugar stealing had stopped. Charity confessed herself baffled. The day after the last theft, Ntoto had handed in a key, found, he said, in the mud alongside the stepping stones that led to Furniver's flat.

Mudenge had scratched his head, equally perplexed, when Charity told him.

"No result, no fee," he said wryly.

Both of the boys knew that it would soon be time for them to move on. Whether or not the mayor was able to pin the blame for his humiliation, sooner or later, motivated by vindictiveness as much as anything, he would track them down and they would be disappeared.

The two teenagers who had never known childhood retreated to their lookout in the eucalyptus trees, sniffed from their glue tubes, drained the last of their *changa*, and drew heavily on their cigarettes of *bhang*. Usually the combination lifted their spirits, taking them into a never-never world in which fantasy ruled over reality.

This time it was different.

"We are too old to play like children," said Rutere, with the wisdom of his 14 years.

Ntoto agreed.

"There will be no more ack-ack," said Rutere.

"It was a stupid game anyway," said Ntoto.

For the next few minutes the boys discussed the merits of ack-ack, devised to pass the time at Harrods, a combination of hide and seek and kick the can.

"A very foolish stupid game," said Ntoto.

Rutere took a closer look at his friend and realised that Ntoto was fighting to hold back tears.

"You were the best player," said Rutere. "Do you remember when Pearson cheated?"

Ntoto grunted.

"Journalist," he said, as if the word both described and explained Pearson's shortcomings.

"We must leave," said Rutere, "I am sure. Even if the pump boy says nothing, I think Guchu will come and pick us when we are sleeping." He looked about him nervously. "And before Mrs Charity can help us, we will have been disappeared. Mrs Charity herself, she knows this."

The boys looked around. They took in the dam in which they had splashed; the State House security fence through which Fatboy Mlambo had scrambled; the new Zimbabwe toilets, clad in gleaming new sheets of corrugated iron; and the railway track that ran through the slum and which was the nearest thing Kireba had to a road.

"Have you got your shoes?"

Charity had given Ntoto a pair of handsome black shoes, resoled and as good as new, for his last birthday. He wore them only on special occasions.

Ntoto nodded.

"In the box."

"It was a good present from Mrs Charity," said Rutere.

Ntoto agreed.

"Very good."

From the Pass Port to Heaven Funeral Parlour came the sound of hammering as Philimon Ogata tried to keep pace with the ever-increasing demand for his services.

A light burned in the Klean Blood Klinic. Results Mudenge was working late again.

Rutere drained the last of the *changa*.

"Things that are good always must end," he said.

"Have you got our photographs?" asked Ntoto.

Rutere nodded, and pointed to the cardboard box that contained the photos of their heroes.

"They are safe," said Rutere. "We must go back now."

He looked anxiously at his friend, far from convinced that Ntoto was ready for the move that awaited them.

"Mr Furniver says I can learn to be a mechanic."

Ntoto said nothing.

"You too, Ntoto, can learn . . ."

Ntoto shrugged.

"We will go together," he said. "I hear them calling."

The boys made their way across the wasteland, picked a path through the flying toilets and, dragging their feet with exaggerated reluctance, made their way to the *matatu* that would take them, together with Charity and Furniver, to the *shamba*.

They were about to get into the *matatu* when Charity sniffed the air.

"What was the last thing I said to you boys?"

There was no reply.

"I said you must have a very good wash," she said sternly. "You, Rutere, you smell like a dead dog."

Ntoto giggled.

"Yes, Rutere, you smell like a dead dog," she continued.

"And you, Ntoto, you smell like a dead hyena. Go! Wash properly!"

The boys washed, enthusiastically debating what creature was most offensive, dead dog or dead hyena, while Charity and Furniver sat on a nearby bench, looking out over Kireba.

Harrods – or Tangwenya's, according to the freshly repainted sign – would be in good hands during the time they would be away on the *shamba*. Cousin Mercy, whose course in public health was not due to start until the summer, would be an excellent caretaker.

But who could say whether the Kireba they knew would still be there when they returned. Everything, anything was possible. No condition is permanent, as the slogan often emblazoned on *matatus* put it.

And perhaps Charity was right. Ultimately corruption would destroy corruption. Perhaps it would also bring a halt to the Kireba project. The cement shortage continued, and prices were rising by the day. The water supply problem went unresolved, although the mysterious death of a plot owner who had taken his case to court did nothing to help resolve the dispute over upstream water rights of the river that ended up trickling into Kireba's dam.

The source and the cost of the additional power supply the project required remained uncertain. And matters weren't helped by a newspaper investigation which revealed that at least seven Cabinet ministers had claimed ownership of plots in Kireba. Meanwhile the road lobby and railway lobby remained at loggerheads – though both agreed that Kireba should be the country's new transport hub.

Only Anders Berksson was happy as estimates of the cost of the project rose steadily.

For the first time since his arrival in Kuwisha, the UNDP budget had overrun the initial estimates as the suppliers became increasingly brazen in their demands for exorbitant payments, and the claims from the international consultants more imaginative.

Berksson's conversation with Digby had been most productive. The suggestion that Nduka be asked to lend his name to the proposed crèche was brilliant. The orphan choir would sing their hearts out.

The UNDP boss sat down and began composing his monthly report to HQ.

Dusk was falling, and lengthening shadows softened and blurred the hard edges of the tin shanties. The sun slipped below the horizon, and a breeze allowed the fragrance of roasting corncobs to take the place of the usual stench. Candles glowed, and paraffin lamps were lit, and as 6 p.m. came round, the BBC time pips could be heard.

Furniver began to recite lines from a favourite poem.

The pip doth toll the end of parting day,
The lowing goats wind slowly o'er the lea . . .

Charity responded, without missing a beat.

The night guard homeward plods his weary way,
And leaves the world to darkness and to me.

" 'Elegy in a Country Churchyard', Thomas Gray. The missionaries at Wedza secondary school", said Charity, "made sure we learnt it by heart."

They both laughed.

A car backfired, or it could have been a gunshot, and made them start.

"Tell me, Furniver, when will all our nonsense end?"

Didymus and Mildred, dressed in their best, each carrying a small case with their worldly possessions, came into sight.

"All done, Mr K?"

Didymus Kigali waved a fat envelope in the air.

"Ready, suh. We are ready for the *shamba*."

It was Furniver's turn to have cold feet, as he recalled a breakfast exchange with Mr Kigali, nearly a year earlier. Under the impression – false, as it turned out – that Charity was contemplating converting to the faith of the Church of the Blessed Lamb, Furniver had asked his steward to explain a central tenet of the Lambs' doctrine.

Never was a member to go naked, whatever the circumstances.

With Furniver's prompting, and the occasional question, which would prompt a flourish of Kigali's yellow duster, the steward explained. He began by pointing out that Christ himself had retained what Mr Kigali called his smalls, all his life, from baptism to crucifixion.

"With you so far," said Furniver.

"Thank you," said Mr Kigali, clearing the breakfast table. "Do you want more toast?"

Furniver shook his head. Mr Kigali continued.

"In the presence of our Lord, it is essential to be decently dressed."

"Fair enough."

"And is not our blessed Lord all-seeing?"

Kigali snapped his duster as if punctuating his point.

"There is no arguing with that," said Furniver.

There was no reference, Kigali went on, in the entire scriptures to Christ ever divesting himself of his smalls.

"Never. Never," he said firmly.

Furniver posed the question that he'd been too embarrassed to raise until now.

"Man and, er, woman . . . never, um, naked . . . even after, er, marriage?"

"Especially after marriage," said Kigali with a touch of steel in his voice. A true believer would never, he went on, under any circumstances, go naked, always taking care to protect their modesty by retaining their underwear whether in bath, shower or bed.

Furniver's heart sank. Although he was as tolerant as the next man, a chap had to draw the line somewhere. And while he did not favour any particular faith, he could not see himself living happily with a woman who had pledged never ever to go naked, no matter what her merits.

Furniver knew that now was an opportunity to put the record straight.

Mr Kigali got there before him.

"I can see you are worried, Mr Furniver, by the 'never naked' doctrine. You need not worry. Some Christians believe in what you call transubstantiation. You believe that the bread and wine you take at communion become the body and the blood of Christ.

"In your church there are some who do not believe this. I must tell you that we Lambs do not believe in this and some of us find it rather strange. But just as some Lambs will never, ever go naked, I know that some Lambs do not follow this law. However, they are still members of our church. And they are still Christians . . ."

He beamed benignly at Furniver and Charity.

Furniver realised that this was the moment of decision.

He looked at Charity.

She nodded.

The ceremony was as short as it was simple, conducted by Kigali, witnessed by Mildred and Rutere and Ntoto, both smelling strongly of Lifebuoy soap.

As Furniver took Charity's hand, he thought his heart would burst with joy. A huge smile broke across Charity Mupanga's face and Edward Furniver was reminded of dawn in Kuwisha.

EPILOGUE

Never could Boniface Rugiru have imagined that 50 years after he had begun work as a 12-year-old *toto* at the Thumaiga Club, he would be back in the very same room he had once cleaned, performing a sad task for its departed occupant.

There was not much left to sort: the Oldest Member's books that would become part of the Club library; clothes that were to go to Kireba; a graceful hare, cast in bronze and caught in mid-flight was also left to the Club.

All that remained was a single drawer in the writing cabinet, which contained a handful of photographs, a notebook in which the OM had kept an occasional diary and a copy of a book entitled *The Souls of Black Folk*.

The photos of old girlfriends were tossed into the fire in the hearth, which had been lit by Rugiru. One of them had a striking resemblance to Bunty Benton. Rugiru tried to recover it for a closer inspection, but he was too late, and the flames consumed her. After reflecting a while, he followed these with the photograph that had caught his attention that morning, so many years ago, when he was first alone in the room.

The two young men, who were awkwardly shaking hands, with a tray of tea between them, were immediately recognisable as the Oldest Member, then an up-and-coming district commissioner, and Josiah Nduka, dressed in the fatigues of a guerrilla commander.

Rugiru examined the diary. The last entry, dated the day before he had died, had been written with a shaky hand.

"They still work on the principle of Pooh Bear and his hums. Sing the first line loudly enough and quickly enough, said Pooh, and the second will come to you before you know what's happening. I can hear the blighters all singing their hearts out, 'Aid for Africa, aid for Africa'. The problem is they sing the first line with enthusiasm, and often, I still cannot hear the next lines."

Rugiru picked up the book, published in 1903. It was a collection of essays by an African American writer, W.E.B. Du Bois, who looked out from the photograph on the jacket. The book fell open at a page where a passage has been underlined.

Rugiru read it aloud:

Between me and the other world there is ever an unasked question: unasked by some through feelings of delicacy; by others through the difficulty of rightly framing it. All, nevertheless, flutter round it. They approach me in a half-hesitant sort of way, eye me curiously or compassionately, and then, instead of saying directly, How does it feel to be a problem? they say, I know an excellent colored man in my town; or, I fought at Mechanicsville; or, Do not these Southern outrages make your blood boil? At these I smile, or am interested, or reduce the boiling to a simmer, as the occasion may require.

To the real question: <u>How does it feel to be a problem?</u> I answer seldom a word.

Rugiru read again the sentence that had been underlined, presumably by the Oldest Member.

"How does it feel to be a problem?"

The question intrigued Rugiru. For him and for his family, the everyday demands of life were problems: feeding the children, keeping the house warm, meeting medical bills . . . These were problems.

But it seemed these were not the problems the writer had in mind. He was asking Rugiru: how did *he* feel to be a problem. Boniface pondered. Never in his life had he regarded himself as a problem.

Then he recalled a conversation with a nephew, who by dint of hard work and a good mind had won a place at university in Manchester. But the toughest part of his journey was not from village hut to school. Or from school to city. It was the day he landed at Heathrow airport. That, he told Rugiru, was when he began to realise that the world treated him – and Africa – as a problem.

For the last time Boniface Rugiru looked around the room, now bare, shorn of its contents, a plume of smoke from the embers of the dying fire drifting up to the high ceiling. He gently closed the door.

A car horn hooted outside. It was probably Charity and Furniver, who had hired a *matatu*, and invited Mr and Mrs Rugiru to join them on the *shamba* for the weekend.

As he made his way to the car park to meet them, the Club clock struck the hour. Somewhere in the building a guest must have turned on their radio for the Six o'clock news. And down the passage drifted the sound of "Lillibullero", followed by the BBC time signal which echoed along the parquet-tiled corridor:

Peep! Peep! Peep! Peep! Peep! Peeeep!